Anonymous

Statesmen, Past and Future

Anonymous

Statesmen, Past and Future

ISBN/EAN: 9783337186869

Printed in Europe, USA, Canada, Australia, Japan

Cover: Foto ©Andreas Hilbeck / pixelio.de

More available books at **www.hansebooks.com**

STATESMEN

PAST AND FUTURE

CASSELL AND COMPANY LIMITED

LONDON PARIS & MELBOURNE

1894

CONTENTS.

Most of these Sketches were written during the last year of Lord Salisbury's second Administration. Ephemeral productions, they were intended for ephemeral use. Their value, if they have any, lies in recording the impression of the day. Some critical phrases have been softened, and some removed. It is easy to exaggerate the faults and underrate the merits of political opponents.

STATESMEN, PAST AND FUTURE.

THE MARQUIS OF SALISBURY.

THE MARQUIS OF SALISBURY is the head of an ancient
and historic family, which before his own time had
produced no remarkable man since the days of Queen
Elizabeth. He is a conspicuous exception to the
two general rules that the British Peerage is modern
and that its hereditary representatives are undistinguished. Unfortunately for the believers in primo-
geniture, he was a younger son. He succeeded to the
Marquisate on the death of his father in 1868. It was
not till 1865 that the death of his brother made him by
courtesy Viscount Cranborne. But while Lord Robert
Cecil entered the world with immense social and accidental advantages over the vast majority of his fellow-
citizens, his bitterest enemy would not deny that his
talents and ability have proved more than equal to the
foremost place which he holds in the Government of the
British Empire. Opinions may differ as to the wisdom
of his administration and the consistency of his career.
Nobody doubts his capacity for business or his powers
of speech ; and these are the two most valuable qualities

for anyone who hopes to distinguish himself in the
public life of this country. When, as is the case
with Lord Salisbury, he writes as well as he speaks, his
success may be considered assured. It will not be
hampered or delayed if he is also the inheritor of an
old title, the possessor of great wealth, and the owner
of the most splendid residence in a land where country
houses are proverbial for their splendour.

There is thus nothing unusual in Lord Salisbury's
steady and uninterrupted advance to place and power.
That is all in the general order of things. Lord
Robert Cecil entered the House of Commons at twenty-
three, and it is worthy of note that while his eldest son
sits for a populous district of Lancashire, he himself
was returned for the pocket borough of Stamford,
extinguished with his own consent in 1885. At thirty-
six Lord Cranborne was a Secretary of State, having
entered the same office at the same age as Lord Randolph Churchill. A combination of power with opportunity is as much as human beings can expect. There
is another and a curious coincidence between the careers
of the older and the younger politician. Both resigned
their posts and left the Cabinet the year after they had
entered it. Lord Cranborne was driven out by Lord
Derby's leap in the dark, Lord Randolph by the
bloated estimates of the First Lord of the Admiralty
and the Secretary for War. But while Lord Cranborne's secession was followed in a few months by the
resignation of the Government from which he had
seceded, Lord Randolph has watched from outside for

more than five years the well-paid blundering of Lord George Hamilton and Lord Cross.

The really remarkable feature in Lord Salisbury's progress from political journalism to the First Ministry of the Crown is the contrast between his principles and his practice. This is no accusation of dishonesty. His principles are spontaneous. His practice has been forced upon him by the necessities of his position. An aristocrat by conviction rather than by temper, he has been compelled to work through democratic methods, and he is clever enough to succeed. But a very little observation will show how little he likes the job. It is probable that the act of his life which cost him the least previous hesitation or subsequent remorse was his retirement from the Government of 1867. He thought the suffrage quite low enough then, if not too low. He deluged Mr. Disraeli with scornful invective for pandering to the mob. Eighteen years afterwards he accepted household suffrage in counties, and even assisted in arranging the new constituencies. The contradiction is more apparent than real. Mr. Goschen thought that the rural districts were more than twenty years behind the urban, and that their partial disfranchisement should be continued. Lord Salisbury held that both were alike unfit, but as the vote had been given to the one, it might be tossed at the head of the other. Democracy is altogether so hateful to him that he cannot discriminate between its degrees. The more ignorant the elector, the more likely he is to be guided by those who know better than himself.

To say that Lord Salisbury has never courted the favour of the masses would be untrue. In 1885 he angled assiduously for the Irish vote. From 1886 to the present time he has surrendered rather than supported the reform of local government, the payment of fees in elementary schools, the reduction of judicial rents in Ireland, and other points where he had held out as long as he could. But while Lord Salisbury will abandon his principles, he cannot change his nature. He has no sympathy with the people. He does not care to win the cheers of a popular audience. He dislikes crowds. His platform speeches, though models of polished irony and effective declamation, excite no enthusiasm. They are better to read than to hear, and that is fatal to them as oratory. As essays, their merit is of the very highest kind, and considering that they are delivered without notes, their finish is wonderful. They are probably committed to memory beforehand. Lord Salisbury's voice, though clear and resonant, is monotonous and unmusical. With the art of gesticulation he is wholly unacquainted. His sense of humour is exquisitely keen. In society, where he is too rarely to be found, his unassuming courtesy, his ready wit, his genial, albeit somewhat cynical, persiflage make him the most delightful company. But he is exclusive in his tastes. Of political differences he takes no count. The rank and file of his own party do not inspire him with enthusiasm.

If Lord Salisbury does not shine at a public meeting, he reigns supreme in the House of Lords. The Lords do not demand enthusiasm; they like to be amused. Lord Salisbury is a consummately dexterous debater, and an incalculable loss to his party in the House of Commons. In the Lords he is more than a match for any of his adversaries, with the possible exception of Lord Rosebery. But his special delight is turning foolish Peers into ridicule. Towards stupidity he is absolutely merciless, even when it should elicit compassion rather than contempt. There seems to be in Lord Salisbury—at least, when he is on his legs—a curious want of moral taste. To take a single instance : not a hundred years ago, the most laughter-provoking article happened for the moment to be a fire-escape. Any allusion to such a contrivance in public was sure to be received with boisterous hilarity, and music-halls resounded with the word. It might have been thought that if there was a man who would eschew the reference, and a place where the joke would not be made, the man was the Prime Minister, and the place was the House of Lords. But not a bit of it. Out it came on the first night of the Session, from the lips of Lord Salisbury himself. The Peers laughed, of course. But there must have been some who felt that the undignified, almost indecent, jibe was not redeemed by the originality of the treatment or the novelty of the theme. A more favourable instance of Lord Salisbury's cynical wit was afforded by a tiresome nobleman, who proposed, in a long and incoherent speech, that Peers desiring to stand for the House of Commons should be excused from attending the House of Lords. Lord Salisbury gently insinuated, without much circumlocution, that while they would be only too glad to let his "noble friend" out of one House, there was not the slightest chance of his getting into the other. This was at least much better than the dull and commonplace jest about the pettifogging attorneys, on which Mr. Traill has expended so much misplaced ingenuity.

It is as Foreign Secretary that Lord Salisbury will be chiefly remembered; but as Foreign Secretary he cannot yet be judged. Silence and secrecy are his watchwords. His object is to keep foreign affairs within a narrow circle of professional diplomatists, and especially to keep them out of the House of Commons. As Prime Minister, Lord Salisbury hardly counts. For the first time since the Administration of Sir Robert Walpole inaugurated the modern system of Premiers and Cabinets, the control of foreign affairs was in 1885 united with the control of the Government. The union has, with brief intermissions, continued ever since. It is a singular one. It combines the most onerous and important of all offices with the superintendence of that and every other. One of two results was inevitable. If there was a Prime Minister, there would be no Foreign Secretary; if there was a Foreign Secretary, there would be no Prime Minister. Lord Salisbury has buried himself in the Foreign Office, and left his colleagues to their own devices. Nobody doubts that his personal administration has been in some respects successful. The Triple Alliance and the Franco-Russian understanding are a poor substitute for the Concert of

Europe. But Lord Salisbury has worked exceedingly
hard. He has made himself a master of his business,
and his dispatches are among the best ever produced.
When he first went to the Foreign Office, in 1878, he
was not supposed to know much about it, and his
French had the worst reputation. It was said to be
almost as bad as Lord Beaconsfield's, whereas Lord
Granville and Sir Charles Dilke spoke it like natives.
But there are more important qualities for a Foreign
Secretary than a good accent or a copious vocabulary.
One of these is prudence ; and Lord Salisbury's official
utterances have been remarkable for prudence. Rash
and rancorous as his tongue can be, he has almost
always, since 1885, kept a watch upon his lips in talking
of other nations. His chief faults have been two : he
has not trusted Parliament or the country; he has
been timid and irresolute in dealing with Great Powers.
He has not Lord Beaconsfield's moral courage, as Prince
Bismarck discovered at the Congress of Berlin. Firm
and even menacing to Portugal, his subservience to
Germany is exaggerated, and sometimes painful. He
has not cultivated France as much as a British Minister
should. He probably yielded to the Queen in forbid-
ding Lord Lytton to attend the opening of the French
Exhibition ; but he ought to have held out.

Lord Salisbury's foreign policy will be finally
estimated when the secrets of all dispatch-boxes are
made known. His patronage—the one function of the
Premiership he really exercises—has been characteristic.
On no subject is he more cynical. He is credited with

the saying that the clergy of the Church of England
might be exhaustively divided into those who were fit to
be bishops, and didn't want to be, and those who wanted
to be bishops, but were unfit to be. His practice has
been based on the assumption that one man is as good
as another, and therefore political convenience alone
need be consulted. It is said that a notorious judicial
appointment was forced upon the Chancellor, who almost
attained the Christian virtue of resignation in consequence. One would like to know who actually sent Sir
Alexander Miller to India. Perhaps Lord Salisbury
feels, like Carteret, "What is it to me who is a Judge
or who is a Bishop? It is my business to make Kings
and Emperors, and to maintain the peace of Europe."

Lord Salisbury has puzzled some of his critics by
a combination of theological orthodoxy with general
incredulity. But the blend is not so rare as it seems to
be thought. There are many men who, having early in
life taken one particular form of religious faith and
ecclesiastical discipline for granted, find their powers of
belief exhausted, and scoff at everything which is not
within the four corners of their creed. "When I speak
of religion," said the Rev. Mr. Thwackum, " I mean
the Christian religion ; and when I say the Christian
religion, I mean the Protestant religion; and by the
Protestant religion, I mean the religion of the Church
of England." Lord Salisbury, notwithstanding his personal amiability, has led, intellectually, an isolated life.
He prefers to work alone. He is not surrounded with
able assistants. He thinks for himself. His under

secretaries have not been men of mark; his private
secretaries are not likely to argue with him.   His
Cabinet contained only two men of first-rate ability
besides himself.   His mind is original, and his ideas
are his own.   His will is not so strong as his understanding, or the bitter enemy of Mr. Disraeli would not
have become the obsequious follower of Lord Beaconsfield.   But his intellectual independence, probably
strengthened by the scientific studies in which he
delights, has earned for him general and well-deserved
respect.

It is perhaps needless to add that Lord Salisbury's
personal character has been always irreproachable.
Moreover, he is incapable of bearing malice.   His
vitriolic sarcasm is a literary product.   It is primarily
intended not to hurt other people, but to amuse himself.   The most serious blot on his career is his misleading answer to Lord Grey about the Anglo-Russian
Agreement in 1878.   That such a thing should still be
remembered with disapprobation is creditable to the
public life of Great Britain and to the straightforward
characters of British statesmen.   Mr. Traill's defence
of it is overstrained and rickety.   To have admitted the
authenticity of the Treaty stolen by a rascal, and published by an evening paper, would not have been injurious to the country.   A refusal to answer would not
have been tantamount to an admission.   Lord Salisbury
deliberately misled the House of Lords and the country;
but he would not, in the ordinary sense of the word,
tell a falsehood.   He spoke by the card, and yet

equivocation undid him, so that his name was used as an odious synonym. He thought he was right. He acted on a theory, and he could cite great moralists on his side. But the crisis did not justify evasion, if any crisis ever can. It was one of those blunders which are worse than crimes.

Mr. Sexton described Lord Salisbury as a bigot by calculation. The phrase is not only felicitous, but true. Lord Salisbury does not hate Roman Catholics or Irish Roman Catholics. But when people are against him in politics, he " goes for them bald-headed." He does not belong to the highest type of statesmen ; but he is much further removed from the lowest. If he has not much hold upon the masses, he interests leisurely and literary folks. Although intensely Conservative, his conservatism is of the utilitarian type. He has singularly little respect either for the stately traditions of the past or for the solemn plausibilities of the world.

MR. BALFOUR.

AFTER the uncle, the nephew. After the Tory Leader of the House of Lords, the Tory Leader of the House of Commons. This may seem like inverting the proper order, and giving an implied sanction to the use of that inaccurate and unauthoritative phrase, the Upper House. But Lord Salisbury—though people are apt to forget it —is Prime Minister as well as Foreign Secretary, and thus entitled, politically as well as socially, to precedence. Nevertheless, Sir William Harcourt was quite right in congratulating Mr. Balfour upon having attained the highest and most honourable post in the British Empire, or indeed in the world. To lead the House of Commons many men would gladly endure years of arduous labour in subordinate situations. Mr. Balfour succeeded Mr. Smith at the age of forty-three, and Lord Randolph led at thirty-seven. Mr. Balfour, with his usual candour, and more than his usual accuracy, has traced much of his success in Ireland to good luck. He has been a fortunate man. Inheriting large estates in early youth, closely allied by birth and friendship with the acknowledged chief of English Conservatism, he was provided with a pocket borough when he was twenty-five, and entered the Cabinet twelve years afterwards. When, in the autumn of 1891, Mr. Smith died and Mr. Balfour

B

stepped into his shoes, Mr. Courtney stigmatised as a fool anyone who said that the new First Lord of the Treasury owed his advancement to nepotism. That is Mr. Courtney's way of signifying dissent. Accidental advantages of family or station confer, not indeed ability or knowledge, but the power and opportunity of using them. A mute inglorious Milton is a much more difficult conception to grasp, but there are mute inglorious Balfours in abundance.

Lord Salisbury had in 1891 to choose between Mr. Balfour and Mr. Goschen. It is unnecessary to suggest that he was biassed in his choice by the ties of kindred. The rank and file of the Conservative party would not have Mr. Goschen at any price—certainly not at the price of his own Consols. He was not one of them, and they did not like him, and the memory of the Public House Endowment Bill was unpleasantly strong. Mr. Balfour's qualifications were obvious and undeniable. He had always been a Conservative—at least, ostensibly and by profession. He had gained as Chief Secretary for Ireland a reputation which, spurious or genuine, was accepted by Conservatives at large as the source of their strength. He had shown skill and courage in debate. His political opponents, or such of them as came into personal contact with him, regarded him with feelings very different from those which are supposed by distant observers to animate Parliamentary antagonists. Mr. Gladstone once said, with a good deal of exaggeration, that a man of forty could no more be made into a member of Parliament than a woman of forty could be made into a ballet-girl. There are numerous instances to confute Mr. Gladstone's theory. But to enter the House young is a distinct advantage, and this fact was properly reckoned among Mr. Balfour's claims.

If Mr. Balfour owes much to his uncle, he owes more to himself. It is well to have a quick apprehension, a clear head, a full and orderly mind. It is, perhaps, better to be liked; and everybody likes Mr. Balfour. Mr. Labouchere plaintively says he knows it's wrong, but he can't help it. What is the particular secret of Mr. Balfour's fascination it would not be easy to say. He is not very witty. He is not very learned. He is not very wise. If Mr. George Wyndham or Mr. Hayes Fisher is taking down his conversation for the benefit of posterity, posterity will not be much obliged to them. He is not in the best sense of the word a great talker, and his serious opinions—if he has any—are reserved for public occasions. Perhaps it is his unaffected simplicity, his entire freedom from ostentation and pretence, his contempt for cant, and his hearty recognition of intellectual capacity in other men which combine to make him so popular and thoroughly agreeable. Something must be added for natural politeness and a keenness of mental sympathy, which is the most attractive of social virtues, as obtuseness is the most tiresome of social crimes. Mr. Balfour is not a man of heroic mould; but nobody is better provided with the small change of life.

Mr. Balfour has been called a great debater; but that is by people who do not understand the House of

B 2

Commons. He is not in the first class. Setting aside
Mr. Gladstone, who is unapproached and unapproach-
able, Mr. Goschen, Sir William Harcourt, Lord Randolph
Churchill, Mr. Chamberlain, and Mr. Sexton are Mr.
Balfour's superiors. So long as Mr. Balfour was in
Opposition he made no mark at all. While he was
Chief Secretary for Ireland he dealt with questions
which few Englishmen cared to understand, and his
deficiencies were only discovered by close observers of
political events. Now that he is Leader of a great
party in the House of Commons, they are patent
to all the world. His merits have long been conspicuous. He is very keen-witted, very clever, very
well informed. The alertness of his mind is as
unusual as it is interesting. He is always for the
moment very much of his own opinion, and what he
says is transparently clear. That is a formidable list
of qualifications, and quite enough to account for Mr.
Balfour's career. He had, however, many adventitious
aids, the greatest of which was that the Irish members,
with the uniform exception of Mr. Parnell, and the
occasional exception of Mr. Healy, never knew how to
deal with him. Mr. Parnell's ascendency over Mr.
Balfour was remarkable. It was the strength of will
and purpose triumphing over mere keenness of intellect.
Mr. Parnell's fall was the most fortunate incident in
Mr. Balfour's life. The ordinary run of Irish National-
ists could not understand that Mr. Balfour was not
to be disturbed by abuse. He was not merely indifferent to it; he positively throve on it. Part of his

stock-in-trade was to read out vituperative extracts from
United Ireland, and to suggest, adroitly enough, that
such language meant, as it would mean in England or
Scotland, a weak case. The real weapon with which to
fight him was ridicule. When Mr. Healy made fun of
him, he collapsed.

Besides his other advantages, Mr. Balfour has a good,
though not an imperturbable, temper, and a wholesome
abhorrence of humbug. His defects are now coming
out. He is an indolent man, and he has never paid the
House of Commons the compliment of preparing his
speeches. His great fault as a debater is the characteristic sin of a bad advocate. He ignores the strongest
points on the other side. He makes a show of comprehensive reply, sneers at a few of his opponents' most
obvious slips or blunders, enunciates a general line of
policy which was not impugned, and sits down without
having touched the main ground of charge. Such, at
least, was his practice as Chief Secretary. His practice
as First Lord has hitherto been to make the sort of
speech which his adversaries would have made for him
if it had been left to them. Everybody who heard or
read the debates on Coercion must recollect the sort of
thing which used to happen. An Irish member would
call attention on the Irish Estimates to the conduct of
a resident magistrate in dispersing a political meeting,
or to the zeal of a policeman in bludgeoning a peaceful
citizen, and would ask the Chief Secretary whether he
approved of such proceedings. Mr. Balfour would
point out some discrepancies of date, place, and the

number of persons concerned. Then, taking up a pile
of newspaper extracts, he would read to the House every
passage in which an Irish newspaper had prefixed to
his name a silly and vulgar epithet. Finally, in an
energetic peroration, loudly cheered from the benches
behind him, he would declare his fixed resolve to stand
by his subordinates on every emergency. But on the
base mechanic question, whether the dispersed assembly
was unlawful, or whether the men assaulted had done
anything wrong, he would throw no light at all. Politically, that may have been Mr. Balfour's wisest course.
But it was not debate ; it was evasion.

The House of Commons, which even in its col-
lective capacity is not infallible, has made two mistakes
about Mr. Balfour. First, it took him for a trifler ;
secondly, it took him for a man of genius. Until he
became Chief Secretary for Ireland, he was not, to use a
theatrical phrase, " in the bill." Since that epoch he
has never been out of it. Six years ago his suicide
would not have excited any morbid degree of sensation
in the public mind. The other day an evening paper
chronicled for the instruction and amusement of its
readers the thrilling fact that his boots were muddy.
It is characteristic of him that he does not boast of his
own achievements, leaving that operation with well-
founded confidence to others. Indeed, Mr. Balfour has
no love of rhetoric and no appreciation of oratory. He
is never eloquent, and he has no natural gift of continuous speech. He has not Lord Salisbury's literary
faculty and ingenious style. His bent is philosophical,

and in metaphysics he can hold his own with professors. On the platform of a Church Congress he has proved, amid clerical applause, the impossibility of being certain that Christianity is not true. In a delightful address at St. Andrews he criticised a rather pedantic discourse by Mr. Frederic Harrison, and pleaded for general licence in reading of books, thus proving himself, as was wittily said at the time, a Coercionist in politics and an Anarchist in literature. Mr. Balfour is a better politician than his uncle. He now represents a great popular constituency. He has no dread or dislike of the masses. Though not devoid of intellectual arrogance, and by no means suffering fools gladly, he is entirely free from aristocratic hauteur, as people have agreed to call an unpleasant mixture of snobbishness and shyness. William of Wykeham was not such a simpleton as to suppose that manners, except in the sense of character and conduct, make a man. But Mr. Balfour's manners disarm his enemies and attract his friends. They have influenced his critics, and caused him to be taken for a much greater man than he is. There is no originality in his ideas, and little wisdom in his methods. If a thing can be logically defended, he assumes that it may be prudently done. He is a Tory because he disbelieves in progress, not because he believes in tradition or Conservatism. His record would be clearer, and his character would stand higher, if he had not cut bad jokes about the sufferings of the Irish members in prison. But he has no vices. He is not even an early riser or a Sabbatarian.

MR. CHAMBERLAIN.

IF in the year 1879, when Mr. Chamberlain described Lord Hartington as the late leader of the Liberal party, and was rebuked by Mr. Fawcett for his rudeness, anyone had prophesied that in the year 1892 Mr. Chamberlain would be playing second fiddle to the Duke of Devonshire, and dancing to the genteelest of Tory tunes, the prophet would have been set down for a lunatic; and perhaps the description would have been accurate. Only those who watched Mr. Chamberlain most closely detected before 1886 the part of his character which has since become so prominent, and it was only in 1885 that people began to watch him closely at all. In that year he attained the summit of his popularity. As the preacher of the Unauthorised Programme, he became everywhere notorious, and for a short—a very short—time his name excited more enthusiasm than Mr. Gladstone's. The fortune of the Unauthorised Programme was made by the Tory Press. The principal, if not the only, articles of the Birmingham faith were allotments, graduated taxation, and free schools. Two of these principles or watchwords have been more or less adopted by the Tories, and even graduated taxation has been to some extent recognised by Mr. Goschen. The alarm of the

Tories was exaggerated and absurd enough. But they had some excuse in Mr. Chamberlain's language rather than in his proposals. The tone of Mr. Chamberlain's speeches at that period was undeniably rancorous. He breathed out threatenings and slaughter against those "who toil not, neither do they spin," perhaps unconscious of the fact that he was comparing them with the lilies of the field. He assailed the wealthy classes with the doctrine of ransom, and it was six years before he discovered that by this phrase or theory he meant pensions for the aged poor. He was universally and persistently misunderstood at the time by Peers and Proletariats, by paupers and millionaires. To the Conservatives in 1885 Mr. Chamberlain was the most dangerous and revolutionary agitator since Jack Cade. To the Radicals he was the leader of the future. To the working classes, or a large portion of them, he was a political standard-bearer, and the herald of the good time coming, when plutocracy and aristocracy should be no more. If anyone desires to know what the spirit of class hatred means, he should study Mr. Chamberlain's oratorical performances in 1884 and 1885.

There were some who saw very little genuine Liberalism, and still less careful thought, in these wild and whirling words. The despotic intolerance which is at the bottom of Mr. Chamberlain's character, and which makes him perhaps the best hated man of his time, showed itself then, as it shows itself now, though it was not so easy to be seen.. It would be a mistake to suppose that even in 1885 the bulk of the working classes were with Mr. Chamberlain. Many intelligent artisans, especially in London, felt and said that the leader of the new Radicalism promised more glibly than he explained, and that his words were a good deal stronger than his reasons.

To understand Mr. Chamberlain, it is necessary to remember two important dates. In May, 1880, he became President of the Board of Trade. In February, 1886, he became, after refusing the Admiralty, President of the Local Government Board. In each case the office was accompanied with a seat in the Cabinet. The six intervening years had not raised Mr. Chamberlain as much as they ought to have done in the estimation of Mr. Gladstone. Mr. Chamberlain entered the Cabinet less than four years after entering Parliament. Mr. Morley accomplished the journey in three years. But Mr. Morley only remained in the Cabinet six months, whereas Mr. Chamberlain's length of tenure was five years. To Mr. Chamberlain's administrative ability emphatic testimony is borne by the highly-trained experts who served under him. They say that his only rival at the Board of Trade in recent times was the late Lord Cardwell. But Mr. Chamberlain quarrelled with the shipowners, and thus lost the chance of passing his most ambitious attempt at legislation, the Merchant Shipping Bill. He was not loved by his colleagues in the Cabinet. He was a determined opponent of the late Mr. Forster, and he refused to attend the complimentary dinner at which Lord

Spencer was entertained on retiring from the Vice-royalty of Ireland. There was not much love lost between John Bright and the new member for Birmingham. In May, 1880, Mr. Chamberlain received from Mr. Gladstone great and possibly unexpected promotion. In February, 1886, when he considered himself at least the second person in the Liberal party, if not the first, he was offered a post he did not like, and on his refusing it, one rather below than above his former level. From this time his flattery of Mr. Gladstone, which had been more copious than refined, suddenly ceased, and has never been resumed.

Mr. Chamberlain's acceptance of office in February, and his resignation in April, are defensible and consistent. He was entitled to join a Home Rule Government, and to say that he could not support Mr. Gladstone's Home Rule Bill. The abruptness with which he broke up the Round Table Conference in 1887 has, on the other hand, never been completely explained. Its immediate result was a cessation of personal intercourse with Sir George Trevelyan, by which Sir George was certainly not the chief loser. A Parliamentary Return of the old friends with which Mr. Chamberlain is not on speaking terms would be an interesting and voluminous document. It would not, however, include Mr. Gladstone, Sir William Harcourt, or Mr. John Morley. The chief reason why Mr. Chamberlain, with all his ability and ingenuity, has so little weight with the public outside Birmingham is the flagrant contrast between his old and his new self. A man may change

his mind without lowering his reputation. He who
never changes his mind is an obstinate fool, and probably has no mind to change. Mr. Chamberlain could
say without any discredit: "I thought Home Rule
right. On further reflection and consideration, I think
it wrong." Or: "I am a Home Ruler, though I do not
believe in Mr. Gladstone's Home Rule." But when he
jeers at demagogic arts, when he expresses contempt for
votaries of "the People with a big P," when he calls
Radicals Nihilists and extols the House of Lords as a
"stately" institution, the extent of the conversion is
too much for ordinary minds. Such tergiversation,
like the elder Sheridan's dulness, is not in nature.

As a Parliamentary speaker Mr. Chamberlain is
almost faultless. He is not indeed eloquent, if by
eloquence is meant what excites the passions or appeals
to the heart. He never raises the tone of a debate or
the mind of an individual. His literary allusions are
confined chiefly to Dickens, and in Dickens chiefly to
"Oliver Twist." He cannot be persuaded that when
Oliver asks for more he enlists the sympathy of the
reader, or that to dub a prophet Cassandra is to pay
him the highest of all possible compliments. He
attributed to Mr. Bright the ancient classic phrase
about "going over to the majority." But his perfect
command of simple and vigorous English, his admirable
lucidity of statement, his power of incisive criticism,
his adroitness and readiness in reply, give him immense
power in the House of Commons, even among those
who most dislike and distrust him. There is only one

great deficiency in Mr. Chamberlain as an orator, and
that is his total lack of humour. Mr. Chamberlain
came into public life with the same sort of contempt for
education and educated people as is expressed by Mr.
Tomlinson, the rich miller, in "Janet's Repentance."
Early as Mr. Chamberlain retired from business, with
an honourable preference of politics for money-making,
he could, as Mr. Tomlinson says, "buy up most of the
educated men he knew." He was not acquainted, and
did not wish to be acquainted, with the past. The
present and the future were enough for him. He has
since travelled, mixed in fashionable society, and read
French novels. Having been to Washington on a
diplomatic mission, he ought to understand the American
Constitution. But when he tried to turn Professor
Bryce the author against Mr. Bryce the politician, he
showed once more that before you can use a book you
must know something more than how to read. When
Mr. Chamberlain was first taunted for his alliance with
the Tories, he replied that his new friends were English
gentlemen, and not Irish rebels. The phrase was an
unhappy and, considering his former relations with Mr.
Parnell, an ungenerous one. But it has given rise to
an unfounded charge. Snobbishness, the worship of rank
and social position, is not among Mr. Chamberlain's
faults. That odious vice implies self-distrust and self-
contempt, which are not qualities characteristic of Mr.
Chamberlain. He thinks too much of himself to be
a sycophant or a toady. Disappointed ambition and
uncontrollable temper have had more to do with his

change of front than any reverence for the "Upper Crust." Though by birth a Londoner, he came to London in 1876 with a provincial hatred and dread of the metropolis. That he should have overcome these prejudices is praiseworthy, and he would not injure the prospects or lower the dignity of the Right Honourable Joseph Chamberlain for all the dukes and duchesses in England.

MR. SPEAKER.

MR. GLADSTONE is sometimes said, even by his admirers, to be deficient in the art of choosing the best men for offices of high responsibility in the State. Whatever truth there may be in the general charge, it certainly does not apply to the holders of the two most important posts in the Parliament of 1886. Mr. Courtney is held by competent judges to have been the best Chairman of Committees within living memory or extant tradition. And if as much could not be said of the present Speaker by the few veterans who remember Mr. Speaker Lefevre before he became Lord Eversley, it is universally acknowledged that Mr. Speaker Peel need not fear comparison with the most illustrious of his predecessors. When, eight years ago, Mr. Speaker Brand stepped down from the chair and elected to merge the old Barony of Dacre in the new Viscounty of Hampden, the image of no obvious successor presented itself to the political eye or the Parliamentary imagination. It is said that the name of Arthur Peel, youngest son of the great Minister, and member for Warwick, was suggested by a junior member of the Government, whose father had been Serjeant-at-Arms, and who might therefore be held to have an hereditary interest in the

order of the House of Commons.   Mr. Peel was at that
time in his fifty-fifth year, and had been for nearly
twenty years in Parliament.   Between 1868 and 1880
he held several subordinate places in Liberal Administrations, and he had for a few months been principal
Whip.   In 1880 he left the Home Office, not, it was
believed, finding Sir William Harcourt an altogether
congenial chief.   That fact, however—if fact it be—
did not prevent Sir William Harcourt from warmly
supporting his claims to the Speakership in 1884.

To the general public the personality of the new
Speaker was hardly known.   He had been, if not exactly
a silent member, a sparing and infrequent contributor
to debate.   Nor, though his remarks were always sensible and his arguments well expressed, had his speeches
arrested any particular attention either in the House
or in the country.   His brother members held him in
high esteem, and were much less surprised than their
constituents at Mr. Gladstone's choice.   Still, the nomination was not expected, and doubts of its wisdom were
freely expressed.   They did not last very long.   When
Mr. Peel had been proposed, seconded, and unanimously
chosen, he delivered an address which took the House
by storm.   It was not only admirable in taste, temper,
and tone, but clothed in felicitous diction and uttered
with imposing dignity of demeanour.   The perfect
manners of the late Lord Hampden had accustomed
the House of Commons to high-bred courtesy from their
presiding officer.   In the new Speaker they found that,
and something more.   His fine presence and sonorous

voice were accompanied by a certain lofty stateliness, as if this quiet representative of a sleepy Midland borough, since amalgamated with the fashionable watering-place of Leamington, had been preparing himself in a comparatively private station to appear one day in full-blown majesty as First Commoner of the realm. More austere and frigid in deportment than Lord Hampden, Mr. Speaker never forgets his position, and sometimes magnifies his office. There is a man who played a practical joke upon him, and who still lives—nay, even thrives; but it is the unanimous opinion of the jester's friends that he will never try that form of diversion again.

Lord Holland said that he had only known one Speaker of first-rate ability, and that the worst Speaker he had ever known. He referred to Lord Grenville, whom Lord Rosebery, in his "Life of Pitt," describes in unusually disparaging terms. If it be true that Mr. Goschen was only prevented by the defective range of his vision from succeeding Mr. Speaker Brand, the shrewd observation of Lord Holland was within an ace of being strengthened by a new instance. It is seldom, indeed, that anyone of Mr. Goschen's calibre dreams of shrouding his talents and capacities beneath the canopy and the wig. Sir Gilbert Elliot, afterwards first Earl of Minto, was offered the post at the age of thirty-five. But if he ever had any idea of taking it, he was soon laughed out of the notion by his lively and ambitious wife. Cleverness is not an indispensable quality in a Speaker. He is assisted by the clerks in cases of difficulty; he has a counsel to advise him on

c

points of law. Abundance of precedents hedge his
course and preserve him from going far astray. He
has plenty of time in which to make up his mind,
unless very exceptional circumstances should suddenly
arise, and then he has the advantage of being able
to impose his will on all the combatants. The essential
qualities in a Speaker are courtesy, dignity, imperturbability, and fairness of mind. He must be in the
real, not the conventional, sense of the word, a
gentleman. He must be able to detach himself from
party strife and from personal predilections. He must
never let technicalities, so far as he can control them,
stand in the way of justice. He must have the spirit
of a judge, without the mind of a lawyer.

The Speaker has earned for himself in a very short
time a very great reputation. He has made mistakes,
as when he allowed Colonel Saunderson to accuse his
opponents of consorting with men whom they knew to
be murderers, and when he showed that he had read a
foolish attack upon himself by a very inconsiderable
member of Parliament. But his errors have not been
numerous, and they were so clearly the blunders of an
impulsive, generous, high-minded man that they rather
increased his influence and popularity than otherwise.
Not very long after his appointment a number of Tories,
among them the present Lord Chancellor, almost drove
him to resign by voting against the Closure, and nearly
defeating it. That, it must be remembered, was when
the Closure could only be put on the Speaker's initia-
tive, acting on what he conceived to be the general

sense of the House. In the early part of the present Parliament the Speaker came into slight collision with some of the Liberal leaders, especially his old friend, Sir William Harcourt. More recently he caused some resentment by reading the Liberal party a lecture on the impropriety of multiplying Instructions when a Bill goes into Committee.

These are specks on the sun ; and very small specks, too. Nobody—or at least nobody whose opinion is worth having—suspects the Speaker of conscious partiality. His fault is rather that he takes too much interest in things, and makes himself responsible for what really belongs to the jurisdiction of the House itself. The old-fashioned Speaker sat like a stuffed figure, and only moved—if the phrase may be pardoned, —when he was pulled with a string. The present Speaker is extremely jealous for the honour, authority, and decorum of the assembly over which he presides, and of which he is the mouthpiece. If in zeal for the House of Commons he sometimes appears to go beyond his exact functions as the guardian of order, the failing is one which leans to virtue's side. If his sensitive magnanimity has been now and then wounded by incidents unworthy of serious notice, that, again, is the natural weakness of a high and simple character. When the House of Commons has to be represented before the public, the Speaker appears at his best. The debate, or rather the series of wrangles, on the breach of privilege committed by the directors of the Cambrian Railway was not creditable to the House. They began

c 2

in something very like confusion ; they ended in
something very like tumult.   It lay with the Speaker
to redeem the reputation of the mother of Parliaments,
and nobly he performed the task.   The position was a
trying one.   The directors, like everybody else, knew
that they had escaped, and that they could not even be
compelled to reinstate the man they had dismissed.
The Speaker was like a judge who is called upon to
pass sentence, and has no sentence to pass.   Yet he
contrived to save the situation.   No trace of the exciting
conflict which had been surging round him was suffered
to intrude upon his calm and serious sternness.   His
rebuke was a superb performance, which remains on
record while the noise and turbulence have vanished
into space.   Only a great Speaker could on that
occasion have protected the righteous assertion of
Parliamentary privilege from being dragged into an
ignominious farce.

THE DUKE OF ARGYLL.

THAT the Duke of Argyll is one of the foundations of society we have his own implied authority for believing. Whether there can be more than one foundation of the same structure it would perhaps be hypercritical to inquire. Certainly the Duke of Argyll is neither unseen nor unheard. He has been all his life conspicuous, and he has—if anything, a little too obviously—enjoyed the fact. He is a wit among Dukes, in the old-fashioned sense of a degraded word. He is the only Duke who can write, and, except the Duke of Devonshire, the only Duke who can speak. He never forgets that he is a Duke, nor, indeed, do any of his natural or acquired advantages ever for a moment escape from the range of his conscious admiration. It was his ancestor that Burns described as "My Lord, their God, his Grace." It was to him that Lord Rosebery applied his happy phrase, "the portentous political pedagogue." Highly blessed and endowed as he is, the Duke lacks one thing. He has not the most elementary sense of humour, a defect which is, perhaps, the only characteristic he has succeeded in bequeathing to the Marquis of Lorne. As an aristocrat, the

Duke of Argyll despises statesmen and men of science
such as Mr. Darwin and Mr. Gladstone. As a man of
science and letters, he despises the illiterate aristocracy.
His self-adoration is undisturbed by the shadow of
a doubt in his own absolute infallibility. He has
lately told the world that he always hated the Whigs,
although he condescended to accept office from Lord
Palmerston. His political idol is the younger Pitt.
Pitt entered public life as a Whig, and never disclaimed
the title of a party whose principles he claimed to
represent better than Fox. But the Duke of Argyll
thinks little more favourably of the Free Traders than
of the Whigs. He regards himself as almost the only
consistent Free Trader who ever lived, while Cobden,
and Bright, and Mr. Charles Villiers were only plausible
impostors. Ricardo knew no more about political
economy than Darwin knew about natural history, and
Mr. Gladstone's conceptions of politics are fundamentally
erroneous. The Duke's opinion of his contemporaries,
with the exception of the seventh Earl of Shaftesbury
and the eighth Duke of Argyll, is a deplorably low
one. With the death of the eminent philanthropist
departed, in the Duke's opinion, his only rival for
the moral crown. Intellectual rival he never had, nor
social superior. He permitted his eldest son to connect
himself by marriage with the Royal Family. He
bestows his patronage upon the Queen, and when his
Sovereign created him a Duke of the United Kingdom
he made a public speech upon the topic, which was
gracious in the extreme. The Duke deplores the follies

of the world and the ignorance of mankind with a solemn pathos which he, doubtless, means to be sincere. But if everyone were as good and as wise as himself, he would not be so supremely happy as he is. "They'd rather that the Dean should die than their prediction prove a lie," says Swift of the prophets who concerned themselves with the probable date of his demise. The Duke has so often foretold the ruin of his country if it did not follow his advice—and unhappily, it very seldom does—that its continued prosperity sometimes gives him a passing qualm.

The Duke of Argyll resembles in some respects the first Lord Brougham, who was also—or so he flattered himself—a man of ancient descent. Macaulay called Brougham, in language which exactly applies to the Duke, "a kind of semi-Solomon, half knowing everything from the cedar to the hyssop." But Macaulay, who had no love for Brougham, admitted that his Parliamentary speaking was of the highest possible order. So is the Duke of Argyll's. A born orator, with a musical voice of great compass and penetration, he has an easy flow of language, which he regulates with consummate art. It is not easy to be heard in the House of Lords; but the Duke, unless physical weakness restrains him, is always audible and distinct. It is his misfortune that he never sat in the House of Commons, where he would have made his mark, and might have learned some lessons. In the House of Lords his best speeches were made against the political adventures of Lord Beaconsfield. The adventurer himself, who had never heard the Duke before, was quite astonished, and pronounced him at once the best speaker among the Peers. The bitterness with which the Duke of Argyll then attacked Lord Salisbury was unusual even in an Assembly where the Speaker has no power to enforce order. He accused Lord Salisbury of deliberate mendacity, and persisted in the charge. His famous apostrophe to the Peers in the Government, "My lords, you are beginning to be found out," may have been in questionable taste, but it excited much sensation in the House and in the country. On that occasion, as at the time of the American Civil War, the Duke of Argyll, with courage and sagacity, set himself against the prevalent prejudices of his own class. He was a resolute Northerner and a determined foe of Turkish oppression in Europe. With Mr. Gladstone, Lord Russell, and the late Lord Granville, who sat in Lord Aberdeen's Cabinet, and were responsible for the Crimean War, he condemned root and branch the Eastern policy of Lord Beaconsfield. He inveighed against it with his tongue and with his pen only less vigorously and copiously than Mr. Gladstone himself. At that time the Duke of Argyll passed for an advanced Liberal. It was on the delicate question of land and the sacred institution of landlords that he separated himself from Mr. Gladstone and the Liberal party. It was then that he politely compared his old colleagues, including Mr. Chamberlain and the present Duke of Devonshire, with a set of jelly-fish.

Archbishop Magee said of John Bright that he

divided his opponents into knaves and fools, with the third class of bishops, who united the characteristics of both the others. The Duke of Argyll makes no such nice distinctions. Those who differ from him are bad as well as stupid. In his view their blindness is judicial. They are punished by mental obtuseness for not accepting the gospel of Inverary. Mr. Gladstone's case puzzles the Duke extremely. The Duke sets great value upon orthodoxy in religion, and he cannot deny that Mr. Gladstone's religion is orthodox. Perhaps the explanation may be found in the fact that Mr. Gladstone is not a Presbyterian. But that only gets over the least serious part of the difficulty. Mr. Gladstone was not only brought up in the true faith which unites Presbyterians with Episcopalians; he has enjoyed the rich and precious privilege of sitting several times in the same Cabinet with the Duke of Argyll. Every opportunity of learning the truth has thus been presented to him, and nothing short of invincible ignorance can save him from the consequences of disbelieving the ducal message to mankind. Mr. Gladstone's only consolation—and that a poor one—is that those who have successively fallen under the Duke of Argyll's displeasure are numerous in quantity and various in quality. Ricardo wrote a treatise as abstract and as disconnected with morals as Euclid, for the malignant purpose of keeping down wages. Cobden only cared for the interests of his own class. Disraeli was a charlatan. Lord Salisbury told lies. The Duke of Devonshire is a jelly-fish. Mr. Chamberlain is no

better. The members of the present Government are
unspeakably mean and base. Lord Shaftesbury is
dead. If the Duke of Argyll were to be removed from
us, it would be the most tragic event in human history
since the decease of Sir John Falstaff. The late Mr.
Justice Maule, a much cleverer man than the Duke, but
by no means such a model of all the virtues, remarked
that public schools turned out sad dogs, and that private
schools were responsible for poor devils. Neither the
Duke of Argyll, nor Mr. Chamberlain, nor Sir William
Harcourt had the discipline which Maule considered so
bracing. Yet they are not distinguished for embarrass-
ing bashfulness or shrinking timidity. There is a
story told of another Duke, that when he presented
himself to Keate for his second flogging within twelve
hours, the illustrious pedagogue condescended to ob-
serve : " Your Grace is unlucky to-day." It is possible
that some such early correction, if bestowed rather in
sorrow than in anger, might have done the Duke of
Argyll no harm. He never came under the chastening
influence of a university, but burst upon the world in
the full panoply of the MacCallum More. Mr. Froude,
while disclaiming the character of a social leveller,
inclines to think that there should be no Dukes. They
dazzle him, he says. They are too bright and good—
he was, perhaps, thinking of the late Duke of Sutherland or the late Duke of Marlborough—for human
nature's daily food. The Duke of Argyll has dabbled
in science, and in the course of his lucubrations has
called Professor Huxley much what he called Lord

Salisbury. It never seems to have struck him, in bringing wholesale charges of interested motives against legislators and political economists, that he was open to any such suspicion himself. Yet he is a landlord, and the cause of the landlord has no more eloquent advocate. It was on the question of land, not on the question of Home Rule, that he separated himself from the Liberal party. His opposition to the Irish Land Bill of 1881 was an instance of *"Proximus ardet Ucalegon."* He knew it might be his own turn next; and so it was. The Crofter Commission reduced his rents, and decided that his Crofter tenants had been paying him for the improvements they had themselves made upon his land. The Duke has now developed into a thorough-going Tory, and his feudal instincts are almost as strong as Mr. Chamberlain's.

MR. MICHAEL DAVITT.

MR. MICHAEL DAVITT was, with the possible exception of Mr. Edward Blake, the most interesting and remarkable of the new members of this Parliament. His entrance into the House of Commons added little or nothing to his own influence or fame; but, on the other hand, he was one of the most notable figures in that assembly. It is curious that an Irish patriot of such eminence and ability should have been defeated in his first candidature, and should have had a hard fight in his second. The reason, of course, is that he preferred to contest Parnellite strongholds rather than places where his return would have been a foregone conclusion. For Mr. Davitt is an ardent Nationalist, and a loyal member of the Irish Parliamentary party. No more striking tribute has been paid to the strength of the Nationalist cause, and the prudence of its leaders, than the adhesion of Mr. Davitt. Mr. Davitt, as everybody knows, was in youth an active Fenian, and spent some of the best years of his life in penal servitude for treason-felony. His political opinions are much more Socialistic than those of his Parliamentary colleagues, and during the reign of Mr. Parnell he was not on the best of terms with Mr. Parnell's principal lieutenants. For Mr. Parnell himself he had a profound admiration, and never lifted a finger to dispute the authority of the Chief. But when Ireland had to choose between a constitutional alliance with British Liberalism and the desperate struggle of a disappointed man for the recovery of his personal ascendency, Mr. Davitt joined the Constitutionalists without a moment's hesitation. If Mr. Gladstone's Irish policy had achieved nothing else than the conversion of Mr. Davitt, it would not have been fruitless. Before 1886 Mr. Davitt, though he trusted Mr. Parnell, gravely doubted the efficacy of political agitation as a weapon for obtaining Home Rule. It was in frank acknowledgment of Mr. Gladstone's wisdom and sincerity that he fell into line with the general body of Nationalist politicians. Nothing could be more creditable to Mr. Davitt. It was Mr. Gladstone's Government that prosecuted him in 1870; it was Mr. Gladstone's Government that revoked his ticket-of-leave, and sent him back to Portland in 1881. When the interests of his country are concerned, Mr. Davitt is incapable of personal feeling. He may not be always judicious; he may not sufficiently realise the truth of the maxim that if speech is silver, silence is golden; but his keenest and bitterest opponents admit his transparent sincerity, his chivalrous sense of honour, and his absolute devotion to the cause of Ireland. In Ireland the name of Michael Davitt is something more than a household word. Even at the height of the lamentable quarrel to which the deposition of Mr. Parnell gave rise, the cowardly assault upon Mr. Davitt, for which, like Mr. O'Brien, he refused to prosecute, excited universal indignation.

The characteristic qualities of the intellectual and gentleman-like party have been well illustrated in their references to Mr. Davitt. Some of their lower organs in the Press think it dignified and becoming to call him " Davitt." The fact that when he was twenty-four he engaged in a criminal conspiracy to procure the restoration of his country's freedom by force has been made the excuse for denouncing him as unfit for the society of honest men. Chief Justice Cockburn's suggestion, founded on an ambiguous letter, that he had been engaged in a plot to murder somebody is still repeated without the full explanation given by Mr. Davitt himself to the Special Commissioners. Because in 1882, being in gaol for felony, he was ineligible for Parliament, the jurists and pundits who follow the Duke of Devonshire and Mr. Chamberlain gravely argue that, although his sentence expired in 1885, he must be ineligible now. Their way of putting the argument is even more edifying than the argument itself. They describe Mr. Davitt as " disqualified by a vote of the House of Commons." They might as well say that he was disqualified by a vote of the Ulster Convention, for the House of Commons has no more power to disqualify anybody than, as Sir Fletcher Norton elegantly put it, "so many drunken porters." Mr. Davitt used himself, it is believed, to feel scruples about taking the oath of allegiance to the British Sovereign; but that was before Mr.

Gladstone had recognised the rights of the Irish people.

Mr. Davitt's abilities as a speaker are of a very high order indeed. He is fluent—if anything, too fluent. He is in deadly earnest. He is capable, when deeply moved, of genuine eloquence. In describing, before the Special Commission, the scenes of hardship and suffering which he had witnessed as a boy, he drew signs of rare emotion from the impassive countenance of Mr. Parnell. Lord Hannen and his colleagues were delighted with Mr. Davitt. No doubt, being a hostile tribunal, they relished his candid admissions—admissions so candid as to raise the question whether he would not have done better to retire from the case with Sir Charles Russell and the other counsel retained. But there was something about Mr. Davitt's manly, straightforward appearance in the witness-box which favourably impressed even the most bigoted Coercionist. It would probably not be denied by Mr. Davitt's warmest admirers that he was anxious to vindicate his position as the real founder and originator of the Land League. A man who has been three times imprisoned for his political faith can afford to be self-assertive without dreading the charge of egoism; and certainly it would be the height of absurdity and the depth of imbecility to accuse Mr. Davitt of undue personal ambition. More than almost any other Irishman, he has toiled for the advancement and regeneration of the working classes. In pleading for the farmers, he did not forget the artisans, and his relations with

the labour party in England are very close. The
doctrines of Mr. Henry George which he professes, or
at least professed, have not been made popular in
Ireland, even by him. The Irish peasant is an
individualist to the backbone. But as editor of *The
Labour World* he has acquired a good deal of power
among the class which lives by weekly wages on
this side St. George's Channel, and his most recent
speeches have urged his countrymen to co-operate in
obtaining social reforms for Great Britain. Two of
Mr. Davitt's phrases have become commonplaces of the
Irish controversy. One contains the famous image
of the "wolf-dog of Irish vengeance bounding across
the Atlantic," which was at the time he used it as
accurate as it was vivid. The other introduced the
familiar simile of breakfast, dinner, and supper, which
gave the Tories an occasion for saying that Mr. Davitt,
at all events, did not regard Home Rule as final. But
when the context came to be examined, the disestablishment of the Irish Church appeared to be Mr. Davitt's
idea of breakfast, and the Land Acts had supplied
his dinner, leaving the programme to be completed by
a supper of Home Rule.

Mr. Davitt's recollection goes back almost to the
great famine, and probably covers the cruel evictions
which followed it. He exemplifies the truth of John
Bright's familiar saying that the people of Ireland were
anxious to cross the three thousand miles of ocean and
join hands with the great Republic of the West. His
parents emigrated to the United States in his early

youth, and his own ways of thought are in many
respects more American than Irish. As a thorough
Radical, however, he is quite at home among the British
Democracy, and a very popular speaker on English platforms. It would be important that Mr. Davitt should
be in Parliament even if he did not succeed there; for
he is a thoroughly representative man, and nobody else
could exactly fill his place. It is quite true, as Mr.
Lecky says, that in the time of O'Connell, and ever
since, Irish members have given valuable assistance to
the cause of progress and reform. It is also true that
closer intercourse with America has made Ireland more
Democratic than she used to be. But still, Mr. Davitt
does not belong to any ordinary type of Irish Nationalist.
He is more of a philosopher and a theorist, less conventional and provincial than most of his colleagues.
It is a wonderful thing, which may well make the
comfortable classes ashamed of themselves, that a man
kept for years in what the Lord Chief Justice of
England has called a state of slavery should have employed the period of his punishment and seclusion, not
in indulging bitterness and planning vengeance, but in
thinking out schemes for the use and benefit of his
fellow-countrymen. Mr. Davitt's published account of
his life and experience in prison is full of strange and
painful interest. The jury who found him guilty were
probably right on the evidence, and Sir Alexander
Cockburn, who sentenced him, was by no means a
vindictive judge. When Sir William Harcourt, as
Home Secretary, revoked Mr. Davitt's licence in 1881,

D

he very sensibly and humanely directed that Mr. Davitt should be treated as a first-class misdemeanant. It would have been a thousand times better, though quite without precedent, if either the Judge himself or Lord Aberdare, who was then at the Home Office, had given such a direction in 1870. Countries far behind Great Britain in many of the things which make up civilisation put political prisoners on a different level and treat them in a different fashion from other and more sordid criminals. Society is justified in protecting itself from armed attempts at revolution; but the instance of Mr. Davitt, with whom men and women of the highest character are proud to associate, is a valuable warning against the fatal blunder which confounds necessary precautions with degrading penalties.

MR. BRYCE.

Mr. Bryce is probably the best informed and best educated man in the House of Commons. In the array of monsters which *Punch* exhibited as the new Cabinet, Mr. Bryce was considerately consigned to the corner, and disguised in academical costume. He has been Regius Professor of Civil Law at Oxford, and as such has, in excellent Latin, presented many a celebrity for his honorary degree. Years, almost centuries, ago he led up Lord Wolseley—then Sir Garnet Wolseley—to the most dignified Vice-Chancellor Oxford has ever seen. Dr. Liddell sat in his chair of state, himself more dignified and impressive than any outward pomp and show could make him. Professor Bryce referred, in the Latin tongue, to the capture of Coomassie, and the defeat of King Coffee Calcali. *"Urbem incendit,"* he said of the gallant general, and was greeted with cries of mock deprecation. *"Plebi pepercit,"* he added, and there were loud ironical cheers. Why sparing the people should excite laughter, and burning the city approval, the undergraduate conscience must decide. Mr. Bryce went dryly on, without regard for interruption or applause. He has always done the same. He has never quite acted up to his encyclopædic knowledge and

D 2

enormous powers. Mr. Disraeli said that the English
people did not like professors : nobody dislikes Mr.
Bryce. On the contrary, he is universally popular, and
everybody is glad of his success. Even the House of
Commons, with all its ignorance and prejudice, likes
a man of real learning. Mr. Bryce never parades his
information or obtrudes the professor. On the contrary, he makes, if anything, too little of himself.
Somebody at Oxford, being perplexed for a fact or a
date, said : "Look it up in Bryce." He did not mean
any of Mr. Bryce's books, but Mr. Bryce himself. A
reputation of that sort is not lightly acquired at Oxford,
where everybody professes to know a great deal more
than he does.

Mr. Bryce's career offers a fine chance for the astro-
logers. Mr. Bryce was born in 1838. If it could be
proved that between that year and 1892 anyone had
cast Mr. Bryce's horoscope, and predicted that Mr.
Bryce would be Chancellor of the Duchy of Lancaster,
astrology would be justified of her children, and the
Astronomer-Royal would have to take a back seat. Mr.
Bryce entered Parliament in 1880 as member for the
Tower Hamlets. He signalised himself during the
contest by addressing a section of his constituents in
German. But a metropolitan constituency is a difficult
place for a serious politician who has anything else to
do, and in 1885 Mr. Bryce migrated to the good old
city of Aberdeen. It has been said, in one of those
rash and culpable generalisations which disfigure
modern criticism, that a metropolitan member has no

time for politics. He is expected, so these flippant
speculators assert, to attend bazaars on Saturday after-
noons, to have tea with the Dissenters on Wednesday
evenings, and to sup on Sundays with the infidel clubs.
But this category or programme takes no account of
the many calls from Westminster to remote districts
throughout the week. Mr. Bryce sought refuge in
Scotland. He became, in Mr. Gladstone's third Administration, Under Secretary of State for Foreign
Affairs, and the exponent of Lord Rosebery's views in
the House of Commons. But Mr. Bryce is by no
means a type of the " Under Secretary whose chief is in
the Lords." Lord Beaconsfield, in " Endymion," has
given an inimitable description of that class. Walder-
share is so much impressed with his own greatness
when he reaches that stage of political development that
he constructs a gallery for receiving the portraits of
Under Secretaries whose chiefs were in the Lords. He
regards them as the greatest of God's creatures. Everyone knows the type. Mr. Bryce does not belong to it.
He is a hard-headed, keen-witted, half Scottish Ulster-
man, educated to the highest possible level, equally
conversant with ancient and modern languages, whose
place in any Ministry is an accident, whose position in
the world of intellect is secure.

Mr. Bryce is, of course, much more than a simple
politician. He is one of the few men who have
ascended Ararat. He ranks among the greatest
legal and constitutional authorities in Europe. He
has written a book about the United States which

anybody can read, and which a few people pretend that they can remember. In Germany Mr. Bryce would rank even higher than he ranks here. In the House of Commons he has never quite done justice to his great knowledge and capacity. Occasionally, as in his reply to Mr. Chamberlain about the powers of American tribunals, he is admirably neat and precise. Every now and then, as in his speech at the Eighty Club introducing Mr. Blake, he is peculiarly graceful and distinguished. But as a rule, Mr. Bryce speaks below his abilities. He writes better than he speaks. The interest of the reader, as in Gibbon, never flags, because the interest of the author is always sustained. Mr. Bryce, as becomes a man who has seen, or claims to have seen, the ark, is a warm friend of the Eastern population, and a constant enemy of Turkish tyranny. The Armenians owe much to him, and the Greeks are largely in his debt. But Mr. Bryce has not made as much of these interesting nationalities in the House of Commons as would have been made by many inferior persons. Mr. Bryce offers a curious contrast to another well-known member of Parliament, Mr. Chaplin. Mr. Chaplin has a good voice, an impressive manner, and a gesticulation which is a sort of compound of Mr. Gladstone at his best and Mr. Disraeli at his worst; but he has absolutely nothing to say. Mr. Bryce is brimful of information, which he has thoroughly digested, and over which he has entire control. It is the power of bringing it out which occasionally fails, and which makes some of

Mr. Bryce's speeches, like Pindar's odes, only intelligible to the well-informed. But when all is said and done, few men have brought more strength and character to Mr. Gladstone's Cabinet than the member for North Aberdeen.

MR. CAMPBELL-BANNERMAN.

THERE is probably no man living who has talked less nonsense than Mr. Campbell-Bannerman. When that hopeful youth, Branwell Brontë, was asked if he proposed to enter holy orders, he replied that he had no qualification for the Ministry except hypocrisy. That is, perhaps, the one qualification for another sort of Ministry that Mr. Campbell-Bannerman lacks. There is too much *nuda veritas* about him. Like Boileau, he calls a cat a cat and Howard Vincent a bore. He does not, with Tennyson's orator, charm us till the lion looks no larger than the cat. Mr. Campbell-Bannerman's shrinking and sensitive nature must have suffered severely from the notoriety of his famous phrase about " finding salvation." He is not by any means a Salvationist, though in the freedom of conversation he adopted the language of Mr. Booth. Lord Beaconsfield once complained that he had suffered from the " misplaced laughter of another." It is the misplaced seriousness of another of which Mr. Campbell-Bannerman has reason to complain ; for what Mr. Campbell-Bannerman whispered in the ear, the object of his confidence proclaimed on the platform. Hence it is that a comfortable, easy-going man of the world figures in

contemporary history as a sort of fanatical energumen—
an unpleasant mixture of unctuous fervour and professional cant. Mr. Campbell-Bannerman has himself
to thank if he is not better known and better understood. There are very few abler men in the Government
or the House of Commons. But he makes no fuss and
no show. He does not sufficiently sacrifice to the
glorified spirit of self-advertisement which presides over
the new era. He cannot always get up what may,
perhaps, be called, without injuring respectable suscepti-
bilities, the moral steam. He happened to be Secretary
of State for War when the long and bitter agitation
against recognising vice came to its inevitable and
highly desirable close. He disappointed the zealots on
both sides. He refused to be excited or perturbed. He
treated the question from the military and utilitarian
point of view, without adopting the official doctrine of
necessity. The result was that while neither party
cheered him with enthusiasm, both parties listened to
him with respect. When Thwackum and Square have
had their say, Allworthy, prig as he is, strikes in with
considerable effect. Mr. Campbell-Bannerman is not
a prig; but he has a judicial mind—he is free from
prejudice and passion. When he speaks, people listen,
attend, and are convinced.

An eminent statesman said the other day that there
was no office under the Crown for which Mr. Campbell-
Bannerman was not fit. His return to the War Office
gave great satisfaction to the inmates of that rather
chaotic establishment. The War Office requires a strong

hand and resents a rough one. There are a good many
people to be kept in order, from the Duke of Cambridge
downwards. The present Secretary of State is just the
man for the post. Everybody who knows him likes
him, and he is the more liked the better he is known.
He made a superb Chief Secretary for Ireland, though,
unfortunately, his reign was brief. The Irish members
were then at enmity with the Liberal party, and they
"tried it on," half in fun, as their manner is, with Mr.
Campbell-Bannerman. But they found the game so
dull that they very soon left it off. The imperturbable
geniality, the serene good humour, of the Chief Secretary
were too much for them. They gave him up in despair.
You can be angry with a man who laughs at you; a
man who laughs with you is irresistible, and in the long
run unassailable. Mr. Bannerman resembles in some
respects the celebrated Duke of Wharton, that strange
product of the glorious Revolution. The Duke was a
vicious man, and Mr. Bannerman is a virtuous one.
But one is as pachydermatous as the other was.
The wits of Queen Anne's reign tilted at Wharton,
whose manners and excesses afforded them abundant
scope for invective. He only laughed at their
jokes, and cursed them good-humouredly for their
pains. Mr. Parnell, in some interview or other,
enumerated with candid comments the Chief Secretaries he had known. Of Mr. Campbell-Bannerman
he had nothing to say except that nothing could be
made of him. Like the elderly British spinster who
walked unharmed among the lions of Africa, he was

too tough. Yet he did not, like that heaven-born statesman Mr. Balfour, set himself to irritate and annoy the men with whom he had to deal. Being a statesman of a more mundane type, he treated the Irish members in a conciliatory fashion, assumed that their objects were the same as his own, and mildly indicated some unlucky differences of detail. Mr. Balfour's methods may have been very magnificent; but they were not politics, and they were not common sense. Men of Mr. Campbell-Bannerman's type are invaluable in diminishing the friction which accompanies the management of all human affairs. They do not originate anything; they have no great ideas. But the geniuses, of whom there may be three in a century, could not get on without them. Fifty James Watts would not dispense with the need for the man in fustian and his oil-can.

It is believed that nobody has ever seen Mr. Campbell-Bannerman out of temper. This quality or deficiency sometimes produces a kind of counter-irritation in other men. The present Lord Justice-General of Scotland used almost literally to dance with fury when Mr. Campbell-Bannerman poked fun at him. But with more sensible folks the effect is more agreeable, and Mr. Bannerman is almost as popular on the other side of the House as on his own. At Stirling his constituents thoroughly appreciate him, and give him very little trouble about his seat. *The Scotsman* gravely rebukes him; but if *The Scotsman* were not edited by an Englishman, it would go far to justify English calumnies about Scottish lack of humour. Mr. Bannerman is himself a typical Scot—of the hard-headed, unemotional type. The ease and charm of his personal manner are peculiarly his own. The late lamented Professor Henry Smith, so well known in Oxford Common rooms and scientific gatherings, used to say, " Young men will be serious. When they come to my age they will find that seriousness is the worst joke out." The remark was open to criticism, and was not calculated to fill the undergraduate with good desires or lofty aims ; but, like everything Henry Smith said, it contained a spice of truth. Some youthful politicians, especially youthful Liberals, might with advantage take a leaf out of Mr. Campbell-Bannerman's book. Whatever they may think, the eyes of the world are not on them. They should avoid the error—which is not noble, and is not seldom made—of explaining their motives to people who are not concerned in their acts. It is a great mistake to suppose that the population of these islands, or any appreciable part of it, spend their holidays in wondering why Mr. So-and-So had taken such a place, and what effect his taking it would have upon Mr. Gladstone's policy. The brutal world persists in thinking that these young gentlemen have had uncommonly good luck, and will be very glad within altered circumstances to do what Mr. Gladstone tells them. Much to be commended is the answer of him who, when asked why he had accepted a particular office, rejoined, " Did you ever hear of a fellow called Hobson ? " Morbid self-consciousness is new-fangled in politics, and is not English.

Public schools were supposed to eradicate it; but they seem to have failed in this respect, as in so many others. Mr. Campbell-Bannerman may be, as is said, fond of French novels, but he is a type of manly British sense, of straightforward, unaffected vigour and ability.

MR. BURT.

No Liberal will ever forget the month of December, 1890. Committee Room Fifteen has left its impress upon English as well as upon Irish politics. In Scotland, opinion was the more excited and embittered because Mr. Parnell had been recently presented with the freedom of the City of Edinburgh. At the height of the hubbub, when the political atmosphere was full of poisonous miasma, and even the Prime Minister, in the House of Lords, had been joking about a national crisis in the style of a music-hall comedian, the Eighty Club entertained as their principal guest the member for Morpeth, Mr. Thomas Burt. It is the well-known practice of that institution to invite eminent Liberals to dine and to address the club on public affairs. The opportunity has never been abused, except by Mr. Chamberlain, whose violent attack upon his immediate predecessor, Mr. Goschen, was in painfully bad taste. But perhaps nobody ever made a better use of the occasion than Mr. Burt. At that time of acrimonious controversy over a disagreeable subject, in which the lowest type of politician positively revelled, the mere presence and personality of Mr. Burt were wholesome and refreshing. Nothing could be more ludicrously unlike the typical demagogue of the Tory imagination than Mr. Burt. The son of a working collier, once a working collier himself, he was born thirty-three years before compulsory education, and what he learned he taught himself. Yet a more perfect example of all the essential qualities in the character of an English gentleman could not be found in either House of Parliament. His speech to the Eighty Club dealt chiefly with the politics of labour. But it was impossible altogether to avoid the topic of the hour, and Mr. Burt's reference to the great causes which could not be impeded by personal misconduct was exactly the proper medicine for the prevalent complaint.

Mr. Burt has represented the same constituency in the House of Commons for the continuous period of eighteen years, during which he has never had a serious contest, and only once had a contest at all. He succeeded a typical Whig, the late Sir George Grey, whose grandson is one of the rising hopes of the Liberal party. The transition from Sir George Grey to Mr. Burt was an abrupt one. But Morpeth in that respect only illustrated a general tendency, if not a general rule. Mr. Burt entered Parliament at a period of profound political repose. The policy of the late Mr. Forster, and the consequent dejection of the Dissenters, had the curious and rather illogical result of placing Mr. Disraeli in power. He came unpledged to anything in particular, except to leave people alone. There was on the horizon no sign of the foreign troubles which within three years were to convulse the nation, and which drove Lord Beaconsfield from office when he appealed to the country. In those days the two special representatives of the working classes in the House of Commons were Mr. Thomas Burt and Mr. Alexander Macdonald. Mr. Macdonald was a failure. He is long since dead, and it would be useless to inquire now why he did not succeed. But a certain pretentiousness of manner and behaviour on his part served to heighten the effect of Mr. Burt's modest simplicity. The House of Commons judges men on the whole fairly, and without the slightest reference to their political opinions. Mr. Burt from the first commanded an esteem and attracted a regard which Tories feel as much as Liberals, and which have steadily increased since 1874.

Mr. Burt was never seen at greater advantage than in the chair at the Trades Union Congress at Newcastle in the autumn of 1891. The assembly was a very large, a very independent, and not a very quiet one. The chairman had no power to put down a revolt of his authority by penal methods. On the burning question of a legislative eight-hours day he was strongly opposed to the majority. Yet, by keeping his temper, by never losing his head, and by the sparing employment of a dry, sarcastic humour, he guided the Congress through all its difficulties, and enforced his decisions by intimating that if the delegates did not like them they must get another chairman. Mr. Burt is an excellent speaker for those who prefer argument to rhetoric, and who do not demand excitement or gesticulation from a man simply expressing his opinions on his legs. If he does not very often intervene in debate, it is because he never touches a subject with which he has not made himself thoroughly acquainted. His dislike of Parliamentary interference with the hours of labour is well known. It is fully shared by his admirable colleague, Mr. Fenwick, and by Mr. Broadhurst, who, after working as a journeyman stonemason, has been an Under-Secretary of State. In this respect Mr. Burt agrees with his constituents, and does not therefore deserve some of the compliments he has received; but he holds strongly that a regulation of hours implies a regulation of wages.

Mr. Burt has achieved his position in Parliament, in Trades Unionism, and in the country quite as much by moral as by intellectual qualities. Payment of members is by some philosophers denounced as injurious to the character of candidates and legislators. Mr. Burt has since his first election been supported by the voluntary contributions of the Northumbrian miners; yet his integrity and independence are beyond dispute. He is so little disposed to self-assertion that the full powers of his cultivated mind are hardly appreciated. He is a singularly close reasoner. He has read widely. He is familiar not merely with the literature of politics, but with literature properly so called. He is a member of the Wordsworth Society, and a warm admirer of the great poet who moralised nature.

When Mr. Disraeli first heard Mr. Joseph Cowen

E

speak in the House of Commons, Mr. Cowen bitterly
attacked the Tory Premier's Royal Tithes Bill. Asked
what he thought of the performance, Mr. Disraeli
replied that he " didn't understand the lingo." Some
time afterwards Mr. Cowen delivered a powerful speech
in support of Mr. Disraeli's foreign policy, and the
Premier, without waiting to be asked, declared that
nothing had been heard like it since Plunket. Mr.
Burt is not an orator, like Mr. Cowen ; but his strong
Northumbrian accent, once the southern ear has become
accustomed to it, adds richness and raciness to the
shrewd and homely good sense which it clothes. Mr.
Burt is a man of inbred tact and natural judgment.
Finding himself at variance with what is called the
New Unionism, he has been content to differ, and has
carefully abstained from the use of irritating language.
His view is that New Unionism is Young Unionism,
and that there is no more incompatibility between the
two than between an older and a younger generation of
mankind. Mr. Burt is emphatically a Trade Unionist.
His mission to Berlin confirmed him in the view that
the superior condition of the British workman is due to
organised self-help, and would be injured by State
patronage or control. "Leave it to the Unions" is
the substance of his answer to demands for restrictive
statutes. It may be, of course, that he overrates the
power of voluntary association, though very few people
know so much about the matter as he. But in any
case the working classes will never have a more capable,
disinterested, high-minded spokesman than Thomas Burt.

SIR JOHN RIGBY.

Sir John Rigby would be the acknowledged leader of the Chancery Bar if his position were not disputed by Sir Horace Davey. Neither of them belongs to the party which asserts, sometimes in rather bad grammar, that it monopolises the intellect and education of the country. Both can afford to smile at pretensions too ridiculous to be gravely criticised. The contrast between the two men is interesting and piquant. Sir Horace is polished, elaborate, debonair; Sir John is bluff, simple, and downright. Chancery practice does not conduce to making a popular speaker. Judges hate eloquence, and interrupt periods. Even correct English is lost in the Courts, and Mr. Henry Matthews was almost the last advocate who really seemed to care for the turn of his sentences. Certainly Sir John Rigby does not. He is satisfied with the expression of his meaning, and leaves the meaning of his expressions to others. There are those who place him above Sir Horace Davey as a lawyer, believing that, if less ingenious, he is more sound. Perhaps it is scarcely worth while to settle the precedence so diversely constituted, and yet so peculiarly adapted to the interpretation of the law. Sir John Rigby's massive and

E 2

powerful understanding can cope successfully with any
problem presented by the intricacies of equitable jurisprudence. After him and Sir Horace there is a long
interval, though admirers of the past will maintain that
there has been a descent at Lincoln's Inn, as elsewhere,
since the days of Roundell Palmer and Hugh Cairns.
Even now, when an unusually difficult case comes
before the House of Lords or the Judicial Committee,
it is always proposed to enlist the services of Lord
Selborne.

The unfortunate loss of Sir Horace Davey's seat at
Stockton has added to the importance of Sir John Rigby's
position in the House of Commons. Sir Horace, it
ought to be known, was offered the place in the Court
of Appeal left vacant by the resignation of Sir Edward
Fry, and refused to take it, lest the prospects of the
Liberal party should be injured by a change of candidate. There are spheres in which Sir Horace Davey
shines more conspicuously than Parliament or the
platform ; but his steady loyalty to his cause and
his leader is unimpeachable. Sir John Rigby is equally
steadfast, and has equally little to gain by it. His
practice is enormous, and it is a practice of the most
lucrative kind. The House of Lords and the Privy
Council are his favourite hunting-grounds. His cases
are not sensational, and with a large section of the
public his name is less familiar than Mr. Geoghegan's
or Mr. Gill's. But for the small and select circle who
believe that the highest qualities of the human brain
are exhibited in Fearne on Contingent Remainders,

Sir John Rigby's reputation counts for more than Sir William Harcourt's or Mr. Balfour's. It is a far cry from the Cockpit to Forfarshire, and a strong proof of Sir John's unsuspected versatility that he should have been able to oust Mr. Barclay from the representation of a Scottish county. For Sir John is tainted with original sin, and not merely with actual wickedness. In other words, he is an Englishman, as well as a lawyer. The constituency he now represents has lately been made very familiar in England by the delightful writings of Mr. Barrie. Thrums is Kirriemuir, and the little minister, or his son, may have voted for Sir John Rigby. The Forfarshire folk were, no doubt, attracted by the strong sense and sterling honesty of the Liberal candidate. There never was a man of more genuine grit, more entirely free from affectation and pretence, more thoroughly capable of holding his own in any circumstances against all comers.

This was not Sir John's first Parliamentary experience. In the short Parliament of 1885 he had sat for the Wisbech Division of Cambridgeshire. He is a Cheshire man, born at Runcorn nearly sixty years ago, and was educated at an ancient and splendid foundation which Oxford men presumptuously call Trinity, Cambridge. Although he has been for many years immersed not so much in the study as in the practice of the law, Sir John Rigby has read many books on many subjects, and is in particular a thorough master of Constitutional science. Few people realise what a liberal education the proceedings of the Judicial Committee afford. That great

tribunal, which ought to be personally a good deal
stronger than it is, has a wider and a more varied jurisdiction than any other Court in the civilised world.   It
is the last legal resort of her Majesty's subjects in every
part of her Majesty's dominions except the United
Kingdom of Great Britain and Ireland.   Within
these islands, by one of those odd freaks which enliven
the British Constitution, it is restricted to dealing with
matters of ecclesiastical ritual and complaints against
the criminous clerk.   But no one can argue habitually
before it without acquiring a complete knowledge of
our colonial system, and nothing is more likely to make
a man a Home Ruler than thorough acquaintance with
the way in which our kin beyond sea manage their own
affairs.   In the Judicial Committee, as in the House of
Lords, American judgments are often cited, not as binding authorities, but as entitled to respectful consideration.   Hence the necessity that an English barrister
enjoying the highest class of practice should have an
adequate insight into that masterpiece of theoretical
ingenuity, the American Constitution.   An eminent
Queen's Counsel, confronted with a decision given by
the Supreme Court of an American State on a purely
municipal question of State law, contended that it
had been reversed by the Supreme Court of the United
States, which is of course a Constitutional solecism.
Sir John Rigby happened to be on the other side,
and he did not spare his learned friend.

Sir John Rigby's fame as a sportsman is not quite
on a level with his fame as a lawyer; but shooting is

his chief relaxation, and he seeks it on a Scottish moor.
His success in Forfarshire was one more proof that
Scottish constituencies have no invincible prejudices
against an Englishman, provided he understands the
questions in which they are interested, and does his
duty by them in Parliament. It would be rather hard
if they had, considering the number of Scotsmen who
stand and sit for English counties and boroughs.
Besides being a staunch Liberal, Sir John is an ardent
admirer of Mr. Gladstone, whom it takes an intellect of
the first class rightly to appreciate and comprehend.
As a speaker, Sir John lacks form and symmetry. But
the substance of his speeches is always excellent, and
he never shirks a difficulty or evades a point. Hearty
and good-humoured as he is blunt and straightforward,
he is a universal favourite without taking much
trouble to be popular. Like Sir Horace Davey, whom
he resembles in no other respect, he has achieved
distinction as a lawyer, and not as a politician. But
he is far better suited than Sir Horace to the rough-and-
tumble of public life. There is something painful in
the spectacle of a consummately fine and subtle intelligence failing where inferior minds succeed, and this
spectacle was too frequently offered when Sir Horace
Davey, who ought to be a great Judge, spoke from the
Treasury Bench. Sir John Rigby has an imperturbable
solidity of temper and demeanour which his distinguished
friend and rival lacks. He is not the sort of man who
would allow himself to be overcrowed by Sir Edward
Clarke. The term " Honest John," which looks so

clumsy and absurd when applied to a chivalrous and
sensitive man of genius like Mr. Morley, might be used
with some force and point of Sir John Rigby, who as a
lawyer is conventionally supposed to be full of tricks.
It is not, however, the greatest lawyers who resort to
devices, and Sir John's straightforward manner is not,
as has been known, assumed for professional purposes.
It would be impossible to find a sounder thinker, a
more honourable and upright advocate, or a better
example of the Liberalism which springs directly from
rational conviction.

MR. STANSFELD.

WHEN Mr. Gladstone composed his fourth Administration, a good many people were surprisingly confident that they knew exactly what Mr. Labouchere would have, and what Mr. Stuart would have, and what Mr. Stansfeld would have. Then came the official list of appointments, and none of these names appeared there at all. Mr. Stansfeld's friends had sent him back to the Local Government Board. But, unfortunately, the patronage was not theirs, and Mr. Gladstone put Mr. Fowler in Mr. Ritchie's place. Mr. Gladstone used not to be very clear about the locality of the Local Government Board. When it was wrecked with dynamite, he asked where it was. Outrages teach geography as well as wars teach history. Everybody seems now to admit that Mr. Fowler is in the right place. It is less clear why Mr. Stansfeld should have no place at all. He is not a young man, having been born in 1820. But the Prime Minister, if the ordinary sources of information may be trusted, was born in 1809. Mr. Gladstone might say, if he cared to say anything at all, that he could not put everybody in the Cabinet, and that seventeen is too many. Then why?—it might be asked. But that would be an

indiscreet line of inquiry. It cannot be called a personal slight to pass over a man of seventy-two.
Premiers are privileged, and Lord Campbell was raised
to the woolsack on the verge of eighty. But in the
Army, or the Navy, or the Civil Service, a man of
seventy is regarded as altogether impossible, unless he
be a Royal Duke and Commander-in-Chief. Sir Lyon
Playfair, who was only a year older than Mr. Stansfeld,
received a peerage by way of consolation. Probably
Mr. Stansfeld might have been similarly honoured, or
degraded, if he had chosen. But he could hardly,
with his principles and his past, have put the extinguisher of a coronet upon his head. He accepted
the situation with a quiet dignity which did him
infinite honour. Probably he had heard the story of
Cato and the statue. Cato, unlike Sir Henry Edwards,
refused that form of material tribute. "I would
rather," he said, "that men should ask why Cato is
not here than why he is." Mr. Stansfeld has, in that
respect, the advantage over more than one member of
the present Cabinet.

He has also the independence so justly appreciated
by Robert Burns, and the consciousness of a distinguished past. For Mr. Stansfeld was a conspicuous
figure in political life before the present Home Secretary
went to school. It is eight-and-twenty years since Mr.
Stansfeld's relations with Mazzini excited the Tory
party in the House of Commons. In the trial of Greco
and others for conspiring to assassinate the Emperor of
the French, the Procureur Impérial said that Greco's

address in London was 35, Thurloe Square, and he found with sadness that it was the address of a member of the Parliament of England who already, in 1857, had been appointed by Mazzini treasurer to the Tibaldi Plot. Mr. Stansfeld was questioned as to this statement, and made a spirited reply, which Mr. Forster said was quite satisfactory to the country. A little later Sir Henry Stracey gave notice of a resolution declaring that the speech of the Procureur Impérial deserved the serious consideration of the House. Mr. Stansfeld at once resigned, but Lord Palmerston would not hear of resignation. The debate came on, and Mr. Disraeli made one of his most portentous speeches. Mr. Stansfeld, he said, had been the medium of communication between Mazzini and his correspondents. " What correspondents? " asked Mr. Stansfeld. " What correspondents? says the member for Halifax," replied Mr. Disraeli, in his most solemn tones; " why, the assassins of Europe! What correspondents? says the hon. member for Halifax; why, the men who point their poniards at the breasts of our allies! " Mr. Bright made a vigorous reply, vindicating Mazzini, and concluded by saying: " If I were as hungry as the hungriest to take my seat on that bench, I should be ashamed to make my way to it upon the character, the reputation, the happiness, and the future of the last appointed and the youngest member of the Government." The motion was defeated by a majority of ten, and Mr. Stansfeld, anxious not to embarrass the Government, persisted in resigning. The attack had

not only failed, but greatly increased his reputation,
and two years later he became a member of the Government formed by Lord Russell, on Lord Palmerston's
decease. In 1868 he became a Lord of the Treasury in
Mr. Gladstone's Government. While he was at the
Treasury Mr. Forster introduced into his Education
Bill the compromise which so deeply offended the
supporters of undenominational teaching. Sir George
Trevelyan resigned, and it is said that Mr. Gladstone
has never forgiven him. If Mr. Stansfeld had done
the same, he might have become the leader of the
Radicals below the gangway. In the exercise of his
discretion he remained in office, and Mr. Gladstone
made him President of the Poor Law Board when Mr.
Goschen became First Lord of the Admiralty. In this
office he originated the Local Government Board, and
became its first President. But in the Government of
1880 Mr. Stansfeld held no post. New men—notably
Mr. Chamberlain—shouldered him out, and he has since
only for a few brief months in 1886 returned to official
life. The interpretation of the facts may vary; but
the facts are curious, and ought to be instructive.

Mr. Stansfeld has sat for his native town of Halifax
without interruption for thirty-three years. Very few
members of Parliament could say as much. Mr. Villiers
has represented Wolverhampton, now divided, since
1834. But he has not been seen in the town since
1874, and his election must be regarded as rather the
preservation of an ancient monument than the choice
of a popular representative. When Mr. Chamberlain

resigned in 1886, Mr. Stansfeld returned to the Local Government Board, after twelve years of emancipation from the thraldom of office. His Parliamentary experience is almost unsurpassed, and he has not become less Radical with age. In the late Parliament he took the lead in criticising the Local Government Bill from the front Opposition bench, and he was subsequently entrusted with the charge of the Liberal Registration Bill; tasks that he accomplished judiciously. Mr. Stansfeld's exclusion from the Ministry may be explained in various ways. Mr. Gladstone makes mistakes, like other people, and this may be one of them. At the same time, it is possible for a man to outlive his usefulness without surviving his reputation—"*jam rude donatus,*" as Horace says—having received his testimonial, whatever it may be. Mr. Lowe, and even Lord Cardwell, were anxious to come back in 1880. Mr. Stansfeld, however, is not infirm in mind or body. But the controversy to which with admirable courage he devoted so much of his time and energies is closed. He completely succeeded in the crusade which he led against the legal recognition of immorality. On women's suffrage he has lived to see a great reaction in the Liberal party, and a counterbalancing move forward among Conservatives. Mr. Stansfeld remains staunch in that as in other matters. Such a Parliamentary career as his cannot be affected by office, or the want of it. It is to be hoped that Mr. Stansfeld's long, useful, and honourable connection with Halifax may be prolonged through more than one Parliament yet.

THE DUKE OF DEVONSHIRE.

Soon after Mr. Disraeli had been created Earl of Beaconsfield he was congratulated by a brother Peer upon his elevation. "I feel," said Lord Beaconsfield, with the funereal pomposity which marked his later manner—"I feel like one already dead;" then, remembering the status of the congratulator, he added, with a flicker of the old spirit: "and in the realms of bliss." Lord Hartington sat in the House of Commons for five-and-thirty years, almost as long as Mr. Disraeli. For five years he was the nominal leader of the Opposition. For fifteen years he was in office. He took his seat in the House of Lords at the first available opportunity. The change must be very great, and, like the result of the Rossendale election, not the more welcome for having been expected. The late Duke of Devonshire lived to a great age, and devoted a long life, as well as intellectual capacity of a high order, to the good of his neighbours and dependents. He was a lay saint. His son and successor is a very different sort of person. A man of the world, a man of pleasure, of society, of the hunting field, and of the race-course, he has nevertheless played, and may yet play, a considerable part in the history of the world. He was not, like most boys

of his class, sent to a public school; and it would be
interesting if some admirer of those institutions could
point out in which of the qualities they are supposed
to foster the Duke of Devonshire is deficient. At
Cambridge his career was brief and undistinguished,
though an academic toady has sought to prove that it
would have been extremely brilliant if only it had been
a little longer.

Lord Hartington was really forced into politics
against his will, to prevent him from wasting his whole
time in amusement. A valuable essay might be
written on the use of the British Constitution as a
cure for idleness in young men of quality. There are
great advantages in such an apprenticeship to public
life as Lord Hartington's. There was nothing meritorious in his early dislike of politics. On the contrary,
it showed a rather pusillanimous indifference to the
opportunities of his birth and station. But the cant
of the British Philistine denounces ambition as sordid,
and extols indifference as generous. Because Lord
Hartington preferred Newmarket to Westminster, and
found the trammels of office inconveniently restrictive,
he has been compared with Lord Althorp, a simple,
humble-minded, and deeply religious man, who hated
publicity, shrank from fame, and desired only to promote the welfare of the nation. The Duke of Devonshire's political career has been a strictly upright and
honourable one. He has never intrigued; he has
never caballed; he has never made difficulties because
his own claims were imperfectly recognised. But he

has taken the ordinary prizes of Parliamentary life as they came, and up to 1886 he never showed the slightest reluctance to accept them. In 1875 he was offered the leadership of the Liberal party in the House of Commons. He was supported by Mr. Gladstone, by Mr. Bright, and by many Nonconformist Radicals who were dissatisfied with the educational policy of Mr. Forster. Mr. Forster, however, had influential backing, and if Lord Hartington had retired would unquestionably have been elected. Lord Hartington was perfectly justified in allowing himself to be nominated, and Mr. Forster withdrew. An admirer has recently declared that Lord Hartington did the same, but that his withdrawal " characteristically came too late." If unconscious humour be the most amusing, unconscious satire is surely the most severe. In 1880 the Queen sent for Lord Hartington, and directed him to form an Administration. Instead of at once declining a hopeless task, he applied to Mr. Gladstone and to the late Lord Granville. Here, again, he was entirely within his rights. But on both occasions Lord Althorp would have pursued the opposite course.

The Duke of Devonshire is not in any way a remarkable man. His mind and character are of the most ordinary type; but he possesses useful and sterling qualities. He is conspicuously free from meanness or malignity. What he knows he understands thoroughly, and he is well acquainted with the limits of his own knowledge. He came into the House of Commons one of the worst speakers that ever addressed it. A heavy manner, a limited vocabulary, a thick utterance, and an apparent lack of all interest in what he was saying, seemed to conspire against success. But perseverance and a marquisate will overcome many obstacles. Lord Hartington took office, and was forced to speak frequently. He gradually conquered his worst defects, and then his solid ability came out. The Duke of Devonshire is never eloquent, and he is often exceedingly dull. But his meaning is always perfectly clear; his abstinence from exaggeration is in itself a power; and he has the invaluable habit of going straight to the point. What was said of Lord Castlereagh may be said of him. He is a very difficult speaker to answer. When Mr. Gladstone argued that the Plan of Campaign was the consequence of rejecting Mr. Parnell's Land Bill, many indignant and irrelevant comments were made by the Tories. Lord Hartington hit the nail on the head at once. " Is it the legitimate consequence ? " he asked. There was the whole case of his party put in a nutshell, and that a hard nutshell to crack.

As Leader of the Opposition, Lord Hartington only confronted Mr. Disraeli in 1875 and 1876. By the time the Eastern Question became really acute Mr. Disraeli had gone up higher, and Lord Hartington was more fairly matched with Sir Stafford Northcote. Sir Stafford was the cleverer and by far the better educated man of the two. Lord Hartington had more strength of purpose, less sensitiveness, more backbone. The parts, or at least the places, ought to have been

F

reversed. Sir Stafford Northcote was a Conservative-
Liberal; Lord Hartington was a Liberal-Conserva-
tive. Had the Duke of Devonshire belonged to a
Tory family, he would never have left the Tory party,
though he would have done his best to cure it of its
worst prejudices. In the Liberal party he was never
quite at ease, and his final secession from it in 1886
must have come to him with a feeling of relief. It
would be wrong to say that Lord Hartington, like
Lord Selborne, was never in any sense a Liberal at
all. He is, or was, in colloquial language, a "Why
the devil shouldn't he?" sort of Liberal, and that is
not a bad sort, by any means. General tolerance and
licence, easy-going indifference to priggish scruples,
have always characterised him, and the Nonconformists
soon discovered that he had no ecclesiastical bias. His
principal objections to the disestablishment of the
Church are understood to be the trouble it would in-
volve, and the danger to the security of landed estates
which it might possibly bring in its train. If he had
not left Mr. Gladstone on Home Rule, he would
probably have left him on something else before long.
All through the Administration of 1880 to 1885 he
was chafing under Mr. Gladstone's supremacy, and by
some unfortunate mischance the leading Conservatives
knew it. He would have better maintained his
reputation for chivalry—the grounds of which are
not easily discoverable—if he had protested against
the attacks which are still made by his present allies
against Mr. Gladstone as "the murderer of Gordon."

The murderer of Gordon was an Arab fanatic; but if any British statesman could be so described without gross and ludicrous calumny, it would be the Duke of Devonshire himself.

The Duke of Devonshire has always been distinguished for simplicity, directness, and hatred of fuss. Naturally indolent, but thoroughly business-like, he developed in office the great gift of perceiving what, and what only, he must necessarily do himself. That he did, and did uncommonly well. The rest he left to subordinates, who in the British Civil Service can always be trusted. In the House of Commons Lord Hartington seldom showed any sort of feeling, and his stoicism in the terrible year 1882 was marvellous. In one or two instances, however, he was really moved, and the effect was striking. When Lord Randolph Churchill insinuated in the form of a question a silly charge of underhand conduct against the then Secretary for India, Lord Hartington blazed out after a fashion which considerably astonished and rather alarmed the arch mischief-maker below the gangway. When the Tories made their shameful and scandalous onslaught upon Lord Spencer in 1885, Lord Hartington defended him with a spirit and warmth as impressive as they were creditable. But these are rare exceptions. The Duke of Devonshire's disposition is phlegmatic, and he is seldom roused out of it. His manners are not polished. They are too frequently of the kind which causes children to be called " spoilt." Perhaps it is not good for any of the sons of men to have precisely

F 2

what they want all their lives; it engenders satiety, and removes the sense of social obligation. On the other hand, there is nothing affected about the Duke—he gives himself no airs. His behaviour is perfectly natural—sometimes only too natural. It is not that he wishes to be rude, but that he has never had any particular motive for being civil. The Duke of Devonshire is not a man of science, like his father, nor a man of letters, like his former chief. His speeches may be searched in vain for literary quotations or historic allusions. He once candidly admitted in public that he did not know the source of the most familiar line in Terence. His books are of the kind which are made rather than written. Like Sir Henry James, he has much improved as a speaker since he left the Liberal party. It is an undoubted fact that he felt himself overshadowed and slighted between 1880 and 1886. Within the limits of good sense and good taste, he has since shown clearly enough that he enjoys the increased consideration his independent attitude conferred.

MR. SEXTON.

MR. SEXTON's reputation is entirely Parliamentary. On English platforms he is little known. In his own country, except in Belfast and on the Corporation of Dublin, his influence is not for a moment to be compared with Mr. Healy's, or Mr. Dillon's, or Mr. O'Brien's. In the House of Commons none of his compatriots can touch him. He belongs to a different class. Apart from Mr. Gladstone, who is above competition, his only rivals in debate are Mr. Chamberlain, Lord Randolph Churchill, Mr. Goschen, and Sir William Harcourt. But he differs from these eminent statesmen by being a member of Parliament, and nothing more. He has never, from the nature of things, been in office, though few, if any, offices would be too high for his capacity. He has never had any profession, except that sort of journalism which is really a branch of politics. He is not a man of pleasure, or fashion, or sport, or letters. He lives in and for the House of Commons. He knows its rules by heart. He regards its traditions with a respect not shared by many of his colleagues. He is as good a judge of order as the Speaker, and he recently showed that he knew Parliamentary English, such as it is, a great deal better than Mr. Balfour. Mr. Sexton

entered the House of Commons twelve years ago, when
he was thirty-two, a finished debater. Wherever he
learned the art, he had learned it thoroughly. The superstition that all Irishmen are naturally fluent cannot
survive the most meagre acquaintance with the House of
Commons. The Irish Parliamentary party contains
some of the most excruciating orators in the civilised
world. Even Mr. Dillon, who is far above the average,
has not reached the second rate, and it requires excitement in his hearers, as well as in himself, to draw
out the really fine rhetorical gifts of Mr. O'Brien.
Mr. Sexton has never, since his election for Sligo
in 1880, made a bad speech. He has made many
which deserve to be ranked among model specimens of
Parliamentary style.

It was some time before Mr. Sexton's rare and
peculiar powers became known, even in the House itself.
At the beginning of the Parliament in which he first
took his seat there was a disposition among Liberals
and Conservatives alike to lump all the Parnellites
together. The cant of the day assumed that they were
a parcel of obstructives; that they talked either for the
sake of talking or with the object of wasting time;
that it was folly to listen to a word they said; and
that the way in which they said it was a matter of
perfect indifference to everyone except themselves.
"Oh, let him go on!" exclaimed a Liberal member
when Mr. Dillon was giving his reasons—probably very
good ones—why Mr. Forster's Coercion Bill should not
be passed. But affectation always breaks down sooner

or later, and this sham cynicism did not last very long.   Mr. Sexton spoke patiently, frequently, and assiduously.   Gradually it dawned upon his Parliamentary colleagues that listening to him was a more instructive, as well as a more seemly, occupation than interrupting him.   They then discovered that they had amongst them a master of polished sentences and pointed epigrams, who was never slovenly, and always effective.   Mr. Sexton, in those days, cared nothing for the aspect of the House.   He would address a dozen members at four in the morning with as much care and finish as if the House were crowded from floor to roof at five o'clock in the afternoon.   Things are very different now.   It is understood that Mr. Sexton must speak at the beginning of a debate or at the end of it, when the benches are full and the interest general. To the vanity which waits upon success he is not a stranger.   But it ought, in fairness, to be remembered that he worked out his apprenticeship, and in the days of his political youth flung away upon emptiness, in the small hours, pearls which an inferior performer would have preserved for great occasions.   Mr. Sexton must have spent more hours than most men in the precincts of St. Stephen's.   In the good old days, when members of Parliament had not become respectable, and were accustomed to go home with the milkman, Mr. Sexton was at his post early and late.   He did not go into society or frequent London clubs.   At a later period, when Mr. Parnell's principal followers were honoured and genial guests at the festive gatherings of the Liberal party, Mr. Sexton was rarely, if ever, to be seen among them. The House of Commons is to him, as dogs were to the character in Dickens, not a mere amusement, but meat, and drink, and house, and wife, and family.

Mr. Sexton's eloquence is essentially of the Parliamentary stamp. He seldom appeals to the feelings, and never carries people off their feet with enthusiasm as O'Connell and Bright did, as Mr. Gladstone can still do. Mr. Sexton is cool, clear, humorous, argumentative, sometimes bitterly ironical. He has no Hibernian gush, thorough Irishman as he is in mind and speech. He assumes a certain amount of intelligence in his hearers, and has in consequence suffered from some very ludicrous misrepresentations. When Mr. O'Brien is tearing a passion to tatters, the dullest observer can see that something unusual is going on. Mr. Sexton does not play to the gallery. Some of his best things are dropped out, as it were, inadvertently, in a quiet, conversational, almost confidential tone. He is extraordinarily fluent. But fluency is an ambiguous and misleading term. Colonel Nolan is fluent. So far as fluency means carelessness of speech or incontinence of tongue, it has no application to Mr. Sexton. No man weighs his words more thoroughly, or prepares his periods more carefully when he has time and opportunity to prepare them. On the other hand, there are very few who can rise better to an emergency, or whose extemporaneous deliverances will better bear examination. Mr. Sexton's worst fault is of a totally

different kind. He is generally a slow speaker, and not a
quick one. His pauses are sometimes very trying. When
he looks round the House with a complacent smile, as if
congratulating members on the treat he had provided
for them, the gorge of the natural man rises, and he
feels half inclined to be rude. The idea that Mr. Sexton
is simply a word spinner, a proficient in the manu-
facture of phrases without substance, is, as Carlyle would
say, quite curiously the reverse of the truth. Mr.
Sexton is an excellent man of business, an astute tacti-
cian, and a very useful member of important committees. The speech in which he exposed the Irish Local
Government Bill was a capital example of his best style.
He had learned the Bill almost by heart, he had all its
provisions at his fingers' ends, and he turned them into
a ridicule which was fatal because it was founded on
knowledge.

Mr. Sexton has been twice Lord Mayor of Dublin,
and even his enemies admit that his administration of
the office was most successful. He is not a rich man,
and the Lord Mayor of Dublin can save something out
of his allowance if he likes. Mr. Sexton disdained to
take that advantage of his position, and set a high
example of pecuniary disinterestedness. His management of the Corporation's finances was singularly skilful,
and has left permanent results in the shape of municipal
stock at low interest and a premium. Mr. Sexton is
said not to be popular in his own party, and he has not
many friends among English politicians. When he left
Mr. Parnell and followed Mr. McCarthy, it was not

from any fondness for Englishmen and their ways. He is suspected of playing his own game and fighting for his own hand, regardless of the common cause. But in going with the majority after the divorce case, he certainly took the patriotic line; and if Home Rule triumphs, he will have done more than most men to obtain the victory. Mr. Sexton's temper is rather fiery, and he sometimes blazes into wrath on insufficient provocation. When he called Colonel Saunderson a wilful and deliberate liar, Colonel Saunderson had genially told him that he associated with men whom he knew to be murderers. If the Speaker had not felt that he allowed Colonel Saunderson to go too far, he must have named Mr. Sexton to the House. Not a particle of evidence was produced before the Special Commission to connect Mr. Sexton with outrage, or crime, or lawlessness of any kind, and the charge was the figment of an Orange imagination. But if Mr. Sexton did well to be angry then, he has been too often angry since. A man cannot help coming into the world with a thin skin; but he may make it thicker by self-control, as he may make it thinner by self-indulgence. Mr. Sexton is not of the stuff from which leaders of men are constructed; but he is a great member of Parliament, if ever there was one.

SIR RICHARD TEMPLE.

THOSE—and there are too many—who sit in the seat of the scornful say that Sir Richard Temple obtained a baronetcy by inventing a famine. Probably the scarcity was as genuine and also as important as the title. That Sir Richard displayed on that, as on other occasions, unbounded energy, no one who knows him will feel any difficulty in believing. Nor will his friends find it easy to doubt that the Lieutenant-Governor conducted select parties of ladies to see the waggon-loads of provisions which he introduced in such quantities that, according to malicious and probably unfounded rumour, they had to be burned. The Civil Service of India contains some of the hardest workers in the world; but by universal consent Sir Richard Temple rivalled the best of them in that particular. Long before he became Lieutenant-Governor of Bengal he was known as a man of inordinate industry. He did not come into the world with an unusually large stock of brains. He is one of the driest writers of his own or any other age. He does not shine in conversation. He belongs to the plodding order of genius—if genius is, as Carlyle said, an immense capacity for taking pains. He has, however, one quality without

which mere laboriousness is no path to fame.   He
was always careful to employ a trumpeter, and when no
other was to be had, he acted as his own.   Nothing
that he did which could by any possibility conduce to
his immediate or prospective advancement was ever
hidden from the public or the departmental eye.   Is it
a world to hide virtues in ?   Sir Richard Temple's
answer to Sir Toby Belch's question was an emphatic
negative.   The moment he was released from the
function of administering Bengal, he became a candidate
for Parliament.   His most intimate friends had no idea
on which side "Dick Temple" would range himself,
and it is understood that Conservatism owes the honour
of his championship to the eligibility of a vacant seat in
a Conservative district.   But having chosen his party,
Sir Richard stuck to it, as he has always stuck to everything.   Dr. Whewell used to be fond of asserting that
the most valuable of all human qualities was what he
called "stiction," and Sir Richard Temple is an excellent illustration of the rule.   His bitterest enemy could
not deny that he had discharged his Parliamentary
duties with unusual zeal.   He boasts of having never
missed a division during his twelve years of Parliamentary life.   Neither social nor domestic ties are strong
enough to detain him from the lobby.   The approach of
the last General Election inspired him with some distrust in the fidelity of his Worcestershire followers.   He
therefore transferred himself to the Kingston Division
of Surrey, where Mr. Charles Hodgson ran him much
closer than he expected.   His methods of electioneering

were more astute than magnanimous, and much amusement was caused by his sudden discovery that the
gardeners at Kew were under-paid.

The House of Commons soon found it expedient
to make terms with Sir Richard Temple. At first he
showed a desire to take part not only in every division,
but also in every debate. This was plainly intolerable,
and the late ruler of millions had to be coughed
down. But the House is a sensible and tolerant
body. It acknowledged Sir Richard Temple's right
to be heard on Indian subjects, and stipulated that he
should confine his attention—or, at least, his oratorical
efforts — thereto. Sir Richard Temple does not, of
course, know India. Nobody knows India, except a
few tourists who have spent an autumn holiday there.
Sir Richard, however, knows some portions of India
very well, and is perhaps, on the whole, as good an
authority as could be found. His view is always the
official one ; but he expresses it with sense and
moderation. A grotesque and half-unconscious humour
prevents him from being a conventional bore. Nobody
has ever succeeded in more thoroughly convulsing the
House of Commons. Sir Richard Temple plays many
parts. Legislation does not suffice for his energies.
What time he can spare from Westminster, where he
squires many dames, he spends at a lower stage of the
Thames Embankment, where he unfolds the educational
budget of London. For some years he was Vice-
Chairman of the London School Board, and used
literally to sit under the then Reverend Joseph Diggle,

much to the diversion of the idle spectators in the
Gallery; for Mr. Diggle looked for all the world like
the simple and innocent son of the slightly rakish
and comparatively elderly personage below him. The
present Speaker has curtailed, and might with advantage abolish, the absurd practice of putting questions
to members not in the Government about subjects with
which they are concerned in another capacity. Sir
Richard Temple was immensely delighted when in-
quiries were put to him on metropolitan education.
He rose with a more than Ministerial air of consequence,
and he answered in a tone which seemed to combine
the solemn dignity of a judge passing sentence of death
with the tender grace of a gentleman making a proposal
of marriage. He was once asked what would be done
if a certain Teachers' Superannuation Bill did not pass.
He rose with a smile of beatified self-complacency,
holding his hat with one hand and his heart with the
other. "Mr. Speaker," he said, "what will happen if
that Bill does not pass is a question which no man
living can answer." If Sir Richard desired to excite
laughter, he had every reason to be satisfied. The
hilarity was long, loud, and boisterous. There is good
ground for supposing that Sir Richard Temple produces his budgets with zeal and care. He is a strong
partisan of denominational education, which is odd in
an Anglo-Indian. But he gets up his figures, if
he cannot be said to present them, in an intelligible
shape.

Sir Richard Temple's appearance has been made

familiar to the civilised world by the pencil of Mr. Harry Furniss. Wilkes described himself as only half an hour behind the handsomest man in England, and Sir Richard counts himself a terrible lady-killer. Mr. Disraeli used to cite Sir George Campbell as having destroyed his belief in the faculty of government. Sir George and Sir Richard both exercised the faculty in Bengal. Sir George Campbell was a simple, honest man of great ability, who ruined himself in the Parliamentary sense by indulging a tendency to irresponsible chatter. His good points were not such as to strike Mr. Disraeli, who would greatly have enjoyed, had time and fate permitted, the humours (not the humour) of Sir Richard Temple. Anglo-Indians are not wont to charm the House of Commons. Sir James Fergusson is, perhaps, the least unsuccessful of them in that respect, and Sir James Fergusson was a member of Parliament before his connection with India began. Sir Richard Temple is ready at any moment with an address on any aspect of Indian life or politics which may come uppermost in debate. A Mechanics' Institute would find him a good standing dish when more interesting lecturers were not to be had. Sir Richard has obtained a certain sort of reputation, and if he likes it, there is no more to be said. But he would have acquired more durable, and on the whole more respectable, fame if he had waited for the nomination to the Indian Council which he would almost certainly have received. Assiduity and good humour are insufficient qualifications for Parliamentary life. It would

be harsh to say that Sir Richard's imperturbable temper
was the result of crass insensibility. But undoubtedly
his skin is tough, and if he would not rather be noticed
in any way than left unnoticed altogether, his conduct
strangely belies his disposition. To go everywhere,
or rather to be seen everywhere, is apparently his
guiding principle in life. The character is a difficult
one to sustain, and it requires qualities which Sir
Richard Temple conspicuously lacks.

THE EARL OF ROSEBERY.

SPEAKING at Manchester on the 25th of June, 1886, immediately after the defeat of the Home Rule Bill, and just before the General Election, Mr. Gladstone introduced Lord Rosebery, "the youngest member of the Cabinet," as "the man of the future." Lord Rosebery was not then forty years of age, while his brief and brilliant career at the Foreign Office was fresh in the public mind. A good many years have passed since then. Time and sorrow have done their work. But Lord Rosebery is still one of the youngest statesmen of Cabinet rank. The curtains of the future hang, and Mr. Gladstone is happily younger than ever. There is one good reason—perhaps two—why Lord Rosebery should not succeed to the leadership of his party. He sits in the House of Lords, and he will be urgently needed in the direct conduct of foreign affairs. The spectacle of a Prime Minister in a small and perpetual minority of legislators, whose right to legislate his followers denied, would not be dignified. The combination of the Foreign Office with the Premiership is the worst that could be imagined, and means either no Foreign Secretary or no head of the Government. Lord Salisbury's reputation would stand higher

G

than it does if he had contented himself with the duties
he discharged under Lord Beaconsfield.   Lord Palmerston did not attempt the double work, and even Mr.
Canning reluctantly abandoned the ideal which Lord
Salisbury has failed to realise.   The field of European
diplomacy should be wide enough, and the charge of
British interests abroad should be great enough, for the
most inordinate ambition.

Lord Rosebery had the ill luck to succeed his grandfather in the Peerage the year he attained his majority.
He never, therefore, had the chance of entering the House
of Commons, where he would have been improved by discipline, and where he would have won early distinction.
From one supreme calamity he was saved by a circum-
stance as accidental as his earldom.   His grandfather
was a Baron of the United Kingdom as well as a
Scottish earl.   Had he not borne the technically inferior
title, his grandson would have been practically disqualified from sitting in either House of Parliament.
He would have been ineligible for the Commons, and as
a Liberal, the Scottish Peers would never have sent him
to represent them in the House of Lords.   The ingenuity
of Mr. Hunter, M.P., has, however, found him out.   The
Scottish Home Rule Bill introduced by that ardent
Radical would entirely exclude Lord Rosebery from all
share in the government of his country; for it consti-
tutes the Queen and the members for Scottish constituencies the sole legislative authority for Scotland.   The
popular training which Lord Rosebery missed in the
House of Commons has been supplied by the London

County Council. As the first chairman of that miscellaneous and thoroughly representative assembly, he learned more than the House of Lords would have taught him in half a century. How admirably he performed his functions, everybody knows. Lord Rosebery's tact and knowledge of men are almost Napoleonic in their irresistible completeness. His task was a most difficult and delicate one. The body over which he presided was raw and inexperienced, sensitive and independent, amorphous and unruly. His official authority was almost nothing. By personal influence and capacity for business, without any collision, altercation, or disturbance, Lord Rosebery introduced harmony, order, mutual confidence, and respect. It was a remarkable achievement, the more so inasmuch as no more serious complaint could be made against the Chairman than that he was too fond of getting his own way. If he had not got it, the consequences would have been disastrous.

Lord Rosebery did not belong to the class of studious youth. His abilities were very soon discovered and appreciated by his tutor at Eton, a man who, though little known to the public, had a real genius for teaching. At Christ Church he only kept race-horses, and it looked as if he would be chiefly known at Doncaster and Newmarket. But Lord Rosebery was always an early riser, and it is said that he used to read before his friends were up. In 1871 Mr. Gladstone selected him to second the Address; and in 1874 he presided, not without exciting some merriment, over the deliberations of the Social

G 2

Science Congress. He has been Lord Rector of two Scottish Universities, following in one case, with ludicrous incongruity, the late William Edward Forster. Although Lord Rosebery held no very important post until he was appointed Secretary of State for Foreign Affairs, it became gradually known that he had not only keen literary tastes, but immense powers of industry and achievement. Although he wrote for publication very little before his study of Pitt, his clever and amusing review of Mr. Richard Hutton's biography of Scott in *The Academy* showed that he could turn neat sentences with his pen as well as with his tongue. His speaking was thought by the serious to savour of flippancy, and he shares with Lord Melbourne the quality of seeming to know a good deal less than he really knows. He took up with some zeal the subjects of Imperial Federation and reform of the House of Lords. But nothing much came of them; and before much time had passed Lord Rosebery would probably have been almost as glad to withdraw with a decent excuse from the Federation League as to walk out of those doors which, as he once pathetically said, "only open inwards."

In 1886 Lord Rosebery, in the French phrase, "arrived," and since that date he has ranked, by universal consent, among the foremost personages in the country. Lord Rosebery had the good sense to follow his party rather than his class, and to stand by the cause of Home Rule from the first. Personal loyalty, or rather, filial devotion to Mr. Gladstone, may have had something to do with this decision. But Lord Rosebery is a great Opportunist, a singularly shrewd and far-sighted man of the world. "The doom of an aristocracy divorced from the people," he exclaimed in one of his finest speeches, "is written on the ruined palaces of Venice and in every page of history." Not by nature a Radical or a Democrat, he has no strong bias against Radicalism, and a good deal of sympathy with Democracy. He is ambitious, not of pomp, or grandeur, or rank, or dignity—but of power. Knowing where the centre of power is, Lord Rosebery longs to be in the House of Commons, and casts a retrospective glance of envy on Pitt for having been a younger son. He supports, if he did not suggest, Mr. Morley's proposal that the House of Lords should be gradually drained of its available talent by allowing the Peers to renounce their privileges and their disabilities together. In his "Life of Pitt" are to be found sentiments and expressions which might be cited to prove that the writer was something very like a Tory. But that would be a wholly false inference. Lord Rosebery cares no more for Toryism than he cares for Etruscan antiquities. Pitt, or rather the ideal Pitt he has chosen to draw, is for him the embodiment of will, of force, of ascendancy over other men. If Lord Rosebery were to favour the world with his views on Napoleon, it would probably be found that he had an even more questionable hero than Pitt. Lord Rosebery on the wrong side might become a very dangerous man. Lord Randolph Churchill was nearer the truth than he knew when he sportively compared

Lord Rosebery to Machiavelli. Machiavelli was not
a bad man : on the contrary, he was too good for his
age. If Lord Rosebery set his mind on the attainment
of any object, there are few things on the right side of
morality which would stand in his way.

Lord Rosebery is essentially a statesman. He has
at once a large grasp of great subjects and a fine per-
ception of small details. He sees obstacles, but they do
not alarm him. He regards them not as things to be
avoided, but as things to be overcome. As a speaker, he
has many and various merits, especially imperturbability
and humour. But he has lately tried higher flights
with conspicuous success. The vast meeting he harangued in St. James's Hall on the eve of the second
elections for the London County Council was fairly
carried off its feet by his unwonted display of enthusiasm, eloquence, and emotion. As a debater he has unfortunately no opportunity of showing what he can do.
As a talker, he is admirable; with a wit " so nimble
and so full of subtle flame," that one never can have
too much of it. His reading is extensive, and his
knowledge of political history, especially of those
memoirs which are the modern materials for the historian, almost complete. But it is not Lord Rosebery's wit, nor his information—which is not, after all,
out of the way—nor his easy, genial, and gracious
manners which interest people most in him. There
is great charm in mystery, and Lord Rosebery, perhaps as a result of his friendship with Mr. Disraeli,
rather affects the mysterious. It is not, however,

mere affectation. Lord Rosebery's character is not a simple one, and his career may yet puzzle those who think they know him best. As long as he lives he must exercise an important influence on the fortunes of his country, and the stage on which he acts will be well lighted beforehand. Whatever the historian of the nineteenth or twentieth centuries may say of Lord Rosebery, he will have to say a good deal.

*** These pages had already been printed when Lord Rosebery became Premier. It has not been thought necessary to make any alteration in them. Indeed, read in the light of this event, they may gain rather than lose in interest.

MR. GOSCHEN.

GREAT men have their foibles, and Mr. Goschen's pet weakness is an almost passionate readiness to prove, beyond the possibility of doubt or cavil, that he has not a drop of Jewish blood in his veins. His German origin, however, is not to be denied, and cannot be concealed, even if he wished to conceal it, by omitting the modification of the " ö." Although he was educated at Rugby and Oxford, he is less like an Englishman than was the late French Ambassador, who was educated at Rugby and Cambridge. Perhaps it is his foreign descent which makes Mr. Goschen so nervously desirous of emphasising the ardour of his patriotism on every convenient and inconvenient occasion. The ordinary Briton does not talk about making his will and doing his duty, or state in public what precautions he will take when his house is set on fire, merely because the leader of a political party has proposed an important change in the Constitution. This sort of bluster indicates timidity rather than courage, and excites the same kind of feeling in the stolid British mind as Burke excited by throwing a dagger on the floor of the House of Commons. Mr. Goschen does not seem to understand that the military metaphors with which he

garnishes his more ambitious speeches are rather ridiculous
in an elderly gentleman of commercial pursuits, "that
never set a squadron in the field nor the division of a
battle knows more than a spinster." It is indeed sometimes difficult to believe that Mr. Goschen does not
derive his descent from the Pharisees. He is not satisfied with explaining why in his opinion Home Rule
would be bad both for Ireland and for England, nor
even how the Liberal party have become unmindful of
their national obligations. Nothing will serve him but
to claim a monopoly of the cardinal virtues, and to in-
sinuate, often in language almost too direct to be called
insinuation, that Home Rulers are lost to all sense of
morality and decorum. A more complete reversal of
the charity which thinketh no evil than Mr. Goschen's
speeches afford it would not be easy to imagine. Yet
his own skin is of the thinnest, and the least criticism
makes him angry.

The charge of inconsistency as usually brought
against Mr. Goschen is greatly exaggerated, if indeed
it be not wholly unfounded. No doubt Mr. Goschen
entered the House of Commons in 1863 as an advanced
Liberal. No doubt he has been since 1886, if not
before, an intense Conservative. But thirty years ago
Mr. Goschen knew little or nothing about politics.
Indeed, so ignorant was he of public affairs that he
could not even compose without assistance his address
to the electors of the City. He went straight from
Oxford into business, and became a Director of the
Bank of England. He took a first-class in classics;

but it would be difficult to detect the slightest flavour
of classical knowledge in anything he ever said or
wrote; and on a recent visit to his old University
he astonished the not very erudite members of the
Canning Club by attributing to Horace, in a mutilated
form, the most familiar line in all the satires of
Juvenal. It is a curious fact that while on the front
Opposition Bench in the House of Commons there are
at least four good scholars, the Treasury Bench cannot
produce one. Mr. Goschen, however, imbibed in
Austinfriars a more useful form of knowledge than
he acquired at Oriel. No Chancellor of the Exchequer
since the institution of that office has been so thoroughly well acquainted with what Mr. Weller called
"those things that are always going up and down in
the City." When Mr. Disraeli went to the Exchequer
in 1852, he did not know contango from backwardation,
and he would not have known interest from discount
but for the extravagance of his youth. When Mr.
Goschen succeeded Lord Randolph Churchill in 1887,
there was not a denizen of Capel Court who could have
told him anything new. His special training has its
disadvantages. Both his faults and his merits as a
Minister of Finance are essentially those of an expert.
An amateur of equal ability would have failed where
Mr. Goschen succeeded, and succeeded where Mr.
Goschen failed.

John Bright always distrusted Mr. Goschen's
Liberalism, and even denied his claim to be regarded
as a Liberal at all. In later years Mr. Chamberlain

took up and exaggerated Mr. Bright's opinion. When Mr. Goschen joined Lord Salisbury's Cabinet, he astonished his colleagues, especially that most moderate of men, the late Mr. Smith, by the strength and fervour of his Conservatism. It was probably always there. In 1863 the City was Liberal within the Palmerstonian meaning of the word, and was tolerably faithful to its old connection with Lord Russell. Mr. Goschen had the same politics as the City. He has the same politics as the City still. After Lord Palmerston's death he joined Lord Russell's Government, and fell under the influence of Mr. Gladstone, in whose Cabinet he sat from 1868 to 1874. If Mr. Gladstone had never made a speech or passed a Bill, he would nevertheless have exercised upon the minds of his contemporaries a personal effect without precedent or example. Mr. Goschen served his chief zealously and well. He was always an excellent administrator, and he might, if he pleased, have held high office in the Government of 1880. But with an adherence to principle which did him infinite honour, he remained a private member of Parliament, because he did not think the agricultural labourers fit for the political franchise. Imperfect justice has been done to Mr. Goschen for this conscientious firmness. Mr. Goschen had no reason to covet the coarser and more material rewards of power. But he has always been a glutton for work, and for a man of his administrative capacity, five years' deprivation of office in the prime of life was a heavy penalty to pay. He could not have foreseen that a

fresh career would open to him under the patronage
of a Tory Premier.

Mr. Goschen was a Liberal, if a Liberal he was,
because he detested religious disabilities and commercial
restraints. In 1863 the Universities were still practically closed to Dissenters, and Protection was not sufficiently remote to be safely despised. Mr. Goschen's
real inconsistency dates from the year 1887. He was
perfectly justified, from every point of view, in joining
Lord Salisbury's Government. Nothing in his past
history disqualified him for doing so, and it is absurd to
say that sitting on almost equal terms with Lord Salisbury in the Cabinet was "giving a blank cheque" to
that distinguished statesman. On the other hand, Mr.
Goschen's refusal of place in 1880 was in itself a reason
for acceptance in 1887. But a man so ready to make
imputations as Mr. Goschen should be circumspect in
his own behaviour. He should not say that to tamper
with judicial rents in Ireland would be dishonest, and
then proceed within a few hours to tamper with them.
He should not oppose free education as demoralising,
and adopt it to forestall the other side. He should not,
merely because he differs with his former friends on the
government of Ireland, forswear his own doctrines on
the incidence of taxation and the apportionment of
rates. He should not act upon financial principles
which he had denounced as shabby, flabby, and inadequate. Having entered public life the earnest advocate
of religious equality, he should not resist the removal
of religious disabilities from Catholics because the

Leader of the Opposition was the author of the Bill. He should not earn the cheers of Mr. James Lowther and Mr. Howard Vincent by dallying with the errors of reciprocity and retaliation. Even if a man must turn his coat—and Mr. Goschen might plead that he had bought his without looking at it—he should leave his other garments as they were.

Mr. Goschen's reputation as a financier is the subject of acute controversy. It would stand higher if, instead of laboriously correcting every slip made by his minor critics in speeches from rural platforms, he had replied to the careful and exhaustive indictment drawn up in the year 1890 by Sir Thomas Farrer. It is not disputed that while he has removed some burdens which pressed heavily on the shoulders of the struggling classes, he has reduced the Sinking Fund, borrowed without necessity, extended the vicious system of grants in aid, and increased the complexity of the national accounts. His conversion of the National Debt was skilfully performed. But the bribe to the bankers which ensured its success was bad in principle, and made it impossible to ascertain whether the condition of the money market required the reduction of interest. The price of commodities is not set by giving away a new sixpence with a pound of tea. Mr. Goschen's acute and ingenious mind is deficient in grasp and scope. He does not see the wood for the trees. His statements are not lucid, though his arguments are often wonderfully clever.

As a debater Mr. Goschen ranks very high. Quite

as quick and ready as Mr. Balfour, he has the great
superiority over that statesman of dealing instinctively with the strong and not with the weak points of
his adversary's case. Interruption he not only bears,
but welcomes, and even courts. No public man deals
so admirably with the incidental remarks which often
put practised speakers out of their reckoning. Only
once was Mr. Goschen unprovided with a retort. There
was a financial discussion in the House of Commons.
Mr. Gladstone, after a few mild and complimentary
remarks, had left the House. Sir William Harcourt, as
not unfrequently happens, had imparted more warmth
into the debate. Following Sir William, Mr. Goschen
began in his most pompous style: "When the cat's
away the mice will play." An Irish member, sitting
under the opposite gallery, said, "And the rats." Mr.
Goschen paused, and it was well for that Irishman that
the Chancellor of the Exchequer had not the power of
life and death. If Mr. Goschen had succeeded Mr.
Smith as leader of the House, he would in some respects
have done better than Mr. Balfour. But he would
have wrought himself into a fit of righteous indignation three times a week, and the idlest lovers of amusement would have been the principal frequenters of the
Strangers' Gallery. Although Mr. Goschen was not
loved at the Treasury, his private friends are devoted to
him, and he shines at what used to be called the festive
board, in spite of the tendency to make small jokes so
mercilessly satirised by *Punch*. Ambitious of fame as a
wit, he has scarcely realised his ideal. His nickname

of Jacobyns for the Radical party is the stock-in-trade
of the Funny Correspondent, who probably does not
know the difference between Jacobins and Jacobites.
But the existence of the party is too shadowy, and the
personality of Mr. Jacoby too little known, for the
general public to taste the humour.

THE MARQUIS OF RIPON.

LORD RIPON is not the least distinguished of the five Peers who are now necessary members of any Liberal Cabinet. The others are, of course, Lord Spencer, Lord Rosebery, Lord Kimberley, and Lord Herschell. Lord Ripon is certainly the most Radical of the five, and his change of religion involved no change of politics. Nobody has worked harder for his party than Lord Ripon. Few men have been engaged in more of those great historical transactions which will live in the memory of the world when the strife of parties is forgotten. Mr. Gladstone has performed, in the course of his long and laborious life, many notable achievements; but not one of them has been more glorious to himself, nor more beneficial to mankind, than the Treaty of Washington. The moral effect of submitting the Alabama claims to arbitration was incalculable. It proved that England was not afraid to do right. It united the two great English-speaking Powers in a friendship which has never since been broken, and which forms the greatest possible contrast with their uneasy relations in the past. It gave an example of settling international disputes which has been largely followed, which has saved millions of lives, and which has done much to relieve civilisation from the reproach of barbarism. Of the Commission which arranged the Treaty, Lord Ripon, then Lord de Grey, was chairman, Lord Derby and Sir Stafford Northcote being his principal colleagues. The most important post which a subject of the Queen can fill outside the United Kingdom is the Viceroyalty of India. Lord Ripon took up the office at a very critical time. The personal eccentricities and political blunders of the late Lord Lytton had been fruitful in discontentment and disgust. The addition of a tawdry ornament to the simple title of an ancient throne was no amends for the enmity of Russia and the alienation of Afghanistan. Lord Ripon did not forget in India the lessons he had learned at home. He incurred the bitter hostility of those Anglo-Indians who think that her Majesty's Indian possessions should be 'governed for their special behoof; but he earned the undying gratitude of the native races, and he furthered the wise policy of fostering those germs of independence and responsibility which may one day prove the regeneration of India. These are high and splendid services to have been performed by a straightforward man of business, endowed with no more remarkable qualities than an aptitude for statesmanship and an experience of public affairs.

An excellent administrator, equally at home in the chair of his County Council, or at the head of a great Department in the State, Lord Ripon works calmly and accurately, without haste and without fuss. In one sense of the phrase, Lord Ripon was

H

born in the purple. He is understood to be, with
one exception, the only living person who began life at
No. 10, Downing Street. His father, the "transient
embarrassed phantom " of Lord Beaconsfield's satirical
novel, was Prime Minister in 1827, and in 1827 Lord
Ripon was born. Lord Goderich survived his brief
experience of supremacy without power for thirty-two
years, during which he held other offices with respectable competence, like his grandfather, "Prosperity
Robinson," before him.   Few men have been more
rancorously abused than the present Lord Ripon.
From the rabid cliques, who, as Mr. Lang puts it,
" under Eastern skies call Aryan man a blasted nigger,"
venomous scurrility is an honour.   When, in 1880,
Lord Ripon was sent out to succeed Lord Lytton,
objections were raised on account of his religious
opinions.   On this point Mr. Gladstone was peculiarly
well able to meet his critics ; for he had himself five
or six years before attacked Roman Catholicism in a
vigorous pamphlet, contending that Papal Infallibility was a mischievous innovation, which tampered
with the civil allegiance of Catholic subjects to
Protestant Sovereigns. Whether a statesman of Mr.
Gladstone's eminence is wise to embark upon such
controversies is a very doubtful point; but as a matter
of fact, Mr. Gladstone concluded his pamphlet by calling
upon the English Catholics to give an assurance of
their unimpaired patriotism and unabated loyalty. His
Essay naturally provoked many answers, including
one of singular force and beauty from John Henry

Newman. Mr. Gladstone, in replying upon the whole controversy, declared himself satisfied with the declarations he had elicited, and so the dispute ceased. He was therefore perfectly consistent in entrusting Lord Ripon with responsible functions, though it always suits his assailants to ignore the second pamphlet altogether.

Lord Ripon has never flaunted his change of faith, and never concealed it. It compelled him to resign his post as Grand Master of the Freemasons, to the general regret of that Society. But it has not affected in any way his conduct as a public man, and it has never interfered with his devoted attachment to Mr. Gladstone. In early life Lord Ripon was known as a Christian Socialist, and co-operated for philanthropic purposes with Charles Kingsley, Thomas Hughes, and other young Cambridge men of promise. Many are dead. But the only one who remains as sound a Liberal as ever is the only one of high social rank—the only one who sits, or ever has sat, in the House of Lords. Lord Ripon, though an indefatigable speaker, is not an orator. He says what he means, and means what he says. But to eloquence he makes no pretence. He resembles Sir Charles Russell in good-humoured readiness to go wherever he is wanted, and to make a speech whenever a speech is required. Genial, sociable, and unpretending, he is so thoroughly good-natured that no opponent could regard him as an enemy. He learnt public business at the War Office under Sir George Cornewall Lewis, whose grasp and range of mind was almost as much beyond the

H 2

ordinary Cabinet Minister's as Mr. Gladstone's own.
One of the few advantages which a young nobleman still
enjoys consists in the early apprenticeship to great affairs
under great men.   Lord Ripon sat for seven years in
the House of Commons, and fought several contested
elections before he was compulsorily relegated to the som-
nolent atmosphere of the Lords.   At the age of sixty-
five he is as full of fight and energy as ever, with the
same trust in the people and the same belief in the
future which have sustained him throughout his honourable career.   The British public are apt to think that
fidelity and simplicity of character, the preference of
public to private interests, the sense of duty, and even
the discipline of party, are in the long run more valuable
qualities than the dexterous command of a versatile
intelligence.

MR. JAMES LOWTHER.

FEW things are more to be regretted in contemporary politics than the subsidence—one happily cannot say the disappearance—of the Right Honourable James Lowther. There are not many more popular men in the House of Commons. There is not one more straightforward, more honest and upright in word and deed. Though not much over fifty years of age, Mr. Lowther has enjoyed, and occasionally abused, a long Parliamentary experience. He was only twenty-five when he was first returned as member for York, and he represented that city continuously for sixteen years. He was four years member for North Lincolnshire, and has now sat just as long for the Isle of Thanet. It may be doubted whether in the whole of that time he has ever changed an opinion or made an enemy. But when he lost his seat for York in 1880, something seems to have happened to him. He is not quite the same "Jim Lowther" the House used to know. The change is not in all respects to be regretted. Perennial youth is not wholly admirable when the youth has been a stormy one, largely associated with hearing the chimes a good deal later or earlier than midnight. Nobody expects Mr. Lowther, the staid and stolid bachelor, who has sown his wild oats, to go behind the Speaker's chair and crow like a cock, as if Mr. Auberon Herbert were still complaining of the Queen's immunity from income tax. But a good many debates since 1888 would have been far less dreary if Mr. Lowther had struck into them as of yore, hitting out at the Radicals from the shoulder, or aiming a well-planted backhander at the Liberalising tendencies of Ministerial sinners. Mr. Lowther was not included in the Conservative Government of 1885, and has never held office since. Perhaps Lord Randolph Churchill persuaded Lord Salisbury that Mr. Lowther was behind the age, and that it was important to provide for creatures of his own. The result was unfortunate, for the Treasury Bench has been flooded with dismal twaddlers, compared with whom Mr. Lowther is a Demosthenes or a Cicero.

When Mr. Lowther entered the House of Commons, it was led by Lord Palmerston, whose vigour and energy were at last slowly flickering out in listless somnolence. Mr. Disraeli was at the head of an Opposition which became really formidable when, in the following year, the death of the Premier put an end to the truce of Whig and Tory. Mr. Lowther has always been a Tory. He is a genuine Protectionist, who would keep out foreign corn and foreign labourers, if not foreign race-horses and foreign jockeys. Dishing the Whigs has never been in his line; and when, with the rest of his party, he followed Mr. Disraeli into the dark, he relieved himself with a bitter jibe. "What am I to say to my constituents," he exclaimed, "when,

after refusing a small Bill from a good Christian, I
have taken a big Bill from a bad Jew?" Mr. Lowther
was never a Disraelite, though he served in Mr.
Disraeli's Government; and he has always professed
personal admiration for Mr. Gladstone, whose Parliamentary supremacy he is too shrewd not to appreciate.
For Mr. Lowther, though he does not shine as an
abstract thinker, and though his political opinions are
founded rather on prejudice than on reason, has a cool
head, and a ripe judgment on all personal questions and
on all practical points. After holding some minor
appointments, he became Chief Secretary for Ireland in
1878, and brought in a Local Government Bill for that
country, which, if not very far-reaching or thorough-
going, was at any rate better than Mr. Balfour's. His
selection to succeed such a very serious politician as
Sir Michael Hicks-Beach excited a great deal of merriment; but, as a matter of fact, he was far better liked
than his predecessor, partly because, with all his blunt-
ness, he is thoroughly good-humoured, and partly
because his genuine love, not of gambling, but of sport,
is a quality congenial to the Irish people.

Mr. Lowther is by no means a bad speaker. He
does not trouble himself much about literary form, and
might perhaps describe himself, like Mrs. Squeers, as
"no grammarian." But, to apply the famous advice
of the Duke of Wellington, he says what he has to say,
doesn't quote Latin, and sits down. He knows his
own meaning, and never leaves his hearers in any
doubt on the subject. He has a large command of

racy vernacular, and his instinctive sense of fairness gives him a moral authority which is not to be despised. When the disputed votes of the Mombasa Directors were under debate, no speech—not even Mr. Gladstone's—was more effective than Mr. Lowther's. He at least could not be accused of priggish Puritanism on the one hand, or of a wish to damage the Government at all costs on the other. When, in a few grave, weighty, sensible words, he pronounced that, in his opinion, the directors were personally interested, and so ought not to have voted, the House of Commons felt that this unpretending sportsman was a better judge than the brilliant and paradoxical philosopher who found it impossible to distinguish between various motives for voting, which all seemed to him more or less inadequate and absurd. Mr. Lowther has, indeed, much of the judicial faculty in his mental composition. When he sat as a steward of the Jockey Club, with two ornamental colleagues, to hear the complaint of Lord Durham against Sir George Chetwynd, he displayed a mixture of dignity and astuteness which amused and rather astonished the Bar. People sometimes forget that it is much easier to be a good judge than a good advocate. A judge need not say anything until the case has been exhaustively argued, and he is not hampered in the process of investigation by the fear of injuring his client. But, considering his want of legal training, Mr. Lowther's performance in the Courts of Justice was very remarkable.

In sport, as in politics, Mr. Lowther has always

been perfectly straight.   He is not a betting-man, but
a sportsman pure and simple.   If all owners were like
him, the Turf would be cleared of its present disre-
putable associations.   Not long ago Mr. Lowther went
to support the claims of a Parliamentary candidate.
The audience was not composed exclusively of ardent
politicians, and he was interrupted by cries of " Come,
Jimmy, give us a tip for the Grand National."
" Jimmy " was equal to the occasion.   " Gentlemen,"
he said, in his most solemn tones, " I never made a bet
in my life.   But if you take my advice, you'll give
three to one against the field, including my friend
the Grand Old Man ; and he's a rank stiff 'un ! "   With
which most oracular response these anxious inquirers
after truth had to be content.   Mr. Lowther appears
to find the atmosphere of the House of Commons less
congenial than it was before the enlargement of the
county franchise.   But it is probably the Treasury
Bench that agrees with him the least.   Some of the old
gang are familiar to him.   The Stanhopes and Hamil-
tons, with the other Tite Barnacles of the age, he must
have known that he would find there.   The Queen's
Government could not, at least in their own opinion, be
carried on without them.   Mr. Chaplin he can contem-
plate with a not wholly unsympathetic smile.   But
who is Mr. Ritchie ? who is Mr. Matthews ? why
in the name of decency should Mr. Goschen be glaring
at his old friends and flattering his old enemies ?   Mr.
Lowther's sentiments towards Mr. Pitt and the Act
of Union are doubtless orthodox.   But it must have

sometimes crossed his mind that if the Union could not be saved without Mr. Henry Matthews, those abominable Separatists have something to say for themselves, after all. And Mr. Chamberlain! If ever a human being enjoyed himself in this world, then did Mr. Lowther taste pure delight when Mr. Gladstone so lovingly, so gently, with such consummate and inimitable art, chastised Mr. Chamberlain in Committee on the Small Holdings Bill.

MR. JOHN MORLEY.

IT is often said, and sometimes believed, that when Mr. Gladstone retires from the political arena there will be no public man left to touch the sentiment and thrill the moral fibre of the masses. This is to reckon without Mr. John Morley, whose hold upon the affections and convictions of the people is second to Mr. Gladstone's alone. Whatever may be thought of Mr. Morley by Parliamentary hacks and placemen, there can be no doubt that the working classes, especially in the north of England, are enthusiastically devoted to him, and would rather follow him, with the exception aforesaid, than any one else. The fact, of which any one may certify himself by a visit to Newcastle, is equally creditable to both the parties concerned. Mr. Morley never flatters the masses. He often tells them unpalatable truths. He is a man of indomitable courage, and as little like the typical demagogue as can well be imagined. His attitude towards the Eight Hours Bill and other developments of modern Socialism has been censured by tacticians and time-servers as too stiff and obstinate. But nobody who did not want to make himself ridiculous would accuse Mr. John Morley of subservience to the jumping cat. Mr. Morley's faults as a statesman—if faults they are—lie in the opposite direction. He is so determined not to be misled by self-interest or bullied by scheming agitators, that pressure hardens him, and his beliefs are intensified by attack.

The friend, and in some respects the disciple, of Mill, Mr. Morley entered public life as a philosophic Radical. But he came into Parliament, being then about forty-five, under the immediate auspices of Mr. Chamberlain, and with an especial sense of attachment to Mr. Bright. Mr. Bright and Mr. Chamberlain had not enough philosophy between them to endanger the soul of a tomtit. They were, however, practical men, and Mr. Morley, like most literary students, has an exaggerated respect for practical qualities. In 1886, when, three years after taking his seat (and the oath), Mr. Morley suddenly became a Cabinet Minister, he fell under the influence of a far greater personality : one which unites with singular fulness the capacity for business with the enthusiasm for ideals. The steady growth of warm personal friendship between Mr. Morley and Mr. Gladstone has exercised— as it could not fail to exercise—a remarkable influence upon Mr. Morley's view of men and things. Mr. Gladstone is the embodiment of Christian statesmanship, and his creed is at the root of his life. He cannot be appreciated without understanding it, although of course understanding does not imply acceptance. But it is difficult to know Mr. Gladstone and to believe that Christianity is a demoralising superstition.

Mr. Morley, like Mr. Balfour, has never taken very kindly to the House of Commons. The House respects

him a good deal more than he respects the House.
Most members of Parliament are rather ignorant, and
Mr. Morley's knowledge, though he takes more pains
to conceal it than most people do to display it, is encyclopædic. Parliamentary tactics are his aversion, and he
despises the small arts of the lobby. But supreme
success in the House of Commons is rarely obtained by
men who are not imbued with its corporate spirit, who
do not share its thoughts, prejudices, and habits. Mr.
Mill said that if a philosopher went into society he
should go as an apostle. Mr. Morley in society is
beyond criticism and above praise. A more fascinating
companion does not, and could not, exist. But in the
House of Commons he is, perhaps, a trifle too apostolic.
The epithet "austere" applied to him by the foolish
convention of the uninformed is absurd; but he has
principles, and, unlike many men of the highest personal
character, he does not leave them in the cloak-room before
going into the House. Then, again, Mr. Morley is not
a very ready debater. His speeches—eloquent, interesting, characteristic, abounding in flashes of epigram
and sparks of genius—require, as they justify, preparation. Sometimes, and more often of late than in
previous years—there have been instances the other
way. Mr. Balfour's Local Government Bill for Ireland
was a tempting theme, and Mr. Morley made the
best of it. He has never done anything better in
Parliament than his instantaneous dissection of that
astonishing measure.

Mr. Morley and Mr. Balfour have often been

contrasted and compared. For real knowledge, for literary
power, for width of mental range, they cannot, of course,
be mentioned in the same week. In Parliament Mr.
Balfour's position is, largely owing to accidental circumstances, higher. On a platform Mr. Morley is infinitely
superior to his rival, and that not merely in moral
earnestness, but in the oratorical faculty. Few seem
now to remember that in the autumn of 1890, just before an undefended divorce case convulsed the politics
of the Empire, Mr. Morley had got Mr. Balfour into the
tightest of all possible corners. Mr. Morley had made
his famous visit to Tipperary. Mr. Balfour, who is not
deficient in courage, though he has never been in any
serious danger, went to Newcastle and attacked its
illustrious representative. Mr. Morley's reply was crush-
ing and triumphant, not only in itself, but on account
of the enthusiasm it evoked. Mr. Morley, however, is
the most polished of antagonists, and Mr. Balfour, when
he is not dealing with Irish members, imprisoned by his
orders, fights like a gentleman, as well as a philosopher.
Probably no two public men are on better terms, and
Mr. Balfour's respect for Mr. Morley is sincere.

It is Mr. Morley's character, even more than his
intellect, which has given him the great influence and
ascendancy he exercises over his fellow-men. Honesty
is not so rare among British politicians as to make a
man eminent and influential. Even the mental integrity which is proof against sophistry does not put a
statesman upon the pinnacle occupied by Mr. Morley.
What his constituents and admirers rightly believe

about him is that he cares neither for place nor power nor party, except as means to the furtherance of social and moral ends. Moreover, the ends must be, not the passing fashions of the day, or the burning question of the hour, but the definite objects which his own reason and conscience approve. Mr. Morley is, in the philosophical jargon affected by Mr. Herbert Spencer's disciples, an Individualist. He believes that the greatness and prosperity of this country are largely due to the enterprise and public spirit of its private citizens. Holding this view, he has stoutly resisted the recent tendency to repose trust in the ubiquitous interposition of an omniscient State, and his attitude of manly independence is respected by those of his opponents whose respect is worth having.

Mr. Goschen once called Mr. Morley "the St. Just of our English Revolution." He might as well, while he was about it, have said the Calvin of our English Reformation. Both would have been alike nonsense. But it is more decorous to compare your adversaries with bigots than with thieves. The idea that because Mr. Morley has written some brilliant sketches of French history, and some charming studies of literary Frenchmen, he must therefore be a bad Englishman is even more ludicrous than the famous line :

"Who drives fat oxen should himself be fat."

Even as a man of letters, Mr. Morley is at his best, not in depicting Rousseau nor in criticising Voltaire, but in rendering to Robert Walpole and Edmund Burke a tribute worthy of their genius and patriotism. Mr. Morley's style, though abounding in power, beauty, and illumination, is not an equal one. When he writes on French subjects he falls into French idioms, which are apt to irritate even those who understand them. When he writes of English statesmen, as one of themselves, he not only enriches the great storehouse of our literature by work which the world would not willingly let die, but infuses a moral tonic into the somewhat exhausted veins of our body politic. Whether as an administrator and a man of business Mr. Morley will complete the tale of his public services, and justify the historic sense of his worshippers, time must show. But while Mr. Morley has exerted the influence of his vivid and awakening personality upon hundreds who never saw his face or heard his voice, those only who have been under the wand of the magician can thoroughly appreciate the high-minded chivalry and essential greatness of the man. In Mr. Morley's presence the meannesses, the trivialities, the futilities of life disappear. The spell of his magnanimity disperses them, and their haunting presence is laid. One may live, like Isaac D'Israeli, in a library, and yet be immersed in one's own concerns. But Mr. Morley has extracted from books a safeguard against the lowering and deadening forces of the world. His independence and elevation of mind are impervious to the corrupting and debasing elements of party politics. " Great," says Carlyle, "is the combined voice of men; the utterance of their instincts,

which are truer than their thoughts. It is the greatest
a man encounters amid the sounds and shadows which
make up this world of time. He who can resist that
has his footing somewhere beyond time." Mr. Morley's
high courtesy, refined dignity, and delicate sympathy
are not the whole secret of the personal devotion he
inspires. Even "the man who has no cause but himself" bows, perhaps in unconscious reverence, before
"the man who has no self but his cause."

EARL SPENCER.

"I EXHORT them," said Gibbon of the Spencers, "to consider the Faery Queene as the most precious jewel in their coronet." Lord Spencer does not follow the exhortation. He has other views. The owner (until recently) of the finest private library in England, if not in the world, prefers a Blue Book to a first folio, and is a greater dab, as the schoolboys say, at riding than at reading. Lord Melbourne—perhaps the most omnivorous reader of his time—declared that he did not believe in education because "the Pagets got on so devilish well without it." Lord Melbourne did not mean what he said. He seldom said what he meant, and was much misunderstood, in consequence, by fools. But Lord Anglesey, the head of the Pagets, would undoubtedly have governed Ireland with great success, if only the Duke of Wellington had let him alone. Lord Spencer has many of the qualities of his distinguished uncle, the first leader of the reformed House of Commons, and of his no less distinguished grandfather, the ablest Administrator in the Government of Mr. Pitt, after the accession of the Portland Whigs. The second Earl Spencer, Pitt's First Lord of the Admiralty, collected the library. The third—better known as Lord Althorp

—was a mathematician of some repute before he became a politician of great celebrity. The present Lord Spencer, who is the fifth Earl, was regarded till the momentous year 1882 as an hereditary Whig, rather more Liberal, and better affected to Mr. Gladstone than most of his class, who discharged ceremonial functions with ease, grace, and dignity. For a few months before the death of his father he sat in the House of Commons as member for South Northamptonshire. After succeeding to the Peerage, he was appointed on the Households of the Prince Consort and the Prince of Wales. Through the whole of Mr. Gladstone's first Ministry he was a useful and popular Lord Lieutenant of Ireland. For the first two years of Mr. Gladstone's second Ministry he was President of the Council, and nominally responsible for the system of national education ; but the real work was done by the Vice-President, Mr. Mundella.

So far Lord Spencer's life had been, for a man of his class, singularly uneventful. If little known to the general public, he was universally respected by all who knew him. Weak health had kept him from taking an active part in politics from 1874 to 1880, when his party were in Opposition, and he was never a man to push himself forward. The offices he had held were not in the circumstances of the first importance, and the robust thoroughness of his Liberal principles was only known to a few. In 1882 occurred a crisis which gave Lord Spencer his opportunity, and enabled him to win for himself a high place in the front rank of

public men. Lord Cowper, one of the faintest and
most ineffectual Viceroys who were ever ruled by their
Chief Secretaries, retired from Dublin Castle, having
" suffered the manners " of Mr. Forster with exemplary
endurance for two years. Immediately afterwards Mr.
Forster himself resigned, disgusted with the conditional
—or, as he sometimes put it, with the unconditional—
release of Mr. Parnell from Kilmainham. Lord Spencer
went back to Ireland as Lord Cowper's successor,
accompanied by his kinsman, Lord Frederick Cavendish, as Chief Secretary. They entered Dublin on the
morning of the 6th of May with signs of public re-
joicing as the harbingers of reconciliation and peace.
The same evening Lord Frederick and the permanent
Under-Secretary, Mr. Burke, were murdered in the
Phœnix Park, almost under Lord Spencer's eyes. The
Government acted with the utmost promptitude and
energy. Sir George Trevelyan and Sir Robert Hamilton succeeded the martyrs of duty. Sir William Harcourt, as Home Secretary, introduced a stringent
Coercion Bill, and for nearly three years Lord Spencer
administered it with mingled firmness and gentleness,
but with unflinching justice and vigour. No English
statesman has ever worked in more constant peril of
death, nor been more rancorously and mendaciously
assailed with libels upon his public and private
character. Lord Spencer never showed resentment
or fear. He simply stayed at his post and did his
duty, until Ireland was freed from the terror and disgrace of the "Invincible" conspiracy. In days when

Mr. Goschen's fulsome adulation of "brave Mr. Balfour" passes for patriotic discernment, it is refreshing to think of a statesman whose courage would have deserved the panegyrics Mr. Balfour receives. Lord Spencer's reward was very different. When he retired, after Mr. Gladstone's defeat in June, 1885, Mr. Chamberlain refused to attend the banquet in his honour, and in the infamous " Maamtrasna Debate " the Tories attacked him with a virulence the more discreditable because it was not even sincere. Mr. Chamberlain did hate Coercion at that time. The Tories delighted in it, and were jealous of Lord Spencer's success. They only dropped it to catch the Irish vote at the General Election of 1885, after which they at once proposed to resume it.

Lord Spencer left Dublin Castle the second time with a good deal of material for thought. He had put down crime, and refused to interfere with political agitation. The criminals had been hanged, imprisoned, or dispersed. The political agitators—the men who really represented the large majority of their countrymen—were stronger than ever. His Tory successor, Lord Carnarvon, a man of many accomplishments but little wisdom, was substituting, with Lord Salisbury's approval, conciliation for the strong hand. Lord Spencer's most trusted colleagues and advisers in Ireland made no secret of their belief that the game of Coercion was up, and that the only cure for Irish disaffection was Home Rule. Mr. Gladstone, as the Duke of Devonshire afterwards acknowledged, had been for some

years tending towards a drastic reform in Irish government. Mr. Chamberlain had denounced "Castle rule"
as rivalling in tyrannous injustice the treatment of
Venice by Austria and the treatment of Poland by
Russia. A few weeks before the General Election,
Lord Salisbury, whose secret communications with Mr.
Parnell, through Lord Carnarvon, were not then known,
spoke of the "Irish leader" in terms of high respect,
and expressed a pious hope that it were practicable
to give Ireland the same independent position as
Hungary.

When Mr. Gladstone declared for Home Rule, Lord
Spencer, whose authority was unique, became one of his
strongest and staunchest supporters. He adhered to
his chief and to his principles at enormous personal
sacrifice. The society which he frequented was almost
unanimous against him, and declared its intention of
boycotting Home Rulers without mercy. Lord Spencer
was regarded with peculiar aversion by those of his own
order who had estates in Ireland, and who had reckoned
upon him to maintain the ascendancy of their
caste. He felt deeply the conduct of his former
friends ; but he bore it with the same courageous dignity
which had carried him through more material troubles.
He did what he believed to be right ; and notwithstanding his reverence for Mr. Gladstone, it was not Mr.
Gladstone who converted him. It was the facts of the
case. Having discovered that the old methods of ruling
Ireland were mistaken and could be no longer followed,
he preferred conscience to consistency. He declared in

a simple and touching speech that he would have been
"the most despicable individual" if he had taken any
other course. He pursued the fresh path with ardour.
Though far from being a natural orator, he pleaded on
many platforms with a simple and persuasive earnestness
for the cause of justice and peace. Meanwhile, he
hunted the Pytchley hounds with untiring enthusiasm ;
and in 1889 was unanimously elected the first Chairman
of the Northamptonshire County Council. A master of
business, familiar with every detail of local administration, he was, quite apart from his rank and position, the
best choice that could possibly have been made. The
simple manliness and transparent honesty of Lord
Spencer's character have extorted from his bitterest
opponents the tribute of their reluctant esteem.

LORD HERSCHELL.

LORD HERSCHELL, as was said of a far greater personage, is not redeemed by a single vice. There was, indeed, a moment when he promised to rise above his reputation, and to elicit the sympathies of erring humanity. That was in 1886, when Sir Henry James refused the Woolsack, and Sir Farrer Herschell grasped the bauble which Sir Henry was too virtuous or too prudent to accept. But the General Election took away that bauble, and the intensely decorous respectability of the new Chancellor was fatal to his chances of wider fame. Sir George Trevelyan says somewhere that the British public like their ministers of religion to believe rather more than themselves, and their representatives in Parliament to believe rather less. Wickedness was once associated with keeping the conscience of the Sovereign. But Lord Hatherley, Lord Cairns, and Lord Selborne so sanctified the office that the chair of St. Augustine became by comparison almost secular. Lord Herschell has not edited a hymn-book, and at prayer meetings, if he attends them, he does not lift up his voice; but he is an orthodox member of the Established Church, and a rigid observer of the moral law. He never indulges in unseemly jests, nor even in jests which have the merit

of seemliness. If Sir Charles Russell had been eligible
for the post held by Lord Westbury, a good deal would
have been said by the Tories about Irish adventurers
and legal flexibility. It was not the least of Sir Farrer
Herschell's many eminent qualifications for presiding
over the administration of justice that to accuse him of
political or any other form of profligacy would have been
not so much unfair as ludicrous. No set of opinions
could fail to become respectable if Lord Herschell held
them. No one has been more loyal to his party or to
his leader. Lord Herschell did not, and could not,
excite himself, or become enthusiastic for Home Rule or
anything else. But when the clamours of faction were
loudest, when the self-constituted rulers of London
society were threatening all Liberals with ostracism and
disgrace, when foul and calumnious charges of complicity
in murder were hurled by frantic partisans against
political antagonists more honourable than themselves,
Lord Herschell's nerves were calm and his courage
unshaken. Intellectually convinced that the Irish case
for self-government was made out, he declined to be
moved from his course by the wild and whirling
words which created the demand for such wares as
Richard Pigott supplied.

Lord Herschell's progress at the Bar was slow, or at
least it began late. It is said that he was briefless for
seven years. The first person to discover his great
legal abilities was the late Mr. Justice Quain, then a
leader of the Northern Circuit, which Farrer Herschell
had joined. As soon as he got his opportunity, Mr.

Herschell knew how to make good use of it. Accurate, painstaking, clear-headed, and laborious, he acquired and preserved a large practice of the best sort, being retained in almost every commercial cause of importance at Manchester and Liverpool. Before a jury he was nowhere with Sir Charles Russell; but he was an infinitely better lawyer, and his arguments in banc were as powerful as his opinions were authoritative. When his rise once began, it was steady, in politics as well as in law. He was still quite a young man when the city of Durham returned him to Parliament, and he soon made his mark in the House of Commons by his masterly denunciation of the Slave Trade Circular. It is a singular proof of adaptability which prevents Lord Herschell from being exactly like every other man with brains and knowledge, that he should at once have discovered how to address the House of Commons. It was said of him at the time, by an acute observer, that he was the only barrister in the House whose profession could not be detected the moment he began to speak. He has since, however, found an audience which suits him even better than the House of Commons. Very few people have really enjoyed the privilege of talking to the House of Lords, except for a guinea a minute, at the Bar. The late Lord Grey, who was not given to strong language, said that it was like speaking to dead men by torchlight. The Duke of Argyll revels in it. But, in the first place, he is a consummate orator; in the second place, he never sat in the House of Commons; and in the third place, the sound of his own voice

is to him the sweetest music in the world. Lord
Herschell, like Lord Mansfield, has tried both Houses,
and prefers, or appears to prefer, the Lords. Everybody
remembers Macaulay's contrast of Murray and Pitt
with Chatham and Mansfield. In the Commons, a
flash of the Great Commoner's eye or a wave of his
arm cowed the aspiring lawyer. In the Lords,
Chatham's brilliant but histrionic oratory was far less
effective than the calm reflection and luminous order
with which the great Chief Justice discussed and
decided public affairs. It has been said that if a man
can speak in the House of Lords, he can speak anywhere. But he may not be able elsewhere to speak
so well.

What damps the ardour of the young Peer is the
attitude of frigid attention, sometimes varied by the
freedom of private intercourse, with which his remarks
are received. Applause is extremely rare, and is reserved rather for Toryism than for eloquence. Lawyers
are accustomed to speak for hours without a cheer, and
with the knowledge that a cheer would be instantly
"suppressed." Lord Herschell is the last person in
the world who would be embarrassed by the absence of
audible approval. All he wants is listeners, and the
Peers listen to him open-mouthed. Although he is
usually on political questions in a minority of about
one to ten, the ascendancy he has acquired over the
House is something marvellous. The Tories take his
law for gospel. Lord Halsbury, the late Chancellor, is
too indolent to dispute his supremacy. Even the Marquis

himself condescends to meet him with an argument
instead of a sneer.   Lord Herschell is as free from all
suspicion of genius, or even of originality, as anyone
can be; yet his position—his unique position—is well
deserved.   His speech on the second reading of the
Special Commission Bill was as able, as conclusive, as
convincing, as anything which the Lords have heard in
this generation.   It was unanswerable, and has certainly never been answered.   Lord Ashbourne shouted
some self-contradictory contradictions; the English
Chancellor tried his hand at a little special pleading;
but if any future Government should be minded to pack
a tribunal for the trial of their political opponents on
political issues, they would do well first to consult Lord
Herschell's speech, and consider whether any of his
predictions have been left unfulfilled.   Lord Herschell
has, of course, proved a notable addition to the Supreme
Court of Appeal.   Lord Halsbury has become a good
lawyer, except so far as legal instinct was concerned,
since he took the seals.   Lord Herschell brought to
the judicial bench not only a judicial mind, but a
thorough knowledge of jurisprudence, as well as of
case law.   His industry is omnivorous, and he regards
presiding over a Royal Commission as a holiday when
out of office.   The receipt of five thousand a year for
doing nothing [impelled him not to idleness, but to
exertion.

SIR HENRY JAMES.

Sir Henry James, though no longer young, is a gay bachelor, and a frequenter of Marlborough House. Known for several years as the man who refused the Woolsack, he has since received the particular form of consolation which must have been most grateful to his feelings by becoming Attorney-General to the Prince of Wales. From a professional point of view, it may have seemed odd that Sir Henry James should succeed Sir Charles Hall. But that only shows how limited the professional point of view is. Sir Henry James, though, as he once candidly confessed, he was not born in the atmosphere of aristocracy, has taken very kindly to it, and made himself very much at home there. His conversational shop is not legal. His talk is of Princes and Rothschilds rather than of Byles and Benjamin. Nevertheless, Sir Henry James is quite affable, and never forgets his manners if he chances to find himself in plebeian company, which cannot in these democratic and inclusive days always be avoided. Sir Henry received a great deal of well-merited and some rather exaggerated praise for preferring the Union to the Woolsack in 1886. But his subsequent career

has not been unenviable.   His position in the House of
Commons is much better than it was before.   His position at the Bar is unique.   From 1880 to 1885 he led
the life of a slave.   In those days the House sat to any
hour, sometimes through the night.   There was a
famous occasion in that Parliament when the Treasury
Bench was packed, Mr. Gladstone sitting in the middle
of his colleagues at one o'clock on Sunday morning.
Through those crowded and stormy years Sir Henry
James was Attorney-General—not to the Prince of
Wales, but to the Queen.   He set a good example to
his successors by almost entirely dropping his private
practice.   But the work was terrible, and told seriously
upon his health.   It was not unnatural—it was very
right and proper—that before Mr. Gladstone went out
of office in 1885 he should have conferred upon his
Attorney-General the unusual distinction of a seat in
the Privy Council.   The social precedence of a Privy
Councillor is far higher than that of a knight,
so that Sir Henry James had every reason to be
gratified.

Since the memorable night in June, 1885, when the
Liberal Government was defeated on the Budget of
Mr. Childers, and Lord Randolph Churchill jumped
upon the bench in the exuberance of his joy, Sir Henry
James has enjoyed comparative leisure.   Unable as a
Privy Councillor to practise before the Judicial Committee, he has appeared from time to time in almost
every other court, taking as many briefs as he wanted
of the kind that he liked, and earning a handsome

income with a very moderate amount of personal exertion. If this be martyrdom to principle, it is an easy
cross and a comfortable crown. The Prime Minister,
as in duty bound, offered the man who might have
been Chancellor the first legal vacancy in the House of
Lords. Sir Henry refused a place for which he would
not have been particularly well fitted; but if a Peerage
were bestowed upon him without any conditions, he
might possibly not decline it.

The year 1886 made the reputation of Sir Henry
James. Before that time his fame was purely forensic
and fashionable; but the British public, in the slang
of the day, "tumbles" to a man who refuses anything
good, and is for some reason or other especially dazzled
by the Woolsack. When Mr. Gladstone offered Sir
Henry the post, he had probably not read the electioneering speeches of the member for Bury, which
made acceptance practically impossible. Sir Henry had
broken Walpole's advice to his young men, and used
the fatal word "never." He had been bitterly
opposed by the Irish population of Bury, and also
by the Tory vicar of the town. He had been inso-
lently called Mr. Gladstone's lackey, and told that
he would do whatever Mr. Gladstone told him. Sir
Henry James replied to this impertinence with becoming
warmth of temper. He spoke enthusiastically and sin-
cerely of his devotion to Mr. Gladstone, but he said
there was one thing he would never do for Mr. Gladstone or anybody else: and that was to vote for an
Irish Parliament. He is also reported to have declared

that he would not accept the Chancellorship if he were
elected. Sir Henry had thus burned his boats, and
was compelled to remain on Lord Hartington's side
of the stream. It must have been a source of satisfaction to so honourable and amiable a man that the
place which might have been his fell into such competent hands as Lord Herschell's.

The long and close friendship between Sir Henry
James and Sir William Harcourt has survived political
differences and Parliamentary contentions. It would,
indeed, not be easy to quarrel with Sir Henry James.
Opinions may vary about the delicacy of his breeding
or the fineness of his taste; but his civility is undeniable, and the weary length of the Parnell Commission
was constantly lightened by his good-humoured banter.
Sir Henry James is not a wit, and his acquaintance
with literature is slight; he carries, however, the small
change of society about with him, and keeps people
gently amused without any strain upon his mental
resources or theirs. A rather cynical man of the world,
with a contemptuous tolerance of religious controversy,
he revived in his speech to the Commissioners the
vehemence with which years before, in the House of
Commons, he had fulminated against the Galway priests
in defence of Mr. Justice Keogh. If Sir Henry James
denounced the Toryism of the British as he denounces the
Nationalism of the Irish clergy, he would be absolutely
consistent on at least one great question of public policy.

Since he left the Liberal party, Sir Henry James has
greatly improved as a Parliamentary debater. He was

wont to bring with him into St. Stephen's the style of Westminster Hall, and to address the Speaker as if he had only a few minutes to spare before appearing in another court. Lately he has adopted a more deliberate tone, and his rhetorical powers, which are considerable, have full play. He stood, however, no chance against Mr Chamberlain, who, though a far less popular man, is also a far more powerful enemy. At the Bar Sir Henry James has always been distinguished for courtesy, and for disdaining the arts of intimidation. A masterly cross-examiner, he never attempts to browbeat or confuse a witness, but rather leads him unawares into a trap or pitfall. In this artistic self-restraint he formed a striking contrast before the Parnell Commissioners with Sir Richard Webster, who relied chiefly upon a loud voice and a blustering demeanour. By no means a great or learned lawyer, Sir Henry James has made a remarkably skilful and successful advocate, a singularly judicious and capable adviser. It was the general belief of those who knew him that if he had led the case against the Irish members "and others," the forgeries of Pigott would never have been produced in court. Sir Henry James's faults as a politician are timidity and an inclination to magnify the strength of his opponents. On the other hand, he never loses his head, and is never induced by excitement to ignore difficulties, or to imagine that the victory is won before the battle has been fought. His favourite amusement is shooting, and his favourite guest is the Prince of Wales. Judges who do not aim

J

at shining in society, or whose social aspirations have not been gratified, are heard to complain that Sir Henry James is supercilious.   But young barristers who have been brought into contact with him speak of him as the best and most generous of friends.   Entirely devoid of moral or religious pretence, Sir Henry James has probably done more acts of thoughtful and unselfish kindness than most of the bishops.   His early services to liberty in promoting the protection of trades unions and the enfranchisement of the working classes from the fetters of the law are well known.   In the Corrupt Practices Act he made an unwise concession to the Tories by allowing the use of private carriages for the conveyance of voters to the poll.   His public utterances since the unfortunate secession of 1886 have been almost uniformly courteous, and, unlike some of his political friends, he has spoken of Mr. Gladstone without appearing to resent the obligations under which that statesman had laid him.

LORD HALSBURY.

Mr. DISRAELI's astonishment when he first saw Sir
Hardinge Giffard has passed into history. Whatever
may have been the precise terms in which the Prime
Minister expressed his opinion of his Solicitor-General,
there can be no doubt that he entirely failed to appreciate a man who never really has been appreciated,
except by lawyers. The circumstances of Sir Hardinge's
introduction to the House of Commons were peculiar.
No Law Officer of the Crown—at least, in that part of
the United Kingdom called England—ever had so much
difficulty in finding a seat. When at last he discovered
one in the now disfranchised borough of Launceston,
he came up to take the oath without bringing a certified
copy of his return, and this trivial coincidence fixed
his unfortunate adventures upon the public memory.
Lord Halsbury's career has been peculiar, if not unique.
His quaint personality adds point and zest to the
genial and unaffected good humour which make him
a universal favourite. But the curious and interesting
feature of his life is that he obtained a post for
which he has proved himself eminently qualified by
means which would have been equally successful if he
had had no qualifications at all. Lord Salisbury's

J 2

disregard for fitness in any public appointment which
is neither clerical or diplomatic is notorious. He did
not know in 1885—and if he had known he would not
have cared for the knowledge—that he was promoting
to the Woolsack a man who, if not as learned as Lord
Selborne or as brilliant as Lord Cairns, would establish
in the House of Lords a character for judicial breadth
and soundness of view which has rarely been equalled,
and still more rarely surpassed. Yet this is the simple
fact about Lord Halsbury, as lawyers most strongly
opposed to him in politics will testify. A clear head,
a quick apprehension, a mind which instinctively grasps
what is essential and rejects what is accidental, a
common sense almost amounting to genius, and a
thorough knowledge of the world, make a strong Judge.
Lord Halsbury possesses all these qualifications, and
there have been few stronger Judges than he.

In politics the Lord Chancellor hardly counts. His
opinions are understood to be those of his grandmother.
They have probably not changed by a hair's breadth
since he went to school. He is an accomplished man,
and what time he has been able to spare from the law
has—perhaps wisely—been spent on literature or astronomy rather than on Hansard or Burke. With an
Irish origin and an Oxford training, Mr. Giffard
selected the English Bar as his profession, and South
Wales as his circuit. His progress was not very rapid.
But he gradually became an advocate of almost the
highest order. The mental indolence which unexpect-
edly shows itself in so many men of strong and

vigorous understanding must have stood to some extent
in his way. An eminent contemporary, some years his
senior at the Bar, described him as far better in reply
than in opening his case, because at the end of the trial
he had read his brief and mastered the facts. The
same thing must be more or less true of most barristers
in large practice. With Sir Hardinge Giffard it was
sufficiently peculiar to be noticeable. He thoroughly
understood the ways and peculiarities, the manners and
prejudices, of a British jury. He began his practice in
that excellent school of miscellaneous training, the
Mayor's Court, and after that for some years his business was largely criminal. He became exceedingly
astute in dealing with witnesses, and infallible in
keeping the attention of the twelve men to whom his
client's fortunes were committed. Perhaps the greatest
mistake of his forensic career was his inability to appreciate Mr. Bradlaugh. Theological and political prejudice may have been at the bottom of the blunder; but
it was a blunder, and Mr. Bradlaugh took every
advantage of it.

In the House of Commons Sir Hardinge Giffard
did not shine. He never acquired the Parliamentary
manner, and St. Stephen's does not like the style of
nisi prius or of the Old Bailey. He was out of his
element there, and never did himself justice. His
colleague, the late Sir John Holker, concealed under a
drowsy manner and a heavy exterior an acuteness and
adroitness in debate that extorted the admiration of Mr.
Gladstone, who afterwards selected him to be a Lord

Justice of Appeal. Mr. Solicitor has not the same
senatorial opportunities as Mr. Attorney; but Sir
Hardinge Giffard never approached the position of Sir
Farrer Herschell in the Commons. It is the same in
the Lords when they sit as a political assembly. Lord
Herschell is everything, the Chancellor nothing. Lord
Herschell may almost be said to "run" the Standing
Committees, and Tory Peers, ignoring the Woolsack,
listen to him with bated breath. This suits Lord
Halsbury very well. He is inclined to be lazy, and his
ambition was abundantly satisfied—as well it might be—
when he received the Great Seal. Where legal reforms
are concerned he is, considering his crusted and in-
veterate Toryism, Liberal enough. No one is a
stronger advocate for the examination of prisoners, and
his Land Transfer Bill was, at least, too drastic for the
House of Lords. He astonished a good many people
by the fervour with which he vindicated Mrs. Jackson's
legal independence of her husband. But in ordinary
matters of legislation nothing gives him greater pleasure
than to announce that "the Not-Contents have it."

The crisis in Lord Halsbury's otherwise rather tame
existence came when Mr. Gladstone's Government was
defeated in June, 1885. Who was to be Lord Selborne's
successor? Lord Cairns and Sir John Holker were dead.
The general opinion was favourable to the Master of
the Rolls, now Lord Esher, then Sir Baliol Brett. He
had a great reputation as a lawyer; he had sat in the
House of Commons; he had held legal office under
Mr. Disraeli. But Sir Hardinge Giffard perceived that

it was now or never, and he did not hesitate. The late Lord Chancellor and the late Attorney-General having passed away, he claimed the Woolsack as the late Solicitor-General's right. It was said by the gossips of the hour that he refused to leave Lord Salisbury's presence until his application was granted. At all events, he succeeded in his object, and the Master of the Rolls was consoled, though not appeased, with a Peerage. At that time Sir Hardinge Giffard had no reputation for knowing anything except the criminal law, with which his acquaintance was admitted to be unique. Grave apprehensions were felt and expressed at his promotion to preside over the Court of last resort for all causes within the United Kingdom. These fears proved to be entirely groundless. Every day Lord Halsbury sat to hear appeals his knowledge and judgment improved, until the gloomiest of the croakers were at length forced to admit that they had misunderstood the man.

It is a positive calamity that Lord Halsbury could not be confined to the discharge of his judicial duties. His abuse of patronage has been exaggerated for sensational purposes, as all such things are ; but it is gross as a mountain, open, palpable, all the same. When the worst instance of it occurred two years ago, and shocked even the most callous partisans, Lord Halsbury's friends declared that he had struggled against the appointment, and only yielded to irresistible pressure. But this is no defence. The puisne Judges are appointed by the Crown upon the nomination, not of the Prime Minister,

but of the Lord Chancellor. It is absurd to suppose
that the Premier would have ventured upon such a
step as dismissing Lord Halsbury for not allowing an
improper interference with his legitimate province.
Jobbing is not Lord Halsbury's only failing, though
it is a serious one. If he has not Lord Eldon's habit
of procrastination, the reason is that instead of post-
poning business, he neglects it. In this respect he
contrasts most unfavourably with Lord Selborne and
Lord Herschell. Lord Cairns was perhaps almost as
indolent ; but the extraordinary brilliancy of his parts
and the marvellous rapidity of his intellect enabled him
to overtake in a day what had been accumulating for a
month. Lord Halsbury is a clever man, but he is not
equal to Lord Cairns. He resembles that great lawyer,
however, in the pious fervour of his evangelical orthodoxy, even if he does not provide tea and hassocks for
aspirants to courts above and courts below. It was said
of one Administration that the Lord Chancellor believed
what the First Lord of the Treasury professed; but
the Government alluded to could not, of course, have
been Lord Salisbury's.

MR. HENRY FOWLER.

MR. HENRY FOWLER was Mayor of Wolverhampton at thirty-three. Lord Randolph Churchill was leader of the House of Commons at thirty-seven. Mr. Fowler, however, arrived, in the French sense of the word, a good many years ago, and during the exclusion of his party from office he has advanced, as Mr. Gladstone would say, not so much by steps as by strides. Members of the legal profession—gentlemen of the long robe, as Mr. Disraeli would call them—are supposed to be rather too well represented in Parliament, and to obtain at least their fair share of the few prizes in public life. As a matter of fact, they have hitherto only been able to accept purely political, as distinguished from judicial or forensic, appointments, at the cost of abandoning for ever the work by which they made their living. But the legal profession has two branches, and the one to which Mr. Fowler belongs has been excluded from the Government, even when it secured a place in the House of Commons. Mr. Fowler is the first solicitor who has ever been sworn of the Privy Council. He is the first solicitor to enter the Cabinet. No one grudges him his promotion, which he has earned by hard work and efficient service. Mr. Fowler, besides being a solicitor, is a Nonconformist,

and Nonconformists have not in past times received
either from Liberal or Conservative Administrations an
unduly large share of honours and rewards. If the late
Mr. Samuel Morley had not refused a Peerage he would
have been almost the only Dissenter in the House of
Lords, to which the present Earl of Carlisle had not
then been called up. Mr. Bright and Mr. Chamberlain
were the solitary exceptions to the uniform Church-
manship of Mr. Gladstone's successive Cabinets. Mr.
Fowler has remained something more than staunch to
the religious body in which he was brought up.
He has not become a real or a nominal Churchman.
He is an active, influential, and prominent member
of the Wesleyan Connexion.

The Wesleyans, as everybody knows, are the most
Conservative of English Dissenters, and the least hostile
to Church Establishment. But Mr. Fowler is—and
has been all his life—a strong, advanced, and consistent
Liberal. To call him a Radical would perhaps be going
too far; for he is essentially a moderate man. He
exemplifies as well as any contemporary politician
the solid virtues of the class which the Greek
philosopher described as the salvation of society.
It is not that Mr. Fowler ever shrinks from
defending Nonconformity, or even from pushing its
claims. On the contrary, Dissenters have no steadier
or more persistent advocate when their case is really a
strong one. He led the Parliamentary protest against
the persecution of the Salvationists at Eastbourne, and
to no one is their deliverance more largely due. On

the other hand, it would be difficult to depict his horror
at the obstruction of the Clergy Discipline Bill by two
members from Scotland and one from Wales. Mr.
Fowler is thoroughly loyal to the House of Commons.
He has devoted great ability with excellent results to
proving that Lord Salisbury's Government in general,
and Mr. Goschen in particular, distrust and dislike
the principle of Parliamentary control. The system of
hampering future Parliaments by withdrawing naval
or military expenditure from the Estimates, and putting
it into a statute, has no more strenuous and eloquent
opponent. Equally firm and vigorous have been his
protests against making financial arrangements—as in
the Free Education Act, which cannot be altered without the consent of the House of Lords. But with
perfect consistency he condemns in unsparing terms the
efforts of a tiny faction to defy the House of Commons,
in order that they may damage the Church of England
by preventing the removal of drunken and immoral
clergymen.

It is chiefly, though by no means solely, as a
financier that Mr. Fowler has won his great political
reputation. Mr. Goschen, who is very fond of taking
the high line, and assuming that nobody knows the
difference between interest and discount except himself,
has found that he cannot deal in that way with Mr.
Fowler—it would be too arrogant a jest. Mr. Fowler
has tracked Mr. Goschen through all the intricate mazes
of his complicated system, and has brought out the
plain facts—that his surpluses are fictitious, his

reductions in the taxes made out of borrowed money. There is not a better man of business in the House of Commons than Mr. Fowler—not even Mr. Chamberlain. Mr. Fowler possesses not merely great capacity and experience, but that instinctive grasp of what figures mean, without which the most plodding industry will never make a Chancellor of the Exchequer. Mr. Fowler has already been at the Treasury, where he was Secretary in 1886. If he should ever go back to the same department in a higher rank, the interests of the taxpayer and of the national creditor will be in unusually safe and competent hands.

Mr. Fowler is a debater who can hold his own against any man on the Tory side. His speeches, like himself, are business-like, full of knowledge, abounding in moderation and good sense. When he first came into the House of Commons, twelve years ago, he was a little apt to be pompous, and to use what St. Jude calls great swelling words. Time has toned him down, and his style is now a model of the straightforward, argumentative, practical kind, which, for the purposes of every day, a British Assembly prefers to exalted eloquence. It must not be supposed that Mr. Fowler is nothing but a man of business. His favourite reading on his holidays is said to be Hansard. At all events, he is thoroughly conversant with the political history of the last hundred years, and as diligent a student of Burke as Mr. Gladstone or Mr. Morley. His distaste for extremes has cast upon him—perhaps unjustly—the imputation of political timidity, and he has been suspected of hankering after an alliance with Birmingham. But he fights manfully when he thinks the time for fighting has come; and it was inevitable that he should deeply feel the loss of a man with whom he has so much intellectual sympathy as Mr. Chamberlain. In one respect Mr. Fowler is Mr. Chamberlain's superior, and that is the not unimportant quality of temper. A more courteous and amiable man does not sit on either side of the House, as his political adversaries would be the first to acknowledge. Mr. Fowler likes pleasing people as much as Mr. Chamberlain likes annoying them; and that is saying a good deal. Of course this virtue, like others, has its corresponding vice or defect. There are occasions when a man ought not to care what the enemy think of him; there are even some when he should be indifferent to the opinion of his friends. Mr. Fowler will never initiate a great policy or lead a forlorn hope. But he illustrates and typifies in its best shape a class without which the Liberal party could not hold together for a week.

SIR GEORGE TREVELYAN.

CARLYLE, the countryman of Lockhart, and no great admirer of Macaulay, is reported to have described Sir George Trevelyan's "Life" of his uncle as the best biography in the language. It certainly ranks with the "Life of Johnson" and the "Life of Scott," above all others, if indeed it be below those two. It completely changed the general estimate of Macaulay, who, instead of a book in breeches, was found to have been the most genial, affectionate, generous, and delightful of men. It appeared at a convenient season, before the political lull which followed the General Election of 1874 had been disturbed by the revival of the Eastern Question, which set all Europe by the ears. Perhaps that was the culminating period in Sir George Trevelyan's career. Although he had not attained his fortieth year, he stood remarkably high both as a member of Parliament and as a literary man. It was really due to him and to his courageous crusade against military officialism that the iniquitous system of Purchase in the Army had been abolished by Royal Warrant in the teeth of the House of Lords. He was also the pioneer of the movement for extending House-hold Suffrage from boroughs to counties, which the

next Liberal Government was destined to take up and
carry through. His political verses were universally
admired, and had, indeed, no contemporary rivals. He
possessed the ear of the House of Commons, and a
perfectly safe seat. His personal popularity was immense,
and was not confined either to his own side of the
House or to his own class in society. It seems strange
now to reflect that at that time Mr. Balfour, Mr.
Chamberlain, and Lord Randolph Churchill were almost,
if not entirely, unknown. In the year 1876 Mr.
Trevelyan had as good a chance as any man alive of
succeeding Lord Hartington in the Leadership of the
Liberal party, and of becoming Prime Minister of
Great Britain. He had given a signal proof of disinterested sincerity by resigning office in 1870 because
Mr. Forster's Education Bill recognised the public
endowment of sectarian teaching. Yet when, in 1875,
Mr. Gladstone temporarily withdrew from the task of
leading the Opposition, it was Mr. Forster, and not
Lord Hartington, whom Mr. Trevelyan would have put
in Mr. Gladstone's place.

It is difficult to realise the transformation of the
political world which the last fifteen years have brought
with them. The man who in 1875 wrote to the late
Lord Granville as if his work in this world was over
has since been twice Prime Minister, and commands
the unabated devotion of the Liberal party. Lord
Hartington, as Duke of Devonshire, presides over the
deliberations of a select and dwindling cave of Adullamites. Mr. Forster has passed away. The House of

Commons is led by the languid youth who dawdled
through two Parliaments as member for Hertford.
Sir William Harcourt, the free lance of old days,
stands next in Parliamentary succession to Mr. Gladstone. Beyond, if not within, the walls of Parliament
the most influential name in the Liberal hierarchy
belongs to a man who fifteen years ago was simply a
rising light in the literary world. Lord Rosebery, then
hardly more than a boy, would now, if only he were
in the House of Commons, be the Liberal Elisha. Lord
Spencer, then a political figure-head of the ceremonial
and ceremonious type, has proved himself in moments
of doubt, trial, and danger to be essentially a statesman
as well as every inch a man.

Meanwhile, Sir George Trevelyan's history has been
full of distinction, and, still more, full of interest.
Mr. Gladstone would have done well to include him
in the Cabinet of 1880.   As Secretary of the Admiralty, which he did not become till the month of
November—having at first been left out in the cold
altogether—he was doing congenial work in an excellent
way when his old and intimate friend, Lord Frederick
Cavendish, was murdered in the Phœnix Park.   The
vacant post—vacant almost as soon as filled—was offered
to Sir Charles Dilke, who declined to leave the Foreign
Office without entering the Cabinet.   It was then conferred upon Sir George Trevelyan, who accepted it in
the spirit of duty—not because he liked it, but because
it was dangerous. For two years and a half, as the
subordinate colleague of Lord Spencer, he fought

against a murderous conspiracy, and vanquished the conspirators. All the leading combatants in that campaign of law and order are now Home Rulers :— Lord Spencer, Sir George Trevelyan, Sir Robert Hamil ton, and Sir Edward Jenkinson. This simple fact gives some measure of the baseness and falsehood involved in the statement that Home Rule was a cowardly policy, extorted by fear. All these men went about in daily peril of their lives and the lives of their families. Not one of them ever shrank from his duty or uttered a word of complaint. The iron nerves of Lord Spencer carried him safely through an atmosphere of deadly plots and filthy libels. Sir George Trevelyan was more sensitive. Himself the soul of honour, he could not despise as much as he ought the licence of an irrational scurrility. If Coercion was ever justified, it was when the assassination deliberately planned by the Invincibles had shocked the civilised world. But Sir George Trevelyan was too good a Liberal ever to like it, even when he conscientiously believed it to be necessary. As soon as the Chief Secretaryship ceased, largely through his own exertions, to be a post of danger, he resigned it to Mr. Campbell-Bannerman, and came at last into the Cabinet as Chancellor of the Duchy of Lancaster. He looked ten years older for those thirty months; but the work was done. Ireland was pacified, and civilisation was saved.

Among the distinguished converts made by Coercion to Home Rule, Sir George Trevelyan was the last. Everybody knows how he resigned office with Mr.

K

Chamberlain in 1886, how he voted against Mr. Gladstone's Bill, and how, at the General Election of that
year, he lost what had always been considered one of
the safest Liberal seats even in Scotland. The Round
Table Conference, from which Mr. Chamberlain petu-
lantly broke off, and Mr. Balfour's Coercion Bill, introduced not to suppress murder, but to help landlords in
collecting their rents, brought him back to the party
which he should never have left. Sir George Trevelyan
honestly, though erroneously, believed that Lord Hartington and the other seceders could and would remain
a separate and independent wing of the Liberal army,
true to their old convictions, if hostile to Mr. Gladstone's
Home Rule. He soon discovered his mistake. The
meetings he was asked to address consisted almost
exclusively of Tories, who hissed the name of Mr.
Gladstone and cheered the name of Lord Salisbury.
His new associates abhorred the very idea of Liberalism, and did not conceal their abhorrence. Sir George
Trevelyan might give up Parliament, though the priva-
tion was for him perhaps severe ; he could not give up
his Liberal principles. He came back, as member for
Glasgow, to the old cause and the old chief. Politics
have no mercy on even the appearance of vacillation
and indecision. But Sir George Trevelyan's motives
were suspected only by those whose suspicion is a
compliment.

Sir George Trevelyan is an admirable speaker, especially at a public meeting, to which his eloquence is,
perhaps, better suited than to the House of Commons.

As a debater, he is not so ready and not so precise as some inferior men. No one in politics, unless it be Mr. Gladstone, has a better memory or a more richly-stored mind. No one in England is a better judge of a book in any department except physical science and theology. No better classical scholar, except Professor Jebb, and perhaps Mr. Roby, sits in the House of Commons. No civilian ever had a greater passion for military history. Even his uncle, whom in so many respects he resembles, had not a more insatiable appetite for reading. There is no reason why Sir George Trevelyan should not be member for Glasgow for the rest of his life, and introduce his three sons con-secutively to the Speaker. But many will regret that the biographer of Macaulay should for ever desert the paths of authorship. That men of ample means and leisure should devote themselves entirely to politics is meritorious on their part and an advantage for the State; but the House of Commons does not yet sit all the year round, nor every day in the week. Only a unique combination of knowledge, talent, and opportunity could produce the book which fascinated Carlyle. But there is a famous fragment on Fox, which ought not to remain a fragment much longer, especially as it breaks off at the point where Fox had begun to see the error of his way.

K 2

SIR CHARLES RUSSELL.

"THERE has been nothing like it since Follett," was the comment of a high judicial authority on Sir Charles Russell's speech before the Parnell Commission. "A great speech, worthy of a great occasion," was the judgment of the President, now Lord Hannen. It placed the orator incontestably at the head of the English Bar, where, indeed, he was before in the opinion of all competent critics. It is curious that Ireland should have sent to the English courts in our time two such consummate advocates as Charles Russell and Hugh Cairns. On opposite sides of politics, in different branches of the profession, they resembled each other in nothing but eminence and nationality. The first Lord Cairns was incomparably superior to Sir Charles Russell as a legal authority and a Parliamentary debater. After electrifying the House of Commons by his eloquence, he became Lord Chancellor in the prime of life, and shone no less as a judge than as a statesman. It may be doubted whether he ever entered a criminal court, and it was very seldom that he addressed a jury. He was too clever a man not to distinguish himself, even in novel circumstances and uncongenial surroundings. But he would have had no chance at *nisi prius* against

Sir Charles Russell. Cairns was stiff, cold-blooded, puritanical, austere. He seemed to hold himself aloof from ordinary humanity, and to remember his fellow-creatures only in his prayers. His one weakness was hunting; and it was believed that he hunted health as much as the fox. Sir Charles Russell's geniality, vitality, and force of character are at the root of his success. With him it is the man who makes the advocate, and not the advocate who makes the man. If Sir Charles were to accost the first male passenger he met in the street, and order him to take off his hat, the order would probably be obeyed; the power would be felt before there was time to realise the absence of what John Austin called sanction.

Sir Charles Russell, keen, adroit, and full of resource as he is in the conduct of his business, remains the most genuine of men. There is nothing theatrical about him, except the instinctive sense of tone, and manner, and gesture which only the very greatest actors possess. His fine presence and natural dignity of bearing assist the operation of his forensic gifts. But his triumphs are due to himself, and not to his training. Macaulay said that Chatham was the solitary instance of a really great man who had no simplicity of character. In the active pursuit of a calling which encourages every form of menacing or persuasive, of sentimental or dialectical artifice, Sir Charles Russell is at all times and for all purposes himself. He is always an Irishman, always a sportsman, always a Catholic, always a Democrat. When he was Attorney-General he astonished and shocked a good many comfortable prigs by remarking,

almost casually, that a starving person had a right to
take a loaf of bread. Sir Charles was only talking
Catholicism, and it probably never occurred to him that
anyone could think otherwise. When, again, the outcry
against the Prince of Wales for playing baccarat was
at its height, Sir Charles Russell did not put on the
amazement he showed. It was simply incredible to him
that people should see any moral wrong in playing
cards for money. It was impossible for him to take the
purely legal view on the right of public meeting in open
spaces. His democratic sympathies forbade. To be on
the side of the people is as natural for him as to be on
the side of rank and fashion is natural for Sir Henry
James. And when at the close of that magnificent
address, which will be read when the Report of the
Commissioners has sunk into oblivion, he declared that
he was pleading for the land of his birth, he explained
at once the motive of his advocacy and the sources of
its strength.

In the House of Commons Sir Charles Russell is
seldom quite at his best. The atmosphere does not
suit him, and he prefers a larger and more democratic
assembly. But on the platform of a public meeting
he is superb. His opponents complain, naturally
enough from their point of view, that there is
some lack of novelty both in subject and treatment.
For Sir Charles usually speaks about Ireland, and
shows how much more loyal are people who
manage their own affairs. Yet there is something in the
commanding authority and transparent sincerity of the

speaker, the personal conviction and contagious energy of the man, which impress themselves upon a popular audience better than a more elaborate rhetoric and a more paradoxical originality. Sir Charles never seems to be tired of public meetings. Unlike many inferior performers, he will go to the smallest and remotest places, fifteen miles from a lemon or a reporter, if he can help to promote what with him is the sacred cause of Home Rule. There was never a more striking disproof of the calumny, that lawyers only care for politics as a means of selfish advancement, than the career and conduct of Sir Charles Russell. Devoted to Mr. Gladstone and to the Liberal party, he will go anywhere, and do anything, for the purpose of restoring his old chief to office and a native Legislature to Ireland.

Sir Charles Russell's manner in court has sometimes been said to be domineering and dictatorial. One can imagine a judge begging him, as Mr. Justice Maule begged Sir Cresswell Cresswell, to "recollect that I am a vertebrate animal." Yet in private life Sir Charles is singularly unassuming. His perfect freedom from vanity and self-consciousness is as rare as it is attractive. Nobody could be less pompous, or more anxious to put himself on a footing of entire equality with the company in which he may be thrown. No one, on the other hand, is less inclined to flatter or court the conventionally great. Sir Charles is a thorough Democrat, in things social as well as in things political.

The abolition of those convenient "Attorney-General's pillows," the Chief Justiceship of the Common

Pleas and the Chief Barony of the Exchequer, has left
some eminent lawyers in a position vulgarly described
by the epithet " stranded "—men who will not accept
the drudgery of the Bench in Courts of First
Instance, and may never sit on the Bench at all.
Sir Charles Russell is not so learned a lawyer as
Sir Horace Davey and Sir John Rigby. Even on
a question of common law, their opinion would
be better worth having than his. As a speaker
he is, of course, beyond all comparison, their superior, as in other respects besides. He and Mr.
Morley are the two politicians who have been made
by Home Rule on one side, just as Mr. Balfour and
Mr. Goschen have been made by it on the other. Sir
Charles Russell, however, is not one of those morbidly
and wearisomely virtuous persons who knew better than
their neighbours, and were Home Rulers all along.
He sat through the Parliament of 1880, and gave a
general support to Mr. Gladstone's Government, without discovering that an Irish Parliament was necessary
to the land of his birth. It is indeed strange that when
he became a Home Ruler he had ceased to sit for the
Irish constituency of Dundalk, and was member for the
English constituency of South Hackney. There could
hardly be a better guarantee of good faith or a more
obviously natural one.

LORD RANDOLPH CHURCHILL.

SINCE the days of Sir Robert Walpole, if not before, Eton has been a successful nursery of British statesmen. But it may be confidently affirmed that never since the time of Henry VI.—"most patient and hapless of star-crossed kings"—has the greatest of public schools turned out a less conventional product than Lord Randolph Churchill. Lord Rosebery, Mr. Balfour, and the present Viceroy of India were his schoolfellows. He was Lord Edmond Fitzmaurice's fag. Scholastic and academical distinction were not in his line. His career at Oxford is chiefly remembered by the obscure story of a policeman's helmet, which perplexed the magistrates then, and has not since been elucidated by the historian. At the General Election of 1874 a certain Mr. Barnett retired from the representation of the Duke of Marlborough, facetiously called Woodstock in the Parliamentary handbooks. Lord Blandford passed for a Liberal in politics, and was not in other respects favourably known to the public. So his brother, a young man of five-and-twenty, was chosen by the owner of Blenheim to fill the vacancy. Nobody, except his immediate friends and relatives, knew anything about Lord

Randolph Churchill. The helmet had in the course
of five years become a legend, and the Randolph
Hotel was much more famous than the younger son
of an unpopular landlord. Lord Randolph's return
was regarded as a certainty. But a dauntless patriot,
who was afterwards to beard the Parnell Commissioners
in their den, stepped into the breach. Mr. George
Brodrick, now Warden of Merton, Lord Randolph's
college, and a pillar of "Liberal Unionism," came
forward as a candidate. He was supported by Mr.
Goldwin Smith, the most brilliant writer and the most
incapable electioneerer of the day. Mr. Brodrick himself harangued the few agricultural labourers who
could be enticed out of their houses on a wintry
evening (to find the Duke's agent carefully identifying
them) in the style of the college lecture-room. Mr.
Goldwin Smith fired over their heads brilliant epigrams,
which he might as well have delivered in Greek, but
which were appreciated by the few Oxford men who
happened to be present. Mr. William Sidgwick, who
has also gone over to the minority, thundered away as
if he had been Cicero and the Duke had been Verres.
It was a remarkable coruscation of talent, and very
good fun while it lasted. When it was over the
labourers were driven to the poll, and voted for
Blenheim Palace, blankets, unfair rents, and comparative fixity of tenure. Mr. Goldwin Smith announced
that he should go to Canada—"the evil shadow of the
British aristocracy will fall on me no more"—and
everybody went to bed.

Scarcely a thought was given to the Tory candidate. Mr. Brodrick had a future before him; he was to be the great land reformer of the age. Mr. Goldwin Smith was to remove from the new world the effete superstitions of the old. Mr. Sidgwick—but this is not an Oxford Calendar. Lord Randolph Churchill was regarded as his father's son—a shocking example of what rotten boroughs could do to lower the intellectual standard of the House of Commons. During the Parliament of 1874 the member for Woodstock only once distinguished himself, and that was by a rather rude attack upon Mr. Sclater-Booth, now at peace where nobody but Lord Salisbury is permitted to make personal remarks. There is more insolence than wit in saying that a double-barrelled name implies mediocrity. When Parliament was dissolved in the spring of 1880, Lord Randolph Churchill had no reputation for anything more valuable than impertinence.

With the commencement of Mr. Gladstone's second Administration, in May of that year, began Lord Randolph Churchill's career. He started with a very small amount of preparation and a very slender stock of materials. At school and college he had learnt scarcely anything. He was ignorant to an almost incredible degree. His conduct was usually reckless; his statements were usually baseless. But he was found to have unbounded audacity, unsparing industry, immense practical shrewdness, with animal spirits and a freedom from scruple which almost amounted to genius. Sir Henry Wolff, Sir John Gorst, and Mr. Balfour supplied

him with as much information as he could assimilate—
perhaps with a good deal more. He dominated them
all, and it must be admitted that he provided for them
well. " Three of us sworn to-day, and all on the same
cushion," he is reported to have said when the Fourth
Party was dissolved by office. What was the secret of
Lord Randolph's success? He devoted himself to the
House of Commons. The House cares not two straws
for what a man is, says, or does " out of doors."
It forms its judgments at first hand, and once they are
formed, it rarely alters them. [In the Parliament of
1880, the most turbulent of modern times, Lord
Randolph attended almost every sitting and spoke in
almost every debate. It was only by slow degrees
that he acquired his admirable Parliamentary manner,
his readiness of resource, his adroitness in reply. In
1880 he was something very like a buffoon; in 1885
he was something very like a statesman.

That Mr. Gladstone had something to do with Lord
Randolph's rapid rise cannot be denied. Lord Randolph made a point of attacking the Liberal Premier
on every possible occasion, and Mr. Gladstone almost
always allowed himself to be drawn. Mr. Gladstone
has never quite got rid of the old-fashioned prejudice
that it is rather good of a nobleman to feel an interest
in anything, and he paid his youthful assailant the
compliment of taking him seriously. It should be said
on the other hand, that few people have a stronger
sentiment of admiration for Mr. Gladstone, or appreciate his Parliamentary supremacy better, than Lord

Randolph Churchill. For his own leaders Lord Randolph showed from the first the most absolute and unconcealed contempt. Collectively, they were "the old gang." Individually, they were " Marshall & Snelgrove." Lord Randolph culminated, so to speak, in 1886, and then came the crash. He had survived many blunders, and some performances which could not be set down to honest error. At last he made the fatal mistake of supposing himself to be indispensable. He resigned office because he was not allowed to cut down the cost of the spending departments, and to his own amazed bewilderment his resignation was accepted. His kingdom was divided, and given to Mr. Goschen and Mr. Smith. He was left out in the cold, where he has ever since remained. It is the strongest possible tribute to his capacity for business and his knowledge of mankind that he should have left behind him at the India Office, and even more at the Treasury, the reputation of a most able and brilliant administrator. He never introduced a Budget. But the Budget he had prepared is the theme of almost hyperbolical praise among those who were officially acquainted with it. His principal opponents are all agreed that during the brief second Session of 1886 he led the House of Commons with consummate dexterity and tact.

There are reasons why Lord Randolph Churchill is not likely to achieve the highest prize of public life. To lead the House of Commons, intellectual qualities, properly modified and directed, may suffice ; but the House, though it represents the country, is

not the country, except, perhaps, in constitutional
fiction. Some solidity of character, some moral ballast,
is required in the Prime Minister of Great Britain. A
man may change his mind, and change it completely,
on the gravest and most important subjects, without
losing the confidence of the English people; but there
must be reasons for the change, and it must be obviously sincere. Lord Randolph excites interest because
nobody can predict what he will do next. It is not,
however, a very respectful interest, and it commands
more attention than votes. Moreover, a statesman of
the first rank cannot afford to be ridiculous, and there
was much scope for merriment in Lord Randolph's
African adventures. We cannot have a Premier *pour
rire*; though if Lord Randolph is ever again in a
Cabinet without being Premier, there will be few to
envy his chief.

In the House of Commons, Lord Randolph, whenever he chooses to exert himself, must always be a
powerful personage. Mr. Balfour's initial failure as
Leader, which has been redeemed, is understood to
have filled him with unspeakable delight. Mr. Chamberlain, on the contrary, appears to inspire him with
sincere admiration, not untempered with awe. It is
disagreeable to come upon a man cleverer than your-
self, and quite as free from inconvenient bondage to
principle. When Mr. Morley referred to these two
worthies as "wandering stars," he probably did not
mean to suggest that for them was reserved the
blackness of darkness for ever. Their future is difficult

to forecast; it can hardly fail to be conspicuous. Lord Randolph's temper, and his unrestrained indulgence of it, has made him many enemies; yet very few men can be better or more agreeable company than he. One of the brightest and wittiest talkers in London, he criticises friend and foe with an acute discrimination and an entire absence of reserve. A Radical and Democrat—so far as he is anything at all—he is obliged to keep a store of pompous platitudes at command for the ceremonies of the Primrose League and other kindred occasions. His attack upon the London County Council was saturated with insincerity, but his disbelief in Home Rule may perhaps be genuine. What he was like as a colleague may be gathered from Lord Salisbury's undisguised willingness to part with him, and the obvious substitution of a reign of geniality for a reign of terror on the Treasury Bench when Mr. Smith stepped into his shoes. That Lord Randolph has steadily lost ground since 1887 is a plain and palpable fact. How far he can regain it in a new Parliament is among the most curious personal questions of the immediate political future.

MR. HENRY MATTHEWS.

Lord Randolph Churchill's Home Secretary very soon parted company with his political creator. It is said that when Lord Randolph found his resignation accepted at the end of 1886, he expected Mr. Matthews to follow him into retirement. If so, he showed more genuine simplicity of character than has been usually attributed to him by either friend or foe. If the Chancellor of the Exchequer did not know when he was well off, the Home Secretary was by no means in a similar state of ignorance. So Mr. Matthews remained, and did as much harm to the Government of which he was a member as a clever man well could. Few Ministers have been subjected to a larger amount of unjust criticism than Mr. Matthews; but he has brought a great deal of it upon himself by arrogance, pedantry, and want of tact. It is worse than absurd to charge him with vindictive cruelty in the exercise of the royal prerogative. He considers the cases of murderers with laborious and conscientious humanity. Yet, when he is asked questions about them in the House of Commons, he resorts to technical quibbles and to a fine show of virtuous constitutionalism, which make the public suppose that he is indifferent to the prisoner's fate. He went into the case of the Aylesbury poachers with almost painful minuteness. He discussed it with the Lord Chancellor, he discussed it with the Attorney-General, he discussed it with an eminent lawyer on the other side of the House. Whether his ultimate decision was right or wrong, it was formed with the most anxious desire to do justice. If he had given the House of Commons a fair account of the impression produced upon his mind by a perusal of the evidence, he would have silenced much of the outcry against him. But Mr. Matthews would rather be misunderstood than communicative, and his preference was abundantly gratified.

Mr. Matthews had a bad training for political office, and it says much for his ability that his failure has not been more complete. When his name was first mentioned in the summer of 1886 as Lord Randolph's nominee, the public were astounded. They had hardly recovered from their amazement at Lord Randolph's own rapid elevation, when a man wholly unknown outside the Law Courts was pitchforked into the Home Office by an obsequious Premier, at the request of his too powerful colleague. It is true that Mr. Matthews had just been returned for East Birmingham—the first Tory who ever sat for that once Radical town. It is true that nearly twenty years before he had been member for the little Irish borough of Dungarvan—which, however, got rid of him at the first opportunity. He was not, like Sir Richard Webster in 1885, new to Parliamentary life, and unprovided with

L

a seat. But few people remembered that he had ever
been in the House of Commons, and when the circumstances came to be investigated they did not increase
the general confidence in his character. It is, of course,
a picturesque exaggeration to say that Mr. Matthews
was in 1868 a Fenian candidate. But he undoubtedly
eulogised some of the Fenian leaders in eloquent language, and attacked his opponent—now Lord Justice
Barry—for having prosecuted them as the legal representative of the Crown. Moreover, he was at that time
a Home Ruler and a supporter of Isaac Butt. That he
should now come out as a full-blown Tory and step at
once into high place seemed odd and unfortunate. At
that time the name of Mr. Henry Matthews was in
everybody's mouth, on account of his brilliant, vehement and virulent speech against Sir Charles Dilke in
the Divorce Court. He had long been known as an
astute and showy advocate, whose soundness of judgment
was by no means equal to his more plausible and
conspicuous attainments.

Only Lord Randolph Churchill would have thought
of Mr. Matthews as Home Secretary. But Lord Randolph was determined to emancipate the House of
Commons from the control of the " old gang," and in
particular to clap a coronet, by way of extinguisher,
upon the head of Sir Richard Cross. It is understood
that her Majesty refused to part with Lord Cross, who
succeeded Lord Randolph at the India Office. As for
Mr. Matthews, he had attracted the notice of Lord Randolph in 1885. Lord Randolph was then a candidate

for Central, Mr. Matthews for Eastern, Birmingham. Neither of them was successful, though the impression made by the young Secretary of State upon Mr. Bright's majority was a very remarkable event. Mr. Matthews delighted his colleague in the struggle by the liveliness of his personal attacks upon the memory of Cobden and the personality of Bright. Lord Randolph, no doubt, thought in 1886 that he had got hold of a clever speaker—as he had; and of an effective debater—as he had not. Mr. Matthews hardly counts in a serious debate. His adroitness is undeniable, his words are exceedingly well chosen, while in mental cultivation and knowledge of the world he is far above the Ministerial average. But neither his style, nor his tastes, nor his habits of mind and temper are suitable to the House of Commons. He was born in Ceylon. He took a degree in Paris. He has a French exuberance of manner and a thoroughly legal view of political issues. His associations, except at the Bar, are as different as possible from those of an ordinary English member ; and as if to widen the gulf, he is a Roman Catholic, who, though a Minister of the Crown, cannot distribute any patronage in the Church of England. When Mr. Gladstone formed his second Government in 1880, loud and angry protests were made from diverse parts of Great Britain against the inclusion of two Catholics : Lord Ripon and Lord Kenmare. It illustrates satisfactorily the growth of tolerance that the appointment of Mr. Matthews should have passed without a Protestant murmur. But when a strange face

L 2

suddenly appears on the Treasury Bench, every addi-
tional element of strangeness is counted against the
new comer. If Mr. Matthews had been an Irishman,
it would have seemed more natural; as it was, the
eccentricity of the choice could only have been justified
by a striking success.

An eminent counsel past middle life seldom bears
transplanting to the Parliamentary or Administrative
soil. If Mr. Matthews is too much of an advocate for
the House of Commons, he is too much of a lawyer for
the Home Office. The ideal Home Secretary would
know enough law to understand legal opinions, and not
too much to respect them. Mr. Secretary Matthews,
though on the Treasury Bench he professes to be a lay-
man, is regarded in the official world as too self-confident
and too contemptuous of advice. Nor has he contrived
to work harmoniously with able and independent men.
He quarrelled with Sir Edward Jenkinson. He quarrelled with Sir Charles Warren. He quarrelled with
Mr. Monro. Nobody has ever succeeded in quarrelling
with Sir Edward Bradford. Mr. Matthews, in spite of
his forensic training, is a Constitutionalist, and a man
of principle. If he has been fiercely, and sometimes
reasonably, attacked, it should be remembered that the
onslaughts have not all come from the same side.
When he refused to admit the right of public meeting
in Trafalgar Square, the Socialists denounced him as a
Tory. When he declined to interfere with the full right
of combination by the dockers in the great strike, the
Tories denounced him as a Socialist. They even had

the impudence to suggest that he was "unduly influenced," in the spiritual sense, by the late Cardinal
Manning. When he led the Government to defeat in
the stupidly bungled case of Miss Cass, he was technically right in protesting that as the woman had been
acquitted the business was none of his. A prudent
Minister would have managed the House, and soothed
the feelings of Miss Cass's friends. In dealing with
the disturbances at the World's End, Mr. Matthews
showed that he had learned a lesson in place, and
that he could even display tact upon occasion.

In the terrible duty of considering capital sentences
Mr. Matthews has, perhaps, shown more ingenuity than
wisdom. His famous decision that Mrs. Maybrick had
tried to poison her husband, but that Mr. Maybrick
might conceivably have died of something else, was a
miracle of subtlety; but it was too clever by half. On
the other hand, in the case of Lipski he stood firm
against a ridiculous agitation—much firmer than the
Judge, who procured a fruitless respite for which there
was no ground. As a politician, Mr. Matthews is
strongly opposed to the intervention of the State in
matters of trade, and to this now rather unfashion-
able belief he has been faithful wherever he could.
A man in English politics so highly accomplished as
Mr. Matthews has usually been trained at an English
University, in a public school, or both. Statesmen of
Mr. Chamberlain's type are common enough. But Mr.
Matthews is in a class by himself. His reading is
wide, though it seldom shows in his speeches, and he

enjoys the reputation of a learned theologian. There are few more precise purists in the choice of language, and this ought to secure for Mr. Matthews the approval of Mr. Gladstone, of whom he stands in considerable awe.

SIR JOHN GORST.

THE selection of Sir John Gorst to succeed Sir Gabriel
Stokes as member for Cambridge was creditable to
that ancient and splendid University, or rather to
the Tory caucus which controls its political destinies.
They are thoroughgoing Tories at Cambridge. They
do not recognise the people called Liberal Unionists.
They accepted the Duke of Devonshire as their Chancellor partly because he is a duke and partly because
he is really a good deal more Conservative than Lord
Salisbury. But when they were fortunate enough to
secure Professor Jebb to fill the vacancy caused by the
death of Mr. Raikes, they insisted that the new member
should call himself a Conservative, and sit on the
Ministerial side of the House. In choosing Sir John
Gorst they have done well. But inasmuch as Sir
John is at least fifty per cent. more Liberal than most
of the Hartingtonian Adullamites, the Master of Mag-
dalene and Canon Browne exposed themselves to the
reproach of caring more for the name a man gives
himself than for the opinions he holds. If there are
to be University members at all, they ought to be men
of intellectual eminence, and not like the academic
representatives of Oxford. Sir John Gorst was a high

wrangler and a Fellow of John's, where he now holds
an honorary Fellowship. He has seen a great deal of
the world, having been successively Civil Commissioner
of Waikato, in New Zealand, and principal agent of the
Tory party in the best days of Mr. Disraeli. But the
interesting fact about his adoption by Cambridge is that
he belongs to the progressive school of Conservatism,
and is indeed only a Conservative at all because in this
free country a public man must be something.

Various explanations have been offered of Sir John
Gorst's exclusion from the last Tory Cabinet, and they
agree only in being flattering to Sir John Gorst. The
most probable, and the least mysterious, is that Lord
Salisbury loves mediocrities and hates argument. The
only sign of grace the Prime Minister showed was in
raising Sir John to the rank of a Privy Councillor while
still an Under-Secretary of State. Perhaps the capricious
and versatile fancy of Lord Randolph Churchill may have
had something to do with the inadequate recognition
of Sir John Gorst's capacity and powers. When in
1886 Mr. Matthews became a Secretary of State and
Sir John Gorst an Under-Secretary, a duplicate blunder
was committed which may take rank with the grossest in
the history of Administrations. Nor was the folly made
less conspicuous by putting Sir John under the most
incompetent member of the old gang. From 1886
to 1891 it was Sir John Gorst's function to protect
Her Majesty's Indian Empire from the mischievous
fussiness of Lord Cross. For five years he deftly
accomplished his task, and yet avoided quarrelling

with Lord Cross. At last, in the summer of 1891, the fire kindled, and he spake with his tongue. Few more amusing speeches were ever made in the House of Commons than Sir John Gorst's so-called defence of the Indian Government for their dealings with Manipur. The most brilliant invective from the most eloquent opponent would have been far less damaging than the caustic irony which explained to the world from the Treasury Bench how Lord Lansdowne had punished the Senaputty, not for his undoubted vices, but for his equally unquestionable talents and vigour. The ease and self-possession with which this unconventional theory was broached, the air of infantine simplicity which emphasised its most telling passages, delighted the Opposition and disgusted the Ministerialists. Sir John Gorst denied that when he talked of mediocrity he was thinking of Lord Cross, as earnestly and indignantly as Dickens protested that he did not mean Harold Skimpole for Leigh Hunt. But it was difficult to resist the conviction that the speech had been provoked by five years of Lord Cross and the Indian Council.

Those who know everything, or nothing, declare that when the Tory Prime Minister remonstrated with Sir John Gorst, Sir John naïvely replied that he had only said in public what Lord Salisbury said in private. But this is probably too good to be true. Having made himself impossible at the India Office, Sir John Gorst was, in accordance with good old English practice, promoted to a higher sphere, and became Secretary to

the Treasury. He is probably the only man who ever
arrived at this thankless and laborious, but very important, office through the legal service of the Crown.
In 1885, when the Fourth Party was dissolved after
dividing the spoil, Mr. Gorst was knighted on his
appointment as Solicitor-General. If his professional
status hardly warranted so sudden a rise, the scandal
was certainly less than the selection of a briefless
barrister with no knowledge of law to be Lord Chancellor of Ireland. That so clever a man as Mr. Gorst
should not have obtained a larger and more lucrative
practice is rather surprising. But it must be recollected
that he was not called till his return from New Zealand,
and that he devoted himself to politics with intense
assiduity. When the Fourth Party was formed, he
was its shrewdest and most experienced member. Lord
Randolph soon distanced all his companions or com-
petitors in the House of Commons, and the Primrose
League took shape in the chaste imagination of Sir
. Henry Drummond Wolff. But Mr. Gorst knew the
Parliamentary ropes as well as the secrets of the electioneering confessional. The Solicitor-General did not
approve of Lord Salisbury's first legal appointments,
and in 1886, for reasons which could be best explained
by Sir Edward Clarke, Sir John Gorst received a
post of less dignity and emolument. He deserved a
fate which he should have shared with others for the
great blot in his political career, the infamous attack
on Lord Spencer, by which the Tories disgraced the
Session of 1885.

It is a real misfortune to the House of Commons that Sir John Gorst, who has been, among other things, a political journalist, should speak so seldom. He is a debater of the first class, and would have beaten Mr. Balfour hollow if their chances of distinguishing themselves had been equal. He is too fond of sarcasm to expend it all upon the other side, and his convictions are suspected of lacking profundity. But he is quick, ready, dexterous, and good-humoured, with a constant command of excellent English, and a decided turn for felicitous epigram. He does not, however, belong to the class by which the Tories think they ought to be ruled, and it takes a man like Peel or Disraeli to rule them altogether from the outside. Political hewers of wood and drawers of water, like Mr. Ritchie and Mr. Jackson, keep their places and get on very well. Sir John Gorst is too human and too independent to speak when he is spoken to and do as he is bid. Moreover, he is substantially a just and humane man, with a genuine hatred of cruelty and oppression, whether exercised by native princes in India or by British colonists in Australasia. When he was a young man in New Zealand he espoused the cause of the Maories, and he had what a more cynical politician than himself called the taint of philanthropy. His interest in the welfare of the working classes is not purely political. He has been active and useful on the Labour Commission; while at Berlin he excited the warm admiration of so competent and unprejudiced a critic as his colleague, Mr. Burt. In the Parliament of 1880 he refused to

join in factious resistance to the Corrupt Practices Act
and showed an honest determination to put down
bribery.   On the whole, few politicians have a more
honourable record than Sir John Gorst, and the University of Cambridge has shown itself a better judge of his
sterling, straightforward character than either Lord
Salisbury or Lord Randolph Churchill.

MR. COURTNEY.

Mr. Delane is reported to have said that when Leonard Courtney had walked for three hours and written for two he was fit company for ordinary mankind. This superabundant vitality of mind and body makes Mr. Courtney younger and more vigorous at sixty than many men of half his age. When he was Secretary to the Treasury in Mr. Gladstone's second Administration, the House sat from twelve o'clock on Saturday till breakfast time on Sunday morning to finish the Civil Service Estimates, of which he was in charge. But Mr. Courtney showed no signs of physical fatigue, and in the chair of Committees he is equally tough. Of his virtues as Chairman there is only one opinion, except among a few high and mighty youths below the then Ministerial gangway, whose manners and excesses he did not scruple to correct. It is a mistake to suppose that the Irish members liked him. They would have preferred a man who was less just and more sympathetic. Their attitude was one of reluctant admission. They could not deny that he was absolutely impartial, and all his rulings strictly judicial. Our American friends would not stand Mr. Courtney long in the House of Representatives. The first time he was asked to assist in a party manœuvre would be also the last. If he had been Speaker at the

beginning of 1881, the debate on the first reading of
Mr. Forster's Coercion Bill would have been suffered to
reach its normal close. So stiff was Mr. Courtney in
maintaining his neutrality that he would not even con-
form to the traditional usages of the House if they
conflicted with his ideal of indifferent aloofness. On the
comparatively rare occasions when a full-dress debate
was held in Committee, as, for instance, on the policy of
the Mombasa Railway, he refused to accept from the
whips an arranged list of the speakers on either side.
Respect rather than popularity is the reward of this
almost pedantic revolt against conventional practices
and understandings.

As Speaker, with the wig and the mace and the
other symbols of authority, Mr. Courtney might be
thought to have too much roughness and too little
polish. As Chairman of Ways and Means, a post for
which Mr. Gladstone selected him, he was emphatically the right man in the right place; his deficiencies
were unimportant, and his qualities had full play.
He is perhaps the ablest man who ever filled the office,
certainly in our time. His soundness and clearness
of head, his rapid insight and comprehensive grasp, are
marvellous. He is no respecter of persons. As a
general rule, the Speaker or Chairman, when he has
to choose between members desirous of joining in
debate, takes them alternately from either side of the
House. The Speaker usually makes an exception in
favour of the two front benches. Mr. Courtney made
none. Mr. Gladstone once rose to follow a supporter

of his own in a criticism of the Irish Estimates. But
Mr. Forrest Fulton got up simultaneously from the
opposite side, and Mr. Courtney, without a moment's
hesitation, called upon Mr. Fulton. Mr. Gladstone's
face was a study. At first he seemed puzzled. Then
his features relaxed into the well-known smile which
spreads all over them, and he resumed his seat with
amused alacrity. On the other hand, Mr. Courtney has
repeatedly declined to put the closure, even when moved
by the Leader of the House. When Mr. Gladstone
intervened in debate on a Wednesday, the Speaker, who
was about to retire for refreshment, paused with characteristic courtesy and waited until Mr. Gladstone had
finished what he had to say. It is doubtful whether
Mr. Courtney would have done the same. Mr. Courtney
may, perhaps, consider that it is the more essential for
him to emphasise his official impartiality because he
is a controversial politician outside the chair. The
Speaker is precluded by etiquette from making party
speeches, and, on the other hand, there is a general
feeling, which, of course, has no legal or constitutional
validity, that his seat ought not to be contested. The
Chairman has no such privilege, and suffers no such
disability. He mingles in the fray out of doors as
much as he pleases, and has to fight for his political
position like anybody else. It speaks volumes for
Mr. Courtney's freedom from bias that when complaints
have been made of his conduct in the chair, they have,
in nine cases out of ten, come from those with whom
he acts in Imperial questions.

Mr. Courtney is, as everybody knows, a staunch
and sturdy opponent of Home Rule for Ireland. He
has always been a sort of political Nonconformist. The
party system does not suit him. He believes in every
man thinking for himself, which is a very pretty theory,
but which rests on an unverified postulate. If all men
were Courtneys, parties would be luxurious superfluities.
Mr. Courtney has never, during his political career,
been so thoroughly comfortable as when he was dis-
agreeing with his own side. After the General Election
of 1880, when Liberals were wild with delight over the
astonishing magnitude of their triumph, Mr. Courtney
characteristically remarked that he distrusted these big
turnover majorities. From December of that year,
when he succeeded the present Speaker as Under-
Secretary of State at the Home Office, till 1884 he
was in Ministerial harness, proceeding through the
Colonial Office to the Treasury. But in 1884 he had
the great pleasure of resigning because proportional
representation had not been included in the Franchise
Bill. His fidelity to the memory of Mr. Fawcett may
have helped him in taking this step. But it was just
like him. Not one Englishman in a hundred cared
then, or cares now, two straws for proportional representation. Mr. Courtney was not in the Cabinet, and
might probably have obtained leave to vote for his own
crotchet. He had no more responsibility for the Bill
than any other member of the Liberal party. But he
doubtless thought that by resignation he would bring
the priceless blessings of the transferable vote within

the range of the meanest intelligence. Alas for the
imperfections of the human mind! Mr. Courtney was
Second Wrangler and first Smith's Prizeman. He can
scarcely believe that some voters would find the differential calculus puzzling, or that the transferable vote,
even if the element of chance could be eliminated from
it, is quite as hard as the differential calculus. He and
Sir John Lubbock understood it. Mr. Arnold Forster
professes to understand it. Why should the rural
voter pretend that he does not?

Mr. Courtney's hardness of head is accompanied by
great softness of heart, and by an almost gushing
enthusiasm for his favourite reforms. When the
small majority against the Women's Suffrage Bill was
announced by the tellers, no one cheered so lustily as
Mr. Courtney at what he doubtless regarded as a moral
victory. If he does not suffer fools gladly, the amiability of his disposition and the serenity of his temper
are never disturbed, even by those poor creatures who
are ignorant of geometry, and whom Plato would have
excluded from his house. Mr. Courtney is thrown
away upon his present associates. His genuine capacity, so different from the swaggering shallowness
which passes for intellectual superiority among the
Paper Unionists, is far more appreciated by his political
enemies than by his political friends. As a speaker he
suffered by taking the Queen's shilling. When he
stood up below the gangway, and in a genially philosophical way swore at large, the effect was admirable,
and perhaps unique. His luminous lectures to his

M

constituents are still a refreshing contrast to the solemn
platitudes of the Duke of Devonshire and the mock
heroics of Sir Henry James. But when he addresses
the House of Commons from the front Opposition
Bench, whether on a private or on a public Bill, the
general impression is that a chairman without a chair
resembles, as Martinus Scribblerus would say, a lord
mayor without a robe, or a carriage, or a body, or a
soul. Mr. Courtney has been a Professor of Political
Economy, and used to be a dogmatic individualist.
But of late years he has somewhat modified his views,
especially where the control of the liquor traffic is
concerned. The change is, perhaps, not unconnected
with the fact that Mrs. Courtney, a woman of very
strong and original mind, has an extensive knowledge
of the working classes, their habits, tastes, wants, and
temptations. The career of Mr. Courtney, who was
for many years a distinguished journalist, has been a
singularly honourable one. He has pursued his own
straight and independent path, fearing neither Govern-
ments nor mobs, incapable of jealousy or rancour,
placing the good of the people above every other object,
and patriotism above every other motive. His only
weaknesses are to fancy that everyone has the same
intellectual advantages as himself, and to dress in
the evening as if he were employed to advertise the
Edinburgh Review.

MR. BURNS.

Mr. Burns is almost the only new member who has made a real impression upon the House of Commons. There was a time, and that not a hundred years ago, when the House was disposed to regard working men as an interesting novelty, and to pet them accordingly But it has since got used to them, found that they are very like other people—only with rather better manners —and taken them, like other people, on their merits. The aristocratic sentiments of the Right Honourable Jesse Collings sometimes lead him, good-natured man as he really is, to sneer at those who claim to represent the masses, because, as he once put it, in a burst of noble rhetoric, " they worked with their hands in the dim and distant future." " I meant the past, Mr. Speaker," he added, as perhaps the Speaker may have guessed. But Mr. Collings is a peculiarly maladroit personage, and the style of controversy in which he still indulges has become generally obsolete. The Labour Members get their share of attention, and no more. Mr. Keir Hardie has been " taken up " by a smal knot of Tories, who have no definite principles except that their own side ought to be in, and who believe that Mr. Keir Hardie is " agin the Government."

M 2

Others, including that curious and instructive sur-
vival from a past phase of Irish society, Mr. Edward
Carson, made a dead set at Mr. Havelock Wilson, whose
undoubted honesty and ability are not always accompanied by an equal measure of prudence.   But on the
whole the Parliamentary working man has been left to
find his level, and if the level be a high one the credit
is his own.   Mr. Burns had the great disadvantage of
entering the House with a conspicuous reputation
gained outside.   Mr. Chamberlain tells a good story of
an old Parliamentary hand—not Mr. Gladstone—who
advised him to break down in his maiden speech, as the
House would take it for a compliment.   Mr. Chamberlain never did break down—probably could not if he
tried.   Diffidence is not one of Mr. Burns's many
interesting qualities.   The House of Commons had no
terrors for him, and he would not affect the fears he
did not feel.   His maiden speech was delivered with
as much breezy confidence as if he had been on a
Battersea platform.   He had not been long in the
House before a sharp little encounter with Mr. Lowther
showed how remarkably well he could hold his own.
" The honourable member is not in the London County
Council," said Mr. Lowther, with his nearest approach
to a dignified manner.   "Nor is the right honourable
gentleman on Newmarket Heath," was the prompt
rejoinder, which admitted of no rebutter, or, at least,
received none.   After that Mr. Burns was interrupted
no more.   Few men indeed are heard with more attention and respect.   Mr. Burns never talks for the sake

of talking. When he gets up he has something to say, and knows how to say it.

Mr. Burns was one of the first members of the London County Council, being then only thirty years old, so that he is but thirty-five now. Lord Rosebery at once discovered his great ability, and predicted for him a distinguished future. Nevertheless, Mr. Burns has succeeded better at Westminster than at Spring Gardens. He justly despised the reactionary party, who, even granting their opinions to be sound, have always made a miserable show. The result was that he became, in the slang phrase, rather too big for his boots. But in the House of Commons he soon discovered, being a thoroughly sensible man, that the Opposition was strongly and ably led. Mr. Balfour and Mr. Chamberlain, at their best, stand very high in the category of political leaders, in spite of Mr. Chamberlain's temper and Mr. Balfour's indolence. Mr. Burns is full of pluck, and is not afraid of anybody. But he respects a strong enemy, and recognises a good argument. No public speaker is more courageous or less given to flattering the masses. In the debate on the Featherstone Riots he took a very bold line indeed, admitting that dangerous rioters ought to be shot, and even condemning the use of less deadly weapons than the Lee-Mitford rifle. When Mr. Burns took his seat, along with Mr. Keir Hardie, on the left of the Speaker, it was too hastily inferred that he would not support Her Majesty's Government. As a matter of fact, Ministers have had few more staunch and loyal allies.

When a Radical protest is made in the Lobbies, Mr.
Burns almost always gives a Radical vote. But he
never makes mischief, or attempts to organise a revolt.
Why, indeed, should he? Except in one point, the
Government have, on matters affecting the working
classes, stood in with the Trade Unions. They did
not, and having regard to the differences in their own
party they could not, make the Eight Hours Bill for
miners a Ministerial measure. They refused to give
Mr. Woods a day for it after it had been read a second
time. But a day would not have passed it, so that an
opposite decision would have been of no practical use.
On the other hand, the Government have remained firm
against contracting out of the Employers' Liability Bill,
and are, so far as possible, introducing the eight hours
day into Government workshops. These are the chief
questions upon which Mr. Burns has insisted since his
entrance into Parliament. Now, Mr. Burns is not a
dreaming enthusiast, but an essentially practical man,
who prefers getting what he wants without making a
fuss, to making a fuss without getting what he wants.
The principle may look like a truism when stated in
black and white. But many a fine career has been
spoilt by neglect of it.

Mr. Burns has good reason to be satisfied with himself for refusing to despair of Liberalism, and to be led
into the wilderness where the " Independent Labour
Party " seems likely to wander for the next forty
years. He has indeed good reason to be satisfied with
himself generally, as he most unquestionably is.   A

slight tendency to patronise mankind will doubtless be corrected by experience and time. Mr. Burns has done more than enough to be proud of. His fight for the "docker's tanner" was most gallant, most unselfish, and most sagacious. The admirable nature of his work on the County Council is acknowledged by many of his political opponents in Battersea. Perhaps his least successful effort was his interference in the Scotch railway strike of 1890-91, where he was rather out of his element, and which he did not altogether understand. Yet Mr. Burns, though a Londoner by education and residence, is a Scotsman by birth and origin. Indeed, his family is said to be connected with that of the illustrious poet. The House of Commons has done Mr. Burns good. His Parliamentary aptitude is as great as was Mr. Bradlaugh's, and, like Mr. Bradlaugh, he prefers constitutional to revolutionary methods. It is difficult to imagine him ever again acting with such a feather-headed specimen of the sham Democrat as Mr. Cuninghame Graham. Probably it was more the risk than anything else which led Mr. Burns to Trafalgar Square on the unhappily notorious Sunday afternoon. When Mr. Justice Charles had authoritatively, and beyond question rightly, declared the square to be in law the property of the Crown, a Home Secretary of tact and sense would have proceeded to make suitable regulations for meetings to be held there upon convenient occasions. But Mr. Matthews, with all his cleverness, has neither sense nor tact. It was left for Mr. Asquith, Mr. Graham's counsel, to take the prudent course which has been so completely justified by events. Mr. Asquith did not defend Mr. Burns. Mr. Burns defended himself with eloquence and force. But the case was a purely legal one, and the jury could only follow the direction of the judge. Mr. Burns is an excellent speaker of the direct, business-like, and persuasive sort. He does not trouble himself to round his periods. What he cares about is going straight to the point and making his meaning absolutely clear. In neither respect does he ever fail. His controversial weakness is a passion for statistics, which are double-edged tools. His nature is full of geniality and humour, which make him, as he deserves to be, universally popular.

MR. CARSON.

Mr. Edward Carson is the only new member on the Conservative side of the House who has distinguished himself above his fellows. Mr. Scott Montagu created a mild sensation by a clever maiden speech, in which he seemed to hint that Home Rule might not, after all, be quite such a " damnable doctrine and position " as Primrose Leaguers were in the habit rather of asserting than of believing. But nothing more has been heard of him from that day to this. If much speaking made an orator, Mr. Grant Lawson might rank with Cicero. But, alas! it does not, and Mr. Lawson is as little like Cicero as need be. Mr. Carson is neither Ciceronian nor Demosthenic. He does not fill the House, though he does not empty it. His first speech in the House of Commons was an extremely clever one, and Mr. Carson is an extremely clever man. An old Parliamentary hand, on hearing him, compared him with Whiteside, which is understood by an ignorant and oblivious generation to be a high compliment. Although Mr. Carson has not sustained this early level, and although he makes the fatal blunder of letting it be seen that in his own opinion he confers an honour upon the House by taking part in debate, he is an interesting figure. When

M *

George the Third said that, if you wanted an Irishman basted, you could always get another Irishman to turn the spit, he had in his own mind the Carsons of his own day. They were much worse men than the junior member for the University of Dublin. The world improves, and its Carsons improve with it. Mr. Fitzpatrick's terrible book, " Secret Service under Pitt," is a gloomy and poisonous illustration of the royal epigram. " You are a villain," says Brabantio to Iago. " You are a—senator " is Iago's reply. Mr. Carson is not a villain. He is a member of Parliament. He is further removed from the spies and informers of old days than they were from the lowest reptiles that crawled. He has never been anything worse than the ready and willing instrument of Mr. Balfour's coercive policy in Ireland. The story that he introduced himself to the Chief Secretary —then known in Ireland by a silly and opprobrious nickname—as Coercion Carson, and urged this phrase as a title to favour, is doubtless mythical ; but Mr. Carson did render great services to the Tory Government in Ireland, and he has been amply rewarded for it. From the year 1887 to the year 1890 he was in almost every prosecution of importance under the Crimes Act, and he did his work, such as it was, exceedingly well. His language and behaviour would not have been tolerated in an English Court of Justice ; but the Nationalist counsel had certainly no right to complain if Mr. Carson paid them back in their own coin. Neither side gave nor asked for quarter, and Mr. Healy, in particular, is on the most friendly terms with his old antagonist.

Mr. Carson sits for a constituency where there is never a serious contest, and upon which a Tory Administration can always foist a law officer of their own. He succeeded to the Parliamentary vacancy created by the appointment of Mr. Madden to the Bench, and became for a few weeks Irish Solicitor-General. This was not bad for a man of thirty-nine ; for the seat is, of course, a perfectly safe one, unless the University should be disfranchised. But it is understood that Mr. Carson's aspirations are by no means satisfied. When the Tories thought they were coming into office last summer they determined, it is said, to shunt Lord Ashbourne to make Sir Peter O'Brien—better known as Peter the Packer —Lord Chancellor of Ireland, and to appoint Mr. Carson Lord Chief Justice in his room. With such a prize in prospect, Mr. Carson's almost feverish activity in English politics is natural and intelligible. It is a real misfortune for Ireland that the road to fame and fortune in the legal profession should lie almost exclusively through the patronage of the Crown. Mr. Carson's undoubted ability would never have raised him to anything like his present position if his politics had been those of the majority of his countrymen. Mr. Carson, like Sir Richard Webster, took his seat on the Treasury Bench when he first entered the House of Commons. He only occupied it for a very few days before crossing the floor. But to begin Parliamentary life from either Front Bench is an advantage as well as a distinction. Successive Speakers have conformed to the vicious practice, from which Mr. Courtney had the strength of mind to depart, of calling upon late and present Ministers of the Crown in preference to any private member, although it often happens that the private member would be far more gladly heard by the House. Now, a man who can speak whenever he likes has a strong pull over the vulgar herd, who have to wait their turn and take the chance of being called. Considering his possession of this valuable privilege, Mr. Carson's Parliamentary achievements have not been brilliant. Imperturbable assurance never deserts him, and he knows nothing of the temptation to give an independent vote. The House of Commons is accustomed to lawyers, though it is not enamoured of them. But Mr. Carson's brief is too conspicuous and too well marked. It is difficult to listen to him without feeling that he would speak quite as fluently and with the same air of conviction on the other side. Then he has a disagreeable habit of repeating his words, as if he feared that the excellence of his phraseology was not appreciated by the House. Even John Bright's luminous and felicitous flashes of wisdom would have suffered if they had been exhibited twice. Mr. Carson is neither wise, witty, nor eloquent, and the most patient assembly in the world resents hearing twice what was not worth saying once. A stale vocabulary should be aired, as dirty linen should be washed, in private.

The class of Irishman to which Mr. Carson belongs usually flatter themselves on being intensely English. To English eyes they are no more English than the Swiss soldiers of fortune in mediæval times. If Ireland were subject to France Mr. Carson would be French,

and if she were subject to America he would be American. Mr. Carson, besides taking a prominent part in the
festivities of the London season, has got himself called
to the English Bar. He is' a skilful advocate, and his
cross-examination of Mr. Havelock Wilson was justly
admired. In Ireland he is a Queen's Counsel. In England he is a junior, and wears a stuff gown. Mr. Carson
likes a row, and thoroughly enjoyed himself on the night
of the famous disturbance in the House of Commons.
His employers have no reason to be dissatisfied with his
fidelity and zeal. Nobody knew better than he the
weakness of the case against Mr. Morley's Irish Administration; but nobody—not even Mr. T. W. Russell
—attacked the Chief Secretary with greater vigour.
Mr. Carson does not shine in controversy with Mr. John
Morley. Mr. Morley has no legal colleague in the
House, and Mr. Carson often trips him up on points of
law ; yet the essential large-mindedness of the one man
and the essential small-mindedness of the other are too
manifest to be ignored. Mr. Balfour does not like the
spectacle, and his preference of Mr. Morley to a whole
wilderness of Carsons is not always concealed. Mr.
Carson suffers also from comparison with his colleague
in the representation of Dublin University. Mr. Plunket
is a man in whom the whole House of Commons feels a
certain pride. His musical voice, his dignified manners,
and his stately eloquence make him a great member of
Parliament. He is a splendid specimen of a fine type—
an Irish gentleman of the old school. Staunch Conservative as he is, Mr. Plunket listens with genuine and

obvious pride to a fine speech from a Nationalist fellow-countryman. Mr. Carson is a good fighter, and nothing more; but it must be acknowledged that he is a very good one. To reflect upon some of the Irish law officers who have sat in the House of Commons on their way to the Judicial Bench is to understand the general want of sympathy with the administration of the law in Ireland. Mr. Carson at least is no fool. He is a capable debater, a capable lawyer—above all, a man capable of getting on. If there were no Carsons, it would be necessary to invent them. The supply, however, is not likely to fail, and it is artificially stimulated by the present state of the Union between Great Britain and Ireland.

MR. MELLOR.

WHEN Mr. Gladstone became Prime Minister for the fourth time, he had to fill a post quite as important as any of those which are accompanied by seats in the Cabinet. The Chairman of Ways and Means is not a member of the Government, and does not resign office with the Ministers of the Crown. Nominally and formally he is elected by the House when the House first resolves itself into Committee. Really and substantially, he is appointed by the Prime Minister, whose choice has never been—though it might be—disputed by the House of Commons. Mr. Gladstone took plenty of time for consideration. Parliament met in August, and the new Chairman was not elected till February. It was, however, understood almost from the first that the choice lay between Mr. Courtney and Mr. Mellor. Mr. Courtney was by general consent the best Chairman within living memory. Nobody disputed his ability or doubted his impartiality. But it would have been entirely without precedent that a Minister should bestow this valuable piece of patronage upon a member of the Opposition. Mr. Courtney would, in any case, have voted against the second reading of the Home Rule Bill, and his principal duty would have been to preside over the discussion of a measure which he detested and desired to defeat. Two other arguments were sometimes employed which ought not to have weighed, and probably did not weigh, a single ounce with Mr. Gladstone. On the one side, it was said that to muzzle so formidable an opponent, and to prevent him from speaking or voting in Committee, would be plausibly generous and profoundly politic. On the other side it was urged that if the Cornish Liberals were taught to regard Mr. Courtney as an indispensable Chairman, they would come to consider him a necessary representative of the Bodmin Division. The Tories had the benefit of Mr. Courtney's vote, and the Government lost Mr. Mellor's. Lovers of paradox may be heard to contend that Mr. Courtney set too high a standard in what is, after all, a subordinate office. The old-fashioned Chairman, of whom nobody took any particular notice, and who was as likely as not to cry "Ayes to the Noes, Right to the Left," did well enough, and got through his business somehow. Mr. Courtney may have consoled himself, if he required consolation, by reflecting that he suffered the ostracism of Aristides.

Mr. Mellor had deserved well of the Liberal party. He had fought several contests, though it must be said, on the other hand, that he had been rewarded with a safe seat. In Somersetshire, where he resides, and discharges the duties of a country squire, he has been the life and soul of Liberalism. He had held, in the short Liberal Administration of 1886, the post of

Judge-Advocate-General, which has now ceased to be a political appointment. His qualifications were legal training, high character, an imperturbable temper, and a most amiable disposition. But Mr. Mellor took the reins on very onerous terms, and under very grave disadvantages. The times were troublous. Obstruction was rampant, party feeling ran high, and on one occasion a few members came to blows. Mr. Chamberlain devoted all his great Parliamentary ability, never before so conspicuously displayed, to inflaming passion and provoking resentment. Mr. Mellor was an altogether unknown quantity. Most of the new members and many of the old members did not know him by sight. He had not sat in the previous Parliament, in which the new Rules of Procedure were first framed and applied. Most of the faces must have been strange to him, and he had not the royal gift of instantaneous recognition. His good nature stood in his way. Men accustomed to the manners of Mr. Courtney, who ruled with a rod of iron, took Mr. Mellor's politeness for a sign of timidity. He was no sooner in the Chair than Mr. Chamberlain began to patronise him in his most offensive manner, which is very offensive indeed. The noisier Tories made a dead set at him, and Mr. Hanbury, in particular, contradicted him with a rudeness which would not have been tolerated in a parish vestry. It is to Mr. Mellor's credit, and perhaps to Mr. Balfour's also, that these open demonstrations soon ceased. Mr. Mellor is so thorough a gentleman in every sense of the word, he is so invariably courteous

and considerate to everyone with whom he comes
in contact, that attempts to bully or annoy him were
quickly resented by the whole House of Commons. It
is a fine achievement to have presided over some of the
most stormy and acrimonious debates ever held in
Committee without making a single enemy. So much
may certainly be said of Mr. Mellor. He has avoided
all personal encounters, and has never " named " anyone
to the House. His method has been an appeal to
the good feeling of both sides, and to enlist that feeling
on the side of order. It is better, when it is possible,
to ride with a snaffle than to ride with a curb.

Most of the criticisms upon Mr. Mellor's conduct in
the Chair, which have undoubtedly been both numerous
and severe, come from the Liberal party. It is much
to his honour that the most vehement opponents of
Liberals and Liberalism should have been unable to
accuse him of anything like unfairness. Of weakness,
or at least undue mildness, he cannot altogether be
acquitted. There have been occasions when sternness
was imperatively required, and when Mr. Mellor's
gentleness was misunderstood and abused. But the
number of these lost opportunities has been much
exaggerated. Most of the Obstructionists are quite
clever enough to keep within the law, and forbearance
itself has a moral influence which is too apt to be
ignored. The remarkable and unexpected success of
Sir Julian Goldsmid as temporary Chairman has drawn
attention to some of the things which Mr. Mellor leaves
undone. There is a standing order, which Mr. Mellor

has never enforced, against tedious repetition not only of
the speaker's own arguments, but of other people's
arguments also. The necessity for passing many clauses
of the Home Rule Bill without discussion might
perhaps have been avoided if Mr. Mellor had been
willing to enforce the rule which provides for adding
each clause to a Bill after reasonable debate. If
Sir Julian had been in Mr. Mellor's place, he would
have begun by refusing to put the closure when
Mr. Morley moved it the first night the Home Rule
Bill was in Committee; he would next have called
Mr. Gladstone to order for wandering from the point;
he would have proceeded to declare that Mr. Chamberlain was repeating what had been better said by
Mr. Collings ; and finally, he would have refused to put a
motion to report progress made by Mr. Balfour, on the
ground that it was an abuse of the rules of the House.
Then his position would have been secure, and he could
have done anything he pleased. Mr. Mellor preferred
conciliation to coercion, as is no doubt consistent with
the tenets of a Liberal and a Home Ruler. He is
so generally liked and esteemed that it seems
unpleasant and ungracious to find fault with him. But
he has carried too far the famous advice of Lord
Mansfield against giving reasons. A Chairman should
stick to his ruling whatever it is, and should never
condescend to argue. But a Member whose amendment
is ruled out of order is entitled to know why. Mr.
Courtney always gave his reasons, whether they were
good or bad, and that without consulting Mr. Milman.

PRINTED BY
CASSELL & COMPANY, LIMITED, LA BELLE SAUVAGE,
LONDON, E.C.

A SELECTED LIST

OF

CASSELL & COMPANY'S

PUBLICATIONS.

7 G—1.94

Illustrated, Fine Art, and other Volumes.

Abbeys and Churches of England and Wales, The: Descriptive, Historical, Pictorial. Series II. 21s.

A Blot of Ink. Translated by Q and PAUL FRANCKE. 5s.

Adventure, The World of. Fully Illustrated. Complete in Three Vols. 9s. each.

Africa and its Explorers, The Story of. By Dr. ROBERT BROWN, M.A., F.L.S., F.R.G.S., &c. With numerous Original Illustrations. Vols. I. and II. 7s. 6d. each.

Agrarian Tenures. By the Rt. Hon. G. SHAW LEFEVRE, M.P. 10s. 6d.

American Life. By PAUL DE ROUSIERS. 12s. 6d.

Animal Painting in Water Colours. With Coloured Plates. 5s.

Anthea. By CÉCILE CASSAVETTI (a Russian). A Story of the Greek War of Independence. *Cheap Edition,* 5s.

Arabian Nights Entertainments (Cassell's). With about 400 Illustrations. 10s. 6d.

Architectural Drawing. By R. PHENÉ SPIERS. Illustrated. 10s. 6d.

Army, Our Home. Being a Reprint of Letters published in the *Times* in November and December, 1891. By H. O. ARNOLD-FORSTER, M.P. 1s.

Art, The Magazine of. Yearly Volume. With about 400 Illustrations, and Twelve Etchings, Photogravures, &c. 16s.

Artistic Anatomy. By Prof. M. DUVAL. *Cheap Edition,* 3s. 6d.

Astronomy, The Dawn of. A Study of the Temple Worship and Mythology of the Ancient Egyptians. By J. NORMAN LOCKYER, F.R.S., F.R.A.S., &c. Illustrated. 21s.

Atlas, The Universal. A New and Complete General Atlas of the World, with 117 Pages of Maps, handsomely produced in Colours, and a Complete Index to about 125,000 Names. Complete in One Vol., cloth, 30s. net; or half-morocco, 35s. net.

Awkward Squads, The; and other Ulster Stories. By SHAN F. BULLOCK. 5s.

Bashkirtseff, Marie, The Journal of. Translated by MATHILDE BLIND. 7s. 6d.

Bashkirtseff, Marie, The Letters of. Translated by MARY J. SERRANO. 7s. 6d.

Beetles, Butterflies, Moths, and other Insects. By A. W. KAPPEL, F.L.S., F.E.S., and W. EGMONT KIRBY. With 12 Coloured Plates. 3s. 6d.

Biographical Dictionary, Cassell's New. Containing Memoirs of the Most Eminent Men and Women of all Ages and Countries. 7s. 6d.

Birds' Nests, Eggs, and Egg-Collecting. By R. KEARTON. Illustrated with 16 Coloured Plates of Eggs. 5s.

Breechloader, The, and How to Use It. By W. W. GREENER. 2s.

British Ballads. 275 Original Illustrations. Two Vols. Cloth, 15s.

British Battles on Land and Sea. By JAMES GRANT. With about 600 Illustrations. Three Vols., 4to, £1 7s.; *Library Edition,* £1 10s.

British Battles, Recent. Illustrated. 9s. *Library Edition,* 10s.

Browning, An Introduction to the Study of. By ARTHUR SYMONS. 2s. 6d.

Butterflies and Moths, European. By W. F. KIRBY. With 61 Coloured Plates. 35s.

Canaries and Cage-Birds, The Illustrated Book of. By W. A. BLAKSTON, W. SWAYSLAND, and A. F. WIENER. With 56 Fac-simile Coloured Plates. 35s.

Capture of the "Estrella," The. A Tale of the Slave Trade. By COMMANDER CLAUD HARDING, R.N. 5s.

Carnation Manual, The. Edited and Issued by The National Carnation and Picotee Society (Southern Section). 3s. 6d.

Cassell's Family Magazine. Yearly Volume. Illustrated. 9s.

Cathedrals, Abbeys, and Churches of England and Wales. Descriptive, Historical, Pictorial. *Popular Edition.* Two Vols. 25s.

Catriona. A Sequel to " Kidnapped." By ROBERT LOUIS STEVENSON. 6s.

China Painting. By FLORENCE LEWIS. With Sixteen Coloured Plates, &c. 5s.

Chips by an Old Chum; or, Australia in the Fifties. 1s.

Choice Dishes at Small Cost. By A. G. PAYNE. *Cheap Edition,* 1s.

Christianity and Socialism, Lectures on. By BISHOP BARRY. 3s. 6d.

Chums. The Illustrated Paper for Boys. Yearly Volume. 7s. 6d.

Cities of the World. Four Vols. Illustrated. 7s. 6d. each.

Civil Service, Guide to Employment in the. *New and Enlarged Edition,* 3s. 6d.

Climate and Health Resorts. By Dr. BURNEY YEO. 7s. 6d.

Clinical Manuals for Practitioners and Students of Medicine. (*A List of Volumes forwarded post free on application to the Publishers.*)

Cobden Club, Works published for the. (*A Complete List on application.*)

Colonist's Medical Handbook, The. By E. ALFRED BARTON, M.R.C.S. 2s. 6d.

Colour. By Prof. A. H. CHURCH. *New and Enlarged Edition*, 3s. 6d.

Columbus, The Career of. By CHARLES ELTON, F.S.A. 10s. 6d.

Combe, George, The Select Works of. Issued by Authority of the Combe Trustees. *Popular Edition*, 1s. each, net.

The Constitution of Man.	Science and Religion.
Moral Philosophy.	Discussions on Education.
	American Notes.

Commercial Botany of the Nineteenth Century. By J. R. JACKSON, A.L.S. Cloth gilt, 3s. 6d.

Conning Tower, In a. By H. O. ARNOLD-FORSTER, M.P., Author of "The Citizen Reader," &c. With Original Illustrations by W. H. OVEREND. 1s.

Conquests of the Cross. Edited by EDWIN HODDER. With numerous Original Illustrations. Complete in Three Vols. 9s. each.

Cookery, A Year's. By PHYLLIS BROWNE. *New and Enlarged Edition*, 3s. 6d.

Cookery, Cassell's Popular. With Four Coloured Plates. Cloth gilt, 2s.

Cookery, Cassell's Shilling. 110*th Thousand*. 1s.

Cookery, Vegetarian. By A. G. PAYNE. 1s. 6d.

Cooking by Gas, The Art of. By MARIE J. SUGG. Illustrated. Cloth, 3s. 6d.

Cottage Gardening, Poultry, Bees, Allotments, Food, House, Window and Town Gardens. Edited by W. ROBINSON, F.L.S., Author of "The English Flower Garden." Fully Illustrated. Half-yearly Vols., I. and II., 2s. 6d. each.

Countries of the World, The. By ROBERT BROWN, M.A., Ph.D., &c. Complete in Six Vols., with about 750 Illustrations. 4to, 7s. 6d. each.

Cyclopædia, Cassell's Concise. Brought down to the latest date. With about 600 Illustrations. *New and Cheap Edition*, 7s. 6d.

Cyclopædia, Cassell's Miniature. Containing 30,000 Subjects. Cloth, 2s. 6d.; half-roxburgh, 4s.

Delectable Duchy, The. Stories, Studies, and Sketches. By Q. 6s.

Dickens, Character Sketches from. FIRST, SECOND, and THIRD SERIES. With Six Original Drawings in each, by FREDERICK BARNARD. In Portfolio. 21s. each.

Dick Whittington, A Modern. By JAMES PAYN. *Cheap Edition in one Vol.*, 6s.

Dictionaries. (For description see alphabetical letter.) Religion, Biographical, Encyclopædic, Mechanical, Phrase and Fable, English, English History, English Literature, Domestic. (French, German, and Latin, see with *Educational Works*.)

Dog, Illustrated Book of the. By VERO SHAW, B.A. With 28 Coloured Plates. Cloth bevelled, 35s.; half-morocco, 45s.

Domestic Dictionary, The. An Encyclopædia for the Household. Cloth, 7s. 6d.

Doré Don Quixote, The. With about 400 Illustrations by GUSTAVE DORÉ. *Cheap Edition*, bevelled boards, gilt edges, 10s. 6d.

Doré Gallery, The. With 250 Illustrations by GUSTAVE DORÉ. 4to, 42s.

Doré's Dante's Inferno. Illustrated by GUSTAVE DORÉ. *Popular Edition*. With Preface by A. J. BUTLER. Cloth gilt or buckram, 7s. 6d.

Doré's Dante's Purgatory and Paradise. Illustrated by GUSTAVE DORÉ. *Cheap Edition*. 7s. 6d.

Doré's Milton's Paradise Lost. Illustrated by GUSTAVE DORÉ. 4to, 21s.

Dr. Dumány's Wife. A Novel. By MAURUS JÓKAI. *Cheap Edition*, 6s.

Earth, Our, and its Story. Edited by Dr. ROBERT BROWN, F.L.S. With 36 Coloured Plates and 740 Wood Engravings. Complete in Three Vols. 9s. each.

Edinburgh, Old and New, Cassell's. With 600 Illustrations. Three Vols. 9s. each; library binding, £1 10s. the set.

Egypt: Descriptive, Historical, and Picturesque. By Prof. G. EBERS. Translated by CLARA BELL, with Notes by SAMUEL BIRCH, LL.D., &c. Two Vols. 42s.

Electricity, Practical. By Prof. W. E. AYRTON. Illustrated. Cloth, 7s. 6d.

Electricity in the Service of Man. A Popular and Practical Treatise. With upwards of 950 Illustrations. *New and Revised Edition*, 10s. 6d.

Employment for Boys on Leaving School, Guide to. By W. S. BEARD, F.R.G.S. 1s. 6d.

Encyclopædic Dictionary, The. Complete in Fourteen Divisional Vols., 10s. 6d. each; or Seven Vols., half-morocco, 21s. each; half-russia, 25s. each.

England, Cassell's Illustrated History of. With 2,000 Illustrations. Ten Vols., 4to, 9s. each. *New and Revised Edition.* Vols. I. to VI., 9s. each.

English Dictionary, Cassell's. Containing Definitions of upwards of 100,000 Words and Phrases. *Cheap Edition,* 3s. 6d.

English History, The Dictionary of. *Cheap Edition,* 10s. 6d.; roxburgh, 15s.

English Literature, Library of. By Prof. H. MORLEY. In 5 Vols. 7s. 6d. each.

English Literature, Morley's First Sketch of. *Revised Edition,* 7s. 6d.

English Literature, The Dictionary of. By W. DAVENPORT ADAMS. *Cheap Edition,* 7s. 6d. ; roxburgh, 10s. 6d.

English Literature, The Story of. By ANNA BUCKLAND. 3s. 6d.

English Writers. By HENRY MORLEY. Vols. I. to X. 5s. each.

Æsop's Fables. Illustrated by ERNEST GRISET. *Cheap Edition.* Cloth, 3s. 6d. ; bevelled boards, gilt edges, 5s.

Etiquette of Good Society. *New Edition.* Edited and Revised by LADY COLIN CAMPBELL. 1s. ; cloth, 1s 6d.

Europe, Cassell's Pocket Guide to. *Edition for* 1893. Leather, 6s.

Fairway Island. By HORACE HUTCHINSON. With Four Full-page Plates. *Cheap Edition,* 3s. 6d.

Faith Doctor, The. A Novel. By Dr. EDWARD EGGLESTON. *Cheap Edition,* 6s.

Family Physician. By Eminent PHYSICIANS and SURGEONS. *New and Revised Edition.* Cloth, 21s. ; roxburgh, 25s.

Father Mathew: His Life and Times. By FRANK J. MATHEW. 2s. 6d.

Father Stafford. A Novel. By ANTHONY HOPE, Author of "A Man of Mark." 3s. 6d.

Fenn, G. Manville, Works by. Boards, 2s. each ; or cloth, 2s. 6d.

Poverty Corner. | The Parson o' Dumford. } In boards only.
My Patients. | The Vicar's People.

Field Naturalist's Handbook, The. By Revs. J. G. WOOD and THEODORE WOOD. *Cheap Edition.* 2s. 6d.

Figuier's Popular Scientific Works. With Several Hundred Illustrations in each. 3s. 6d. each.

The Insect World. | Reptiles and Birds. | The Vegetable World.
The Human Race. | Mammalia. | Ocean World.
The World before the Deluge.

Figure Painting in Water Colours. With 16 Coloured Plates. 7s. 6d.

Flora's Feast. A Masque of Flowers. Penned and Pictured by WALTER CRANE. With 40 pages in Colours. 5s.

Flower Painting, Elementary. With Eight Coloured Plates. 3s.

Flowers, and How to Paint Them. By MAUD NAFTEL. With Coloured Plates. 5s.

Football: the Rugby Union Game. Edited by Rev. F. MARSHALL. Illustrated. 7s. 6d.

Fossil Reptiles, A History of British. By Sir RICHARD OWEN, F.R.S., &c. With 268 Plates. In Four Vols. £12 12s.

Fraser, John Drummond. By PHILALETHES. A Story of Jesuit Intrigue in the Church of England. 5s.

Garden Flowers, Familiar. By SHIRLEY HIBBERD. With Coloured Plates by F. E. HULME, F.L.S. Complete in Five Series. Cloth gilt, 12s. 6d. each.

Gardening, Cassell's Popular. Illustrated. Complete in Four Vols. 5s. each.

Geometrical Drawing for Army Candidates. By H. T. LILLEY, M.A. 2s. 6d.

Geometry, First Elements of Experimental. By PAUL BERT. 1s. 6d.

Geometry, Practical Solid. By Major ROSS. 2s.

George Saxon, The Reputation of. By MORLEY ROBERTS. 5s.

Gilbert, Elizabeth, and her Work for the Blind. By FRANCES MARTIN. 2s. 6d.

Gleanings from Popular Authors. Two Vols. With Original Illustrations. 4to, 9s. each. Two Vols. in One, 15s.

Gulliver's Travels. With 88 Engravings. Cloth, 3s. 6d. ; cloth gilt, 5s.

Gun and its Development, The. By W. W. GREENER. Illustrated. 10s. 6d.

Guns, Modern Shot. By W. W. GREENER. Illustrated. 5s.

Health, The Book of. By Eminent Physicians and Surgeons. Cloth, 21s.

Heavens, The Story of the. By Sir ROBERT STAWELL BALL, LL.D., F.R.S. With Coloured Plates and Wood Engravings. *Popular Edition,* 12s. 6d.

Heroes of Britain in Peace and War. With 300 Original Illustrations. *Cheap Edition.* Two Vols. 3s. 6d. each ; or two vols. in one, cloth gilt, 7s. 6d.

Hiram Golf's Religion; or, the Shoemaker by the Grace of God. 2s.
Historic Houses of the United Kingdom. With Contributions by the Rev. Professor BONNEY, F.R.S., and others. Profusely Illustrated. 10s. 6d.
History, A Footnote to. Eight Years of Trouble in Samoa. By ROBERT LOUIS STEVENSON. 6s.
Home Life of the Ancient Greeks, The. Translated by ALICE ZIMMERN. Illustrated. 7s. 6d.
Horse, The Book of the. By SAMUEL SIDNEY. Thoroughly Revised and brought up to date by JAMES SINCLAIR and W. C. A. BLEW. With 17 Full-page Collotype Plates of Celebrated Horses of the Day, and numerous other Illustrations. Cloth, 15s.
Houghton, Lord: The Life, Letters, and Friendships of Richard Monckton Milnes, First Lord Houghton. By T. WEMYSS REID. Two Vols. 32s.
Household, Cassell's Book of the. Illustrated. Complete in Four Vols. 5s. each; or Four Vols. in two, half-morocco, 25s.
Hygiene and Public Health. By B. ARTHUR WHITELEGGE, M.D. Illustrated. *New and Revised Edition.* 7s. 6d.
India, Cassell's History of. By JAMES GRANT. With 400 Illustrations. Two Vols., 9s. each, or One Vol., 15s.
In-door Amusements, Card Games, and Fireside Fun, Cassell's Book of. With numerous Illustrations. *Cheap Edition.* Cloth, 2s.
Into the Unknown: a Romance of South Africa. By LAWRENCE FLETCHER. 4s.
Iron Pirate, The. A Plain Tale of Strange Happenings on the Sea. By MAX PEMBERTON. Illustrated. 5s.
Island Nights' Entertainments. By R. L. STEVENSON. Illustrated, 6s.
Italy from the Fall of Napoleon I. in 1815 to 1890. By J. W. PROBYN. 3s. 6d.
"Japanese" Library, Cassell's. Consisting of 12 Popular Works bound in Japanese style. Covers in water-colour pictures. 1s. 3d. each, net. **** List post free on application.*
Joy and Health. By MARTELLIUS. Illustrated, cloth, 3s. 6d. (*Edition de Luxe*, 7s. 6d.)
Kennel Guide, Practical. By Dr. GORDON STABLES. Illustrated. *Cheap Edition*, 1s.
King's Hussar, A. Memoirs of a Troop Sergeant-Major of the 14th (King's) Hussars. Edited by HERBERT COMPTON. 6s.
"La Bella," and Others. By EGERTON CASTLE. Buckram, 6s.
Ladies' Physician, The. By a London Physician. 6s.
Lady Biddy Fane, The Admirable. By FRANK BARRETT. *New Edition.* With 12 Full-page Illustrations. 6s.
Lady's Dressing Room, The. Translated by LADY COLIN CAMPBELL. 3s. 6d.
Lake Dwellings of Europe. By ROBERT MUNRO, M.D., M.A. Cloth, 31s. 6d.
Leona. By Mrs. MOLESWORTH. 6s.
Letters, The Highway of; and its Echoes of Famous Footsteps. By THOMAS ARCHER. Illustrated. 10s. 6d.
Letts's Diaries and other Time-saving Publications are now published exclusively by CASSELL & COMPANY. (*A List sent post free on application.*)
'Lisbeth. A Novel. By LESLIE KEITH. Three Vols. 31s. 6d.
List, ye Landsmen! A Romance of Incident. By W. CLARK RUSSELL. *Cheap Edition*, One Vol., 6s.
Little Minister, The. By J. M. BARRIE. *Illustrated Edition*, 6s.
Little Squire, The. A Story of Three. By Mrs. HENRY DE LA PASTURE. 3s. 6d.
Locomotive Engine, The Biography of a. By HENRY FRITH. 5s.
Loftus, Lord Augustus, P.C., G.C.B., The Diplomatic Reminiscences of. First Series. With Portrait. Two Vols. 32s. Second Series. Two Vols. 32s.
London, Greater. By EDWARD WALFORD. Two Vols. With about 400 Illustrations. 9s. each. *Library Edition.* Two Vols. £1 the set.
London, Old and New. By WALTER THORNBURY and EDWARD WALFORD. Six Vols., with about 1,200 Illustrations. Cloth, 9s. each. *Library Edition*, £3.
London Street Arabs. By Mrs. H. M. STANLEY. Illustrated. 5s.
Lost on Du Corrig; or, 'Twixt Earth and Ocean. By STANDISH O'GRADY. With 8 Full-page Illustrations. 5s.
Man in Black, The. By STANLEY WEYMAN. With 12 full-page Illustrations. 3s. 6d.
Medical Handbook of Life Assurance. By JAMES EDWARD POLLOCK, M.D., F.R.C.P., and JAMES CHISHOLM, Fellow of the Institute of Actuaries, London. 7s. 6d.
Medicine Lady, The. By L. T. MEADE. *Cheap Edition*, One Vol., 6s.
Medicine, Manuals for Students of. (*A List forwarded post free on application.*)

Modern Europe, A History of. By C. A. FYFFE, M.A. Complete in Three Vols., with full-page Illustrations. 7s. 6d. each.
Mount Desolation. An Australian Romance. By W. CARLTON DAWE. 5s.
Musical and Dramatic Copyright, The Law of. By EDWARD CUTLER, THOMAS EUSTACE SMITH, and FREDERIC E. WEATHERLY. 3s. 6d.
Music, Illustrated History of. By EMIL NAUMANN. Edited by the Rev. Sir F. A. GORE OUSELEY, Bart. Illustrated. Two Vols. 31s. 6d.
Napier, The Life and Letters of the Rt. Hon. Sir Joseph, Bart., LL.D., D.C.L., M.R.I.A. By ALEX. C. EWALD, F.S.A. *New and Revised Edition,* 7s. 6d.
National Library, Cassell's. In Volumes. Paper covers, 3d.; cloth, 6d. (*A Complete List of the Volumes post free on application.*)
Natural History, Cassell's Concise. By E. PERCEVAL WRIGHT, M.A., M.D., F.L.S. With several Hundred Illustrations. 7s. 6d.; also kept half-bound.
Natural History, Cassell's New. Edited by P. MARTIN DUNCAN, M.B., F.R.S., F.G.S. Complete in Six Vols. With about 2,000 Illustrations. Cloth, 9s. each.
Nature's Wonder Workers. By KATE R. LOVELL. Illustrated. 3s. 6d.
Nelson, The Life of. By ROBERT SOUTHEY. Illustrated with Eight Plates. 3s. 6d.
New England Boyhood, A. By EDWARD E. HALE. 3s. 6d.
Nursing for the Home and for the Hospital, A Handbook of. By CATHERINE J. WOOD. *Cheap Edition,* 1s. 6d.; cloth, 2s.
Nursing of Sick Children, A Handbook for the. By CATHERINE J. WOOD. 2s. 6d.
O'Driscoll's Weird, and Other Stories. By A. WERNER. Cloth, 5s.
Odyssey, The Modern. By WYNDHAM F. TUFNELL. Illustrated. 10s. 6d.
Ohio, The New. A Story of East and West. By EDWARD EVERETT HALE. 6s.
Old Dorset. Chapters in the History of the County. By H. J. MOULE, M.A. 10s. 6d.
Our Own Country. Six Vols. With 1,200 Illustrations. Cloth, 7s. 6d. each.
Out of the Jaws of Death. By FRANK BARRETT. *Cheap Edition.* One Vol., 6s.
Painting, The English School of. By ERNEST CHESNEAU. *Cheap Edition,* 3s. 6d.
Paris, Old and New. A Narrative of its History, its People, and its Places. By H. SUTHERLAND EDWARDS. Profusely Illustrated. Vol. I., 9s., or gilt edges, 10s. 6d.
Peoples of the World, The. By Dr. ROBERT BROWN. Complete in Six Vols. With Illustrations. 7s. 6d. each.
Perfect Gentleman, The. By the Rev. A. SMYTHE-PALMER, D.D. 3s. 6d.
Photography for Amateurs. By T. C. HEPWORTH. *Enlarged and Revised Edition.* Illustrated, 1s.; or cloth, 1s. 6d.
Phrase and Fable, Dictionary of. By the Rev. Dr. BREWER. *Cheap Edition,* Enlarged, cloth, 3s. 6d.; or with leather back, 4s. 6d.
Physiology for Students, Elementary. By ALFRED T. SCHOFIELD, M.D., M.R.C.S. With Two Coloured Plates and numerous Illustrations. 7s. 6d.
Picturesque America. Complete in Four Vols., with 48 Exquisite Steel Plates, and about 800 Original Wood Engravings. £2 2s. each.
Picturesque Canada. With about 600 Original Illustrations. Two Vols. £6 6s. the set.
Picturesque Europe. Complete in Five Vols. Each containing 13 Exquisite Steel Plates, from Original Drawings, and nearly 200 Original Illustrations. £21; half-morocco, £31 10s.; morocco gilt, £52 10s. *Popular Edition.* In Five Vols. 18s. each.
Picturesque Mediterranean, The. With a Series of Magnificent Illustrations from Original Designs by leading Artists of the day. Two Vols. Cloth, £2 2s. each.
Pigeon Keeper, The Practical. By LEWIS WRIGHT. Illustrated. 3s. 6d.
Pigeons, The Book of. By ROBERT FULTON. Edited by LEWIS WRIGHT. With 50 Coloured Plates and numerous Wood Engravings. 31s. 6d.; half-morocco, £2 2s.
Pity and of Death, The Book of. By PIERRE LOTI, Member of the French Academy. Translated by T. P. O'CONNOR, M.P. Antique paper, cloth gilt, 5s.
Planet, The Story of Our. By the Rev. Prof. BONNEY, F.R.S., &c. With Coloured Plates and Maps and about 100 Illustrations. 31s. 6d.
Playthings and Parodies. Short Stories, Sketches, &c., by BARRY PAIN. 5s.
Poetry, The Nature and Elements of. By E. C. STEDMAN. 6s.
Poets, Cassell's Miniature Library of the. Price 1s. each Vol.
Polytechnic Series, The. Practical Illustrated Manuals specially prepared for Students of the Polytechnic Institute, and suitable for the Use of all Students. (*A List will be sent on application.*)
Portrait Gallery, The Cabinet. *Series I. to IV.,* each containing 36 Cabinet Photographs of Eminent Men and Women of the day. With Biographical Sketches. 15s. each.
Poultry Keeper, The Practical. By LEWIS WRIGHT. Illustrated. 3s. 6d.
Poultry, The Book of. By LEWIS WRIGHT. *Popular Edition.* Illustrated. 10s. 6d.

Poultry, The Illustrated Book of. By LEWIS WRIGHT. With Fifty Exquisite Coloured Plates, and numerous Wood Engravings. *Revised Edition.* Cloth, 31s 6d.

Prison Princess, A. A Romance of Millbank Penitentiary. By MAJOR ARTHUR GRIFFITHS. 6s.

Q's Works, Uniform Edition of. 5s. each.

Dead Man's Rock.	The Astonishing History of Troy Town.
The Splendid Spur.	"I Saw Three Ships," and other Winter's Tales.
The Blue Pavilions.	Noughts and Crosses.

Queen Summer ; or, The Tourney of the Lily and the Rose. Penned and Portrayed by WALTER CRANE. With 40 pages in Colours. 6s.

Queen Victoria, The Life and Times of. By ROBERT WILSON. Complete in 2 Vols. With numerous Illustrations. 9s. each.

Quickening of Caliban, The. A Modern Story of Evolution. By J. COMPTON RICKETT. 5s.

Rabbit-Keeper, The Practical. By CUNICULUS. Illustrated. 3s. 6d.

Raffles Haw, The Doings of. By A. CONAN DOYLE. *New Edition.* 5s.

Railways, British. Their Passenger Services, Rolling Stock, Locomotives, Gradients, and Express Speeds. By J. PEARSON PATTINSON. With numerous Plates. 12s. 6d.

Railways, National. An Argument for State Purchase. By JAMES HOLE. 4s. net.

Railways, Our. Their Development, Enterprise, Incident, and Romance. By JOHN PENDLETON. Illustrated. 2 Vols., demy 8vo. 24s.

Railway Guides, Official Illustrated. With Illustrations on nearly every page. Maps, &c. Paper covers, 1s.; cloth, 2s. .

Great Eastern Railway.	London and North Western Railway.
Great Northern Railway.	London and South Western Railway.
Great Western Railway.	Midland Railway.
London, Brighton, and South Coast Railway.	South Eastern Railway.

Railway Library, Cassell's. Crown 8vo, boards, 2s. each.

Metzerott, Shoemaker. By Katharine P. Woods.	Jack Gordon, Knight Errant. By W. C. Hudson (Barclay North).
David Todd. By David Maclure.	The Diamond Button: Whose Was It? By W. C. Hudson (Barclay North).
The Admirable Lady Biddy Fane. By Frank Barrett.	Another's Crime. By Julian Hawthorne.
Commodore Junk. By G. Manville Fenn.	The Yoke of the Thorah. By Sidney Luska.
St. Cuthbert's Tower. By Florence Warden.	Who is John Noman? By C. Henry Beckett.
The Man with a Thumb. By W. C. Hudson (Barclay North).	The Tragedy of Brinkwater. By Martha L. Moodey.
By Right Not Law. By R. Sherard.	An American Penman. By Julian Hawthorne.
Within Sound of the Weir. By Thomas St. E. Hake.	Section 558; or, The Fatal Letter. By Julian Hawthorne.
Under a Strange Mask. By Frank Barrett.	The Brown Stone Boy. By W. H. Bishop.
The Coombsberrow Mystery. By J.Colwall.	A Tragic Mystery. By Julian Hawthorne.
A Queer Race. By W. Westall.	The Great Bank Robbery. By Julian Hawthorne.
Captain Trafalgar. By Westall and Laurie.	
The Phantom City. By W. Westall.	

Rivers of Great Britain : Descriptive, Historical, Pictorial.
The Royal River: The Thames from Source to Sea. *Popular Edition*, 16s.
Rivers of the East Coast. With highly-finished Engravings. *Popular Edition*, 16s.

Robinson Crusoe. *Cassell's New Fine-Art Edition.* With upwards of 100 Original Illustrations. 7s. 6d.

Romance, The World of. Illustrated. One Vol., cloth, 9s.

Ronner, Henriette, The Painter of Cat Life and Cat Character. By M. H. SPIELMANN. Containing a Series of beautiful Phototype Illustrations. *Popular Edition*, 4to, 12s.

Rovings of a Restless Boy, The. By KATHARINE B. FOOT. Illustrated. 5s.

Russo-Turkish War, Cassell's History of. With about 500 Illustrations. Two Vols., 9s. each ; library binding, One Vol., 15s.

Salisbury Parliament, A Diary of the. By H. W. LUCY. Illustrated by HARRY FURNISS. Cloth, 21s.

Saturday Journal, Cassell's. Illustrated throughout. Yearly Vol., 7s. 6d.

Scarabæus. The Story of an African Beetle. By THE MARQUISE CLARA LANZA and JAMES CLARENCE HARVEY. *Cheap Edition*, 3s. 6d.

Science for All. Edited by Dr. ROBERT BROWN, M.A., F.L.S., &c. *Revised Edition.* With 1,500 Illustrations. Five Vols. 9s. each.

Shadow of a Song, The. A Novel. By CECIL HARLEY. 5s.

Shaftesbury, The Seventh Earl of, K.G., The Life and Work of. By EDWIN HODDER. Illustrated. *Cheap Edition*, 3s. 6d.

Shakespeare, Cassell's Quarto Edition. Edited by CHARLES and MARY COWDEN CLARKE, and containing about 600 Illustrations by H. C. SELOUS. Complete in Three Vols., cloth gilt, £3 3s.—Also published in Three separate Vols., in cloth, viz. :—The COMEDIES, 21s.; The HISTORICAL PLAYS, 18s. 6d.; The TRAGEDIES, 25s.

Shakespeare, Miniature. Illustrated. In Twelve Vols., in box, 12s.; or in Red Paste Grain (box to match), with spring catch, lettered in gold, 21s.

Shakespeare, The Plays of. Edited by Prof. HENRY MORLEY. Complete in Thirteen Vols. Cloth, in box, 21s.; half-morocco, cloth sides, 42s.

Shakspere, The International. *Édition de luxe.*
"King Henry VIII." By Sir JAMES LINTON, P.R.I. *(Price on application.)*
"Othello." Illustrated by FRANK DICKSEE, R.A. £3 10s.
"King Henry IV." Illustrated by Herr EDUARD GRÜTZNER. £3 10s.
"As You Like It." Illustrated by the late Mons. ÉMILE BAYARD. £3 10s.

Shakspere, The Leopold. With 400 Illustrations, and an Introduction by F. J. FURNIVALL. *Cheap Edition*, 3s. 6d. Cloth gilt, gilt edges, 5s.; roxburgh, 7s. 6d.

Shakspere, The Royal. With Exquisite Steel Plates and Wood Engravings. Three Vols. 15s. each.

Sketches, The Art of Making and Using. From the French of G. FRAIPONT. By CLARA BELL. With Fifty Illustrations. 2s. 6d.

Smuggling Days and Smuggling Ways; or, The Story of a Lost Art. By Commander the Hon. HENRY N. SHORE, R.N. Illustrated. Cloth, 7s. 6d.

Snare of the Fowler, The. By Mrs. ALEXANDER. *Cheap Edition in one Vol.*, 6s.

Social England. A Record of the Progress of the People. By various writers. Edited by H. D. TRAILL, D.C.L. Vol. I.—From the Earliest Times to the Accession of Edward the First. 15s.

Social Welfare, Subjects of. By LORD PLAYFAIR, K.C.B., &c. 7s. 6d.

Sports and Pastimes, Cassell's Complete Book of. *Cheap Edition*, 3s. 6d.

Squire, The. By MRS. PARR. *Cheap Edition in one Vol.*, 6s.

Standishs of High Acre, The. By GILBERT SHELDON. Two Vols. 21s.

Star-Land. By Sir ROBERT STAWELL BALL, LL.D., &c. Illustrated. 6s.

Storehouse of General Information, Cassell's. Illustrated. In Vols. 5s. each.

Story of Francis Cludde, The. A Novel. By STANLEY J. WEYMAN. 6s.

Successful Life, The. By AN ELDER BROTHER. 3s. 6d.

Sun, The Story of the. By Sir ROBERT STAWELL BALL, LL.D., F.R.S., F.R.A.S. With Eight Coloured Plates and other Illustrations. 21s.

Sunshine Series, Cassell's. Monthly Vols. 1s. each.
The Temptation of Dulce Carruthers. By C. E. C. WEIGALL.
Lady Lorrimer's Scheme and The Story of a Glamour. By EDITH E. CUTHELL.
Womanlike. By FLORENCE M. KING.
On Stronger Wings. By EDITH LISTER.
You'll Love Me Yet. By FRANCES HASWELL; and That Little Woman. By IDA LEMON.
A Man of the Name of John. By FLORENCE M. KING.
Stephen Wray's Wife; or, Not all in Vain. By LAMBERT SHIELDS.

Sybil Knox; or, Home Again. A Story of To-day. By EDWARD E. HALE, Author of "East and West," &c. *Cheap Edition*, 6s.

Tenting on the Plains, or General Custer in Kansas and Texas. By ELIZABETH B. CUSTER, Author of "Boots and Saddles." With Numerous Illustrations. 5s.

Thackeray in America, With. By EYRE CROWE, A.R.A. Illustrated. 10s. 6d.

The "Belle Sauvage" Library. Cloth, 2s. each.

Shirley.	Adventures of Mr. Ledbury.	Old Mortality.
Coningsby.	Ivanhoe.	The Hour and the Man.
Mary Barton.	Oliver Twist.	Washington Irving's Sketch-
The Antiquary.	Selections from Hood's	Book.
Nicholas Nickleby. Two	Works.	Last Days of Palmyra.
Vols.	Longfellow's Prose Works.	Tales of the Borders.
Jane Eyre.	Sense and Sensibility.	Pride and Prejudice.
Wuthering Heights.	Lytton's Plays.	Last of the Mohicans.
The Prairie.	Tales, Poems, and Sketches	Heart of Midlothian.
Dombey and Son. Two Vols.	(Bret Harte).	Last Days of Pompeii.
Night and Morning.	The Prince of the House of	Yellowplush Papers.
Kenilworth.	David.	Handy Andy.
The Ingoldsby Legends.	Sheridan's Plays.	Selected Plays.
Tower of London.	Uncle Tom's Cabin.	American Humour.
The Pioneers.	Deerslayer.	Sketches by Boz.
Charles O'Malley.	Eugene Aram.	Macaulay's Lays and Se-
Barnaby Rudge.	Jack Hinton, the Guards-	lected Essays.
Cakes and Ale.	man.	Harry Lorrequer.
The King's Own.	Rome and the Early Chris-	Old Curiosity Shop.
People I have Met.	tians.	Rienzi.
The Pathfinder.	The Trials of Margaret	The Talisman.
Evelina.	Lyndsay.	Pickwick. Two Vols.
Scott's Poems.	Edgar Allan Poe. Prose and	Scarlet Letter.
Last of the Barons.	Poetry, Selections from.	Martin Chuzzlewit. Two Vols

The Short Story Library. List of Vols. on application.

Tiny Luttrell. By E. W. HORNUNG. Cloth. *Popular Edition.* 6s.

"Treasure Island " Series, The. *Cheap Illustrated Edition.* Cloth, 3s. 6d. each.
"Kidnapped." By ROBERT LOUIS STEVENSON.
Treasure Island. By ROBERT LOUIS STEVENSON.
The Master of Ballantrae. By ROBERT LOUIS STEVENSON.
The Black Arrow: A Tae of the Two Roses. By ROBERT LOUIS STEVENSON.
King Solomon's Mines. By H. RIDER HAGGARD.
Treatment, The Year-Book of, for 1894. A Critical Review for Practitioners of
Medicine and Surgery. Tenth Year of Issue. 500 pages. 7s. 6d.
Tree Painting in Water Colours. By W. H. J. BOOT. With Eighteen
Coloured Plates, and valuable instructions by the Artist. 5s.
Trees, Familiar. By Prof. G. S. BOULGER, F.L.S., F.G.S. Two Series. With
Forty full-page Coloured Plates by W. H. J. BOOT. 12s. 6d. each.
"Unicode": The Universal Telegraphic Phrase Book. Pocket or Desk
Edition. 2s. 6d. each.
United States, Cassell's History of the. By EDMUND OLLIER. With 600 Illus-
trations. Three Vols. 9s. each.
Universal History, Cassell's Illustrated. With nearly ONE THOUSAND
ILLUSTRATIONS. Vol. I. Early and Greek History.—Vol. II. The Roman Period.—
Vol. III. The Middle Ages.—Vol. IV. Modern History. 9s. each.
Vaccination Vindicated. By JOHN C. McVAIL, M.D., D.P.H. Camb. 5s.
Verses Grave and Gay. By ELLEN THORNEYCROFT FOWLER. 3s. 6d.
Vicar of Wakefield and other Works, by OLIVER GOLDSMITH. Illustrated.
3s. 6d.; cloth, gilt edges, 5s.
Vision of Saints, A. By LEWIS MORRIS. *Édition de luxe.* With 20 Full-page
Illustrations. Crown 4to, extra cloth, gilt edges. 21s.
Water-Colour Painting, A Course of. With Twenty-four Coloured Plates by
R. P. LEITCH, and full Instructions to the Pupil. 5s.
Waterloo Letters. Edited by MAJOR-GENERAL H. T. SIBORNE, Late Colonel
R.E. With Numerous Maps and Plans of the Battlefield. 21s.
Wedlock, Lawful: or, How Shall I Make Sure of a Legal Marriage? By
Two BARRISTERS. 1s.
Wild Birds, Familiar. By W. SWAYSLAND. Four Series. With 40 Coloured
Plates in each. 12s. 6d. each.
Wild Flowers, Familiar. By F. E. HULME, F.L.S., F.S.A. Five Series. With
40 Coloured Plates in each. 12s. 6d. each.
Won at the Last Hole. A Golfing Romance. By M. A. STOBART. Illustrated. 1s.6d.
Wood, The Life of the Rev. J. G. By his Son, the Rev. THEODORE WOOD.
With Portrait. Extra crown 8vo, cloth. *Cheap Edition.* 5s.
Work. The Illustrated Journal for Mechanics. Vols. II. and III., 7s. 6d. each.
Vol. IV., 6s. 6d. *New and Enlarged Series.* Vol. V., 4s.
World of Wit and Humour, The. With 400 Illustrations. Cloth, 7s. 6d.
World of Wonders, The. With 400 Illustrations. Two Vols. 7s. 6d. each.
Wrecker, The. By R. L. STEVENSON and LLOYD OSBOURNE. Illustrated. 6s.
Yule Tide. CASSELL'S CHRISTMAS ANNUAL. 1s.
Zero the Slaver. A Romance of Equatorial Africa. By LAWRENCE FLETCHER. 5s.

ILLUSTRATED MAGAZINES.

The Quiver, for Sunday and General Reading. Monthly, 6d.
Cassell's Family Magazine. Monthly, 7d.
"Little Folks" Magazine. Monthly, 6d.
The Magazine of Art. With Three Plates. Monthly, 1s. 4d.
Chums. The Illustrated Paper for Boys. Weekly, 1d.; Monthly, 6d.
Cassell's Saturday Journal. Weekly, 1d.; Monthly, 6d.
Work. Illustrated Journal for Mechanics. Weekly, 1d.; Monthly, 6d
Cottage Gardening. Illustrated. Weekly, ½d.; Monthly, 3d.
** Full particulars of CASSELL & COMPANY'S **Monthly Serial Publications**
will be found in CASSELL & COMPANY'S COMPLETE CATALOGUE.

Catalogues of CASSELL & COMPANY'S PUBLICATIONS, which may be had at all
Booksellers', or will be sent post free on application to the Publishers :—
CASSELL'S COMPLETE CATALOGUE, containing particulars of upwards of One
Thousand Volumes.
CASSELL'S CLASSIFIED CATALOGUE, in which their Works are arranged according
to price, from *Threepence to Fifty Guineas.*
CASSELL'S EDUCATIONAL CATALOGUE, containing particulars of CASSELL &
COMPANY'S Educational Works and Students' Manuals.
CASSELL & COMPANY, LIMITED, *Ludgate Hill, London.*

Bibles and Religious Works.

Bible Biographies. Illustrated. 2s. 6d. each.
> The Story of Joseph. Its Lessons for To-Day. By the Rev. GEORGE BAINTON
> The Story of Moses and Joshua. By the Rev. J. TELFORD.
> The Story of Judges. By the Rev. J. WYCLIFFE GEDGE.
> The Story of Samuel and Saul. By the Rev. D. C. TOVEY.
> The Story of David. By the Rev. J. WILD.

> The Story of Jesus. In Verse. By J. R. MACDUFF, D.D.

Bible, Cassell's Illustrated Family. With 900 Illustrations. Leather, gilt edges, £2 10s.; full morocco, £3 10s.

Bible, The, and the Holy Land, New Light on. By B. T. A. EVETTS, M.A. Illustrated. Cloth, 21s.

Bible Educator, The. Edited by E. H. PLUMPTRE, D.D. With Illustrations, Maps, &c. Four Vols., cloth, 6s. each.

Bible Student in the British Museum, The. By the Rev. J. G. KITCHIN, M.A. *Entirely New and Revised Edition*, 1s. 4d.

Biblewomen and Nurses. Yearly Vol., 3s.

Bunyan's Pilgrim's Progress (Cassell's Illustrated). 4to. *Cheap Edition*, 3s. 6d.

Child's Bible, The. With 200 Illustrations. Demy 4to, 830 pp. *150th Thousand. Cheap Edition*, 7s. 6d. *Superior Edition*, with 6 Coloured Plates, gilt edges, 10s. 6d.

Child's Life of Christ, The. Complete in One Handsome Volume, with about 200 Original Illustrations. *Cheap Edition*, cloth, 7s. 6d.; or with 6 Coloured Plates, cloth, gilt edges, 10s. 6d. Demy 4to, gilt edges, 21s.

"Come, ye Children." By the Rev. BENJAMIN WAUGH. Illustrated. 5s.

Commentary, The New Testament, for English Readers. Edited by the Rt. Rev. C. J. ELLICOTT, D.D., Lord Bishop of Gloucester and Bristol. In Three Vols. 21s. each.
> Vol. 1.—The Four Gospels.
> Vol. II.—The Acts, Romans, Corinthians, Galatians.
> Vol. III.—The remaining Books of the New Testament.

Commentary, The Old Testament, for English Readers. Edited by the Rt. Rev. C. J. ELLICOTT, D.D., Lord Bishop of Gloucester and Bristol. Complete in 5 Vols. 21s. each.

Vol. I.—Genesis to Numbers.	Vol. III.—Kings I. to Esther.
Vol. II.—Deuteronomy to Samuel II.	Vol. IV.—Job to Isaiah.

Vol. V.—Jeremiah to Malachi.

Commentary, The New Testament. Edited by Bishop ELLICOTT. Handy Volume Edition. Suitable for School and General Use.

St. Matthew. 3s. 6d.	Romans. 2s. 6d.	Titus, Philemon, Hebrews, and James. 3s.
St. Mark. 3s.	Corinthians I. and II. 3s.	Peter, Jude, and John. 3s.
St. Luke. 3s. 6d.	Galatians, Ephesians, and Philippians. 3s.	The Revelation. 3s.
St. John. 3s. 6d.	Colossians, Thessalonians, and Timothy. 3s.	An Introduction to the New Testament. 2s. 6d.
The Acts of the Apostles. 3s. 6d.		

Commentary, The Old Testament. Edited by Bishop ELLICOTT. Handy Volume Edition. Suitable for School and General Use.

Genesis. 3s. 6d.	Leviticus. 3s.	Deuteronomy. 2s. 6d.
Exodus. 3s.	Numbers. 2s. 6d.	

Dictionary of Religion, The. An Encyclopædia of Christian and other Religious Doctrines, Denominations, Sects, Heresies, Ecclesiastical Terms, History, Biography, &c. &c. By the Rev. WILLIAM BENHAM, B.D. *Cheap Edition*, 10s. 6d.

Doré Bible. With 230 Illustrations by GUSTAVE DORÉ. *Original Edition.* Two Vols., best morocco, gilt edges, £15. *Popular Edition.* With Full-page Illustrations. In One Vol. 15s. Also in leather binding. (*Price on application.*)

Early Days of Christianity, The. By the Ven. Archdeacon FARRAR, D.D., F.R.S.
> LIBRARY EDITION. Two Vols., 24s.; morocco, £2 2s.
> POPULAR EDITION. Complete in One Vol., cloth, 6s.; cloth, gilt edges, 7s. 6d.; Persian morocco, 10s. 6d.; tree-calf, 15s.

Family Prayer-Book, The. Edited by the Rev. Canon GARBETT, M.A., and the Rev. S. MARTIN. Extra crown 4to, cloth, 5s.; morocco, 18s.

Gleanings after Harvest. Studies and Sketches. By the Rev. JOHN R. VERNON, M.A. Illustrated. 6s.

"Graven in the Rock;" or, the Historical Accuracy of the Bible confirmed by reference to the Assyrian and Egyptian Sculptures in the British Museum and elsewhere. By the Rev. Dr. SAMUEL KINNS, F.R.A.S., &c. &c. Illustrated. 12s. 6d.

"Heart Chords." A Series of Works by Eminent Divines. Bound in cloth, red edges, 1s. each.

My Father. By the Right Rev. Ashton Oxenden, late Bishop of Montreal.
My Bible. By the Rt. Rev. W. Boyd Carpenter, Bishop of Ripon.
My Work for God. By the Right Rev. Bishop Cotterill.
My Object in Life. By the Ven. Archdeacon Farrar, D.D.
My Aspirations. By the Rev. G. Matheson, D.D.
My Emotional Life. By Preb. Chadwick, D.D.
My Body. By the Rev. Prof. W. G. Blaikie, D.D.

My Soul. By the Rev. P. B. Power, M.A.
My Growth in Divine Life. By the Rev. Prebendary Reynolds, M.A.
My Hereafter. By the Very Rev. Dean Bickersteth.
My Walk with God. By the Very Rev. Dean Montgomery.
My Aids to the Divine Life. By the Very Rev. Dean Boyle.
My Sources of Strength. By the Rev. E. E. Jenkins, M.A.

Helps to Belief. A Series of Helpful Manuals on the Religious Difficulties of the Day. Edited by the Rev. Teignmouth Shore, M.A., Canon of Worcester, and Chaplain-in-Ordinary to the Queen. Cloth, 1s. each.

CREATION. By the late Lord Bishop of Carlisle.
MIRACLES. By the Rev. Brownlow Maitland, M.A.
PRAYER. By the Rev. T. Teignmouth Shore, M.A.

THE MORALITY OF THE OLD TESTAMENT. By the Rev. Newman Smyth, D.D.
THE DIVINITY OF OUR LORD. By the Lord Bishop of Derry.

THE ATONEMENT. By William Connor Magee, D.D., Late Archbishop of York.

Hid Treasure. By RICHARD HARRIS HILL. 1s.

Holy Land and the Bible, The. A Book of Scripture Illustrations gathered in Palestine. By the Rev. CUNNINGHAM GEIKIE, D.D., LL.D. (Edin.). With Map. Two Vols. 24s. *Illustrated Edition.* One Vol. 21s.

Life of Christ, The. By the Ven. Archdeacon FARRAR, D.D., F.R.S., Chaplain-in-Ordinary to the Queen.
POPULAR EDITION, Enlarged and Revised, in One Vol. 8vo. cloth, gilt edges, 7s. 6d.
CHEAP ILLUSTRATED EDITION. Large 4to, cloth, 7s. 6d. Cloth, full gilt, gilt edges, 10s. 6d.
LIBRARY EDITION. Two Vols. Cloth, 24s.; morocco, 42s.

Marriage Ring, The. By WILLIAM LANDELS, D.D. Bound in white leatherette. *New and Cheaper Edition.* 3s. 6d.

Morning and Evening Prayers for Workhouses and other Institutions. Selected by LOUISA TWINING. 2s.

Moses and Geology; or, the Harmony of the Bible with Science. By the Rev. SAMUEL KINNS, Ph.D., F.R.A.S. Illustrated. Demy 8vo, 8s. 6d.

My Comfort in Sorrow. By HUGH MACMILLAN, D.D., LL.D., &c., Author of " Bible Teachings in Nature," &c. Cloth, 1s.

New Light on the Bible and the Holy Land. By BASIL T. A. EVETTS, M.A. Illustrated. Cloth, 21s.

Old and New Testaments, Plain Introductions to the Books of the. Containing Contributions by many Eminent Divines. In Two Vols., 3s. 6d. each.

Plain Introductions to the Books of the Old Testament. 336 pages. Edited by the Right Rev. C. J. ELLICOTT, D.D., Lord Bishop of Gloucester and Bristol. 3s. 6d.

Plain Introductions to the Books of the New Testament. 304 pages. Edited by the Right Rev. C. J. ELLICOTT, D.D., Lord Bishop of Gloucester and Bristol. 3s. 6d.

Protestantism, The History of. By the Rev. J. A. WYLIE, LL.D. Containing upwards of 600 Original Illustrations. Three Vols., 27s.; *Library Edition*, 30s.

"Quiver" Yearly Volume, The. With about 600 Original Illustrations and Coloured Frontispiece. 7s. 6d. Also Monthly, 6d.

St. George for England; and other Sermons preached to Children. *Fifth Edition.* By the Rev. T. TEIGNMOUTH SHORE, M.A., Canon of Worcester. 5s.

St. Paul, The Life and Work of. By the Ven. Archdeacon FARRAR, D.D., F.R.S., Chaplain-in-Ordinary to the Queen.
LIBRARY EDITION. Two Vols., cloth, 24s.; calf, 42s.
ILLUSTRATED EDITION, complete in One Vol., with about 300 Illustrations, £1 1s.; morocco, £2 2s.
POPULAR EDITION. One Vol., 8vo, cloth, 6s.; cloth, gilt edges, 7s. 6d.; Persian morocco, 10s. 6d.; tree-calf, 15s.

Shall We Know One Another in Heaven? By the Rt. Rev. J. C. RYLE, D.D., Bishop of Liverpool. *New and Enlarged Edition.* Paper Covers, 6d.

Shortened Church Services and Hymns, suitable for use at Children's Services. Compiled by the Rev. T. TEIGNMOUTH SHORE, M.A., Canon of Worcester. *Enlarged Edition.* 1s.

Signa Christi: Evidences of Christianity set forth in the Person and Work of Christ. By the Rev. JAMES AITCHISON. 5s.

"Sunday:" Its Origin, History, and Present Obligation. By the Ven. Archdeacon HESSEY, D.C.L. *Fifth Edition.* 7s. 6d.

Twilight of Life, The: Words of Counsel and Comfort for the Aged. By JOHN ELLERTON, M.A. 1s. 6d.

Educational Works and Students' Manuals.

Agricultural Text-Books, Cassell's. (The "Downton" Series.) Fully Illustrated. Edited by JOHN WRIGHTSON, Professor of Agriculture. **Soils and Manures.** By J. M. H. Munro, D.Sc. (London), F.I.C., F.C.S. 2s. 6d. **Farm Crops.** By Professor Wrightson, 2s. 6d. **Live Stock.** By Professor Wrightson. 2s. 6d.

Alphabet, Cassell's Pictorial. Mounted on Linen, with rollers. 3s. 6d.

Arithmetic :—Howard's Anglo-American Art of Reckoning. By C. F. HOWARD. Paper, 1s. ; cloth, 2s. *Enlarged Edition*, 5s.

Arithmetics, The Modern School. By GEORGE RICKS, B.Sc. Lond. With Test Cards. (*List on application.*)

Atlas, Cassell's Popular. Containing 24 Coloured Maps. 2s. 6d.

Book-Keeping. By THEODORE JONES. FOR SCHOOLS, 2s. ; or cloth, 3s. FOR THE MILLION, 2s. ; or cloth, 3s. Books for Jones's System, Ruled Sets of, 2s.

British Empire Map of the World. New Map for Schools and Institutes. By G. R. PARKIN and J. G. BARTHOLOMEW, F.R.G.S. Mounted on cloth, varnished, and with Rollers. 25s.

Chemistry, The Public School. By J. H. ANDERSON, M.A. 2s. 6d.

Cookery for Schools. By LIZZIE HERITAGE. 6d.

Dulce Domum. Rhymes and Songs for Children. Edited by JOHN FARMER, Editor of "Gaudeamus," &c. Old Notation and Words, 5s. N.B.—The Words of the Songs in "Dulce Domum" (with the Airs both in Tonic Sol-Fa and Old Notation) can be had in Two Parts, 6d. each.

Energy and Motion: A Text-Book of Elementary Mechanics. By WILLIAM PAICE, M.A. Illustrated. 1s. 6d.

English Literature. A First Sketch of, from the Earliest Period to the Present Time. By Prof. HENRY MORLEY. 7s. 6d.

Euclid, Cassell's. Edited by Prof. WALLACE, M.A. 1s.

Euclid, The First Four Books of. *New Edition.* In paper, 6d. ; cloth, 9d.

French, Cassell's Lessons in. *New and Revised Edition.* Parts I. and II., each, 2s. 6d. ; complete, 4s. 6d. Key, 1s. 6d.

French-English and English-French Dictionary. *Entirely New and Enlarged Edition.* 1,150 pages, 8vo. cloth, 3s. 6d.

French Reader, Cassell's Public School. By GUILLAUME S. CONRAD. 2s. 6d.

Galbraith and Haughton's Scientific Manuals.

Plane Trigonometry. 2s. 6d. Euclid. Books I., II. III. 2s. 6d. Books IV., V., VI. 2s. 6d. Mathematical Tables. 3s. 6d. Mechanics. 3s. 6d. Natural Philosophy. 3s. 6d. Optics. 2s. 6d. Hydrostatics. 3s. 6d. Steam Engine. 3s. 6d. Algebra. Part I., cloth, 2s. 6d. Complete, 7s. 6d. Tides and Tidal Currents, with Tidal Cards, 3s.

Gaudeamus. Songs for Colleges and Schools. Edited by JOHN FARMER. 5s. Words only, paper, 6d. ; cloth, 9d.

Geometry, First Elements of Experimental. By PAUL BERT. Illustrated. 1s. 6d.

Geometry, Practical Solid. By Major ROSS, R.E. 2s.

German Dictionary, Cassell's New. German-English, English-German. *Cheap Edition*, cloth, 3s. 6d. ; half-roan, 4s. 6d.

German Reading, First Lessons in. By A. JÄGST. Illustrated. 1s.

Hand-and-Eye Training. By G. RICKS, B.Sc. Two Vols., with 16 Coloured Plates in each Vol. Crown 4to, 6s. each.

"Hand-and-Eye Training" Cards for Class Work. Five sets in case. 1s. each.

Historical Cartoons, Cassell's Coloured. Size 45 in. × 35 in. 2s. each. Mounted on canvas and varnished, with rollers, 5s. each. (Descriptive pamphlet, 16 pp., 1d.)

Historical Course for Schools, Cassell's. Illustrated throughout. I.—Stories from English History, 1s. II.—The Simple Outline of English History, 1s. 3d. III.—The Class History of England, 2s. 6d.

Italian Grammar, The Elements of, with Exercises. In One Vol. 3s. 6d.

Latin Dictionary, Cassell's New. (Latin-English and English-Latin.) Revised by J. R. V. MARCHANT, M.A., and J. F. CHARLES, B.A. 3s. 6d.

Latin Primer, The New. By Prof. J. P. POSTGATE. 2s. 6d.

Latin Primer, The First. By Prof. POSTGATE. 1s.

Latin Prose for Lower Forms. By M. A. BAYFIELD, M.A. 2s. 6d.

Laundry Work (How to Teach It). By Mrs. E. LORD. 6d.

Laws of Every-Day Life. For the Use of Schools. By H. O. ARNOLD-FORSTER, M.P. 1s. 6d. *Special Edition* on green paper for those with weak eyesight, 2s.

Lessons in Our Laws ; or, Talks at Broadacre Farm. By H. F. LESTER, B.A. Part I. : THE MAKERS AND CARRIERS-OUT OF THE LAW. Part II. : LAW COURTS AND LOCAL RULE, etc. 1s. 6d. each.

Little Folks' History of England. By ISA CRAIG-KNOX. Illustrated. 1s. 6d.

Making of the Home, The. By Mrs. SAMUEL A. BARNETT. 1s. 6d.

Marlborough Books:—Arithmetic Examples. 3s. French Exercises. 3s. 6d. French Grammar. 2s. 6d. German Grammar. 3s. 6d.

Mechanics for Young Beginners, A First Book of. By the Rev. J. G. EASTON, M.A. 4s. 6d.

Mechanics and Machine Design, Numerical Examples in Practical. By R. G. BLAINE, M.E. *New Edition, Revised and Enlarged.* With 79 Illustrations. Cloth, 2s. 6d.

Natural History Coloured Wall Sheets, Cassell's New. Consisting of 18 subjects. Size, 39 by 31 in. Mounted on rollers and varnished. 3s. each.

Object Lessons from Nature. By Prof. L. C. MIALL, F.L.S., F.G.S. Fully Illustrated. *New and Enlarged Edition.* Two Vols. 1s. 6d. each.

Physiology for Schools. By ALFRED T. SCHOFIELD, M.D., M.R.C.S., &c. Illustrated. 1s. 9d. Three Parts, paper covers, 5d. each; or cloth limp, 6d. each.

Poetry Readers, Cassell's New. Illustrated. 12 Books. 1d. each. Cloth, 1s. 6d.

Popular Educator, Cassell's New. With Revised Text, New Maps, New Coloured Plates, New Type, &c. Complete in Eight Vols., 5s. each ; or Eight Vols. in Four, half-morocco, 50s.

Reader, The Citizen. By H. O. ARNOLD-FORSTER, M.P. Cloth, 1s. 6d. ; also a Scottish Edition, Cloth, 1s. 6d.

Reader, The Temperance. By Rev. J. DENNIS HIRD. 1s. 6d.

Readers, Cassell's "Higher Class." (*List on application.*)

Readers, Cassell's Readable. Illustrated. (*List on application.*)

Readers for Infant Schools, Coloured. Three Books. 4d. each.

Readers, The Modern Geographical. Illustrated throughout. (*List on application.*)

Readers, The Modern School. Illustrated. (*List on application.*)

Reading and Spelling Book, Cassell's Illustrated. 1s.

Round the Empire. By G. R. PARKIN. With a Preface by the Rt. Hon. the Earl of Rosebery, K.G. Fully Illustrated. 1s. 6d.

School Certificates, Cassell's. Three Colours, 6¼ × 4¾ in., 1d. ; Five Colours, 11¾ × 9¼ in., 3d. ; Seven Colours and Gold, 9¼ × 6⅞ in., 3d.

Science Applied to Work. By J. A. BOWER. Illustrated. 1s.

Science of Every-Day Life. By J. A. BOWER. Illustrated. 1s.

Sculpture, A Primer of. By E. ROSCOE MULLINS. Illustrated. 2s. 6d.

Shade from Models, Common Objects, and Casts of Ornament, How to. By W. E. SPARKES. With 25 Plates by the Author. 3s.

Shakspere's Plays for School Use. Illustrated. 9 Books. 6d. each.

Spelling, A Complete Manual of. By J. D. MORELL, LL.D. 1s.

Technical Educator, Cassell's New. An entirely New Cyclopædia of Technical Education, with Coloured Plates and Engravings. In Vols., 5s. each.

Technical Manuals, Cassell's. Illustrated throughout. 16 Vols., from 2s. to 4s. 6d. (*List free on application.*)

Technology, Manuals of. Edited by Prof. AYRTON, F.R.S., and RICHARD WORMELL, D.Sc., M.A. Illustrated throughout.

The Dyeing of Textile Fabrics. By Prof. Hummel. 5s.	Design in Textile Fabrics. By T. R. Ashenhurst. 4s. 6d.
Watch and Clock Making. By D. Glasgow, Vice-President of the British Horological Institute. 4s. 6d.	Spinning Woollen and Worsted. By W. S. McLaren, M.P. 4s. 6d.
	Practical Mechanics. By Prof. Perry, M.E. 3s. 6d.
Steel and Iron. By Prof. W. H. Greenwood, F.C.S., M.I.C.E., &c. 5s.	Cutting Tools Worked by Hand and Machine. By Prof. Smith. 3s. 6d.

Things New and Old ; or, Stories from English History. By H. O. ARNOLD-FORSTER, M.P. Fully Illustrated. Strongly bound in Cloth. Standards I. and II., 9d. each ; Standard III., 1s. ; Standard IV., 1s. 3d. ; Standards V., VI., and VII., 1s. 6d. each.

World of Ours, This. By H. O. ARNOLD-FORSTER, M.P. Fully Illustrated. 3s. 6d.

Books for Young People.

"Little Folks" Half-Yearly Volume. Containing 432 pages of Letterpress, with Pictures on nearly every page, together with Two Full-page Plates printed in Colours and Four Tinted Plates. Coloured boards, 3s. 6d. ; or cloth gilt, gilt edges, 5s.

Bo-Peep. A Book for the Little Ones. With Original Stories and Verses. Illustrated with beautiful Pictures on nearly every page, and Coloured Frontispiece. Yearly Vol. Elegant picture boards, 2s. 6d. ; cloth, 3s. 6d.

Beyond the Blue Mountains. By L. T. MEADE. Illustrated. 5s.

The Peep of Day. Cassell's Illustrated Edition. 2s. 6d.

Maggie Steele's Diary. By E. A. DILLWYN. 2s. 6d.

A Sunday Story-Book. By MAGGIE BROWNE, SAM BROWNE, and AUNT ETHEL. Illustrated. 3s. 6d.

A Bundle of Tales. By MAGGIE BROWNE, SAM BROWNE, & AUNT ETHEL. 3s.6d.

Story Poems for Young and Old. By E. DAVENPORT. 3s. 6d.

Pleasant Work for Busy Fingers. By MAGGIE BROWNE. Illustrated. 5s.

Born a King. By FRANCES and MARY ARNOLD-FORSTER. Illustrated. 1s.

Magic at Home. By Prof. HOFFMAN. Fully Illustrated. A Series of easy and startling Conjuring Tricks for Beginners. Cloth gilt, 5s.

Schoolroom and Home Theatricals. By ARTHUR WAUGH. With Illustrations by H. A. J. MILES. Cloth, 2s. 6d.

Little Mother Bunch. By Mrs. MOLESWORTH. Illustrated. Cloth, 3s. 6d.

Heroes of Every-Day Life. By LAURA LANE. With about 20 Full-page Illustrations. 256 pages, crown 8vo, cloth, 2s. 6d.

Ships, Sailors, and the Sea. By R. J. CORNEWALL-JONES. Illustrated throughout, and containing a Coloured Plate of Naval Flags. *Cheap Edition,* 2s. 6d.

Gift Books for Young People. By Popular Authors. With Four Original Illustrations in each. Cloth gilt, 1s. 6d. each.

The Boy Hunters of Kentucky, By Edward S. Ellis.	Jack Marston's Anchor.
Red Feather: a Tale of the American Frontier. By Edward S. Ellis.	Frank's Life-Battle.
Fritters; or, "It's a Long Lane that has no Turning."	Major Monk's Motto; or, "Look Before you Leap."
Trixy; or, "Those who Live in Glass Houses shouldn't throw Stones."	Tim Thomson's Trial; or, "All is not Gold that Glitters."
The Two Hardcastles.	Ursula's Stumbling-Block.
Seeking a City.	Ruth's Life-Work; or,"No Pains, no Gains."
Rhoda's Reward.	Rags and Rainbows.
	Uncle William's Charge.
	Pretty Pink's Purpose.

"Golden Mottoes" Series, The. Each Book containing 208 pages, with Four full-page Original Illustrations. Crown 8vo, cloth gilt, 2s. each.

"Nil Desperandum." By the Rev. F. Langbridge, M.A.	"Honour is my Guide." By Jeanie Hering (Mrs. Adams-Acton).
"Bear and Forbear." By Sarah Pitt.	"Aim at a Sure End." By Emily Searchfield.
"Foremost if I Can." By Helen Atteridge.	"He Conquers who Endures." By the Author of " May Cunningham's Trial," &c.

"Cross and Crown" Series, The. With Four Illustrations in each Book. Crown 8vo, 256 pages, 2s. 6d. each.

Heroes of the Indian Empire ; or, Stories of Valour and Victory. By Ernest Foster.	By Fire and Sword; a Story of the Huguenots. By Thomas Archer.
Through Trial to Triumph; or, "The Royal Way." By Madeline Bonavia Hunt.	Adam Hepburn's Vow ; A Tale of Kirk and Covenant. By Annie S. Swan.
In Letters of Flame; A Story of the Waldenses. By C. L. Mateaux.	No. XIII.; or, the Story of the Lost Vestal. A Tale of Early Christian Days. By Emma Marshall.
Strong to Suffer; A Story of the Jews. By E. Wynne.	Freedom's Sword; A Story of the Days of Wallace and Bruce. By Annie S. Swan.

Books for Young People. *Cheap Edition.* With Original Illustrations. Cloth gilt, 3s. 6d. each.

Under Bayard's Banner. By Henry Frith.	
The Champion of Odin; or, Viking Life in the Days of Old. By J. Fred. Hodgetts.	Bound by a Spell; or, the Hunted Witch of the Forest. By the Hon. Mrs. Greene.

Albums for Children. Price 3s. 6d. each.

The Chit-Chat Album. Illustrated.	
The Album for Home, School, and Play. Set in bold type, and illustrated throughout.	My Own Album of Animals. Illustrated. Picture Album of All Sorts. Illustrated.

"Wanted—a King" Series. *Cheap Edition.* Illustrated. 2s. 6d. each.

Robin's Ride. By Ellinor Davenport Adams.	Wanted—a King; or, How Merle set the Nursery Rhymes to Rights. By Maggie Browne.
Great-Grandmamma. By Georgina M. Synge.	
Fairy Tales in Other Lands. By Julia Goddard.	

Crown 8vo Library. *Cheap Editions.* 2s. 6d. each.

Rambles Round London. By C. L. Matéaux. Illustrated.
Around and About Old England. By C. L. Matéaux. Illustrated.
Paws and Claws. By one of the Authors of "Poems Written for a Child." Illustrated.
Decisive Events in History. By Thomas Archer. With Original Illustrations.
The True Robinson Crusoes. Cloth gilt.
Peeps Abroad for Folks at Home. Illustrated throughout.

Wild Adventures in Wild Places. By Dr. Gordon Stables, R.N. Illustrated.
Modern Explorers. By Thomas Frost. Illustrated. *New and Cheaper Edition.*
Early Explorers. By Thomas Frost.
Home Chat with our Young Folks. Illustrated throughout.
Jungle, Peak, and Plain. Illustrated throughout.
The England of Shakespeare. By E. Goadby. With Full-page Illustrations.

Three and Sixpenny Books for Young People. With Original Illustrations. Cloth gilt, 3s. 6d. each.

† Bashful Fifteen. By L. T. MEADE.
The King's Command. A Story for Girls. By Maggie Symington.
A Sweet Girl Graduate. By L. T. Meade
† The White House at Inch Gow. By Sarah Pitt.
Lost in Samoa. A Tale of Adventure in the Navigator Islands. By E. S. Ellis.

Tad; or, "Getting Even" with Him. By E. S. Ellis.
† Polly. By L. T. Meade.
† Follow my Leader. By L. T. Meade. "Follow my Leader."
For Fortune and Glory.
† The Cost of a Mistake. By Sarah Pitt.
Lost among White Africans.
† A World of Girls. By L. T. Meade.

Books marked thus † can also be had in extra cloth gilt, gilt edges, 5s. each.

Books by Edward S. Ellis. Illustrated. Cloth, 2s. 6d. each.

The Hunters of the Ozark.
The Camp in the Mountains.
Ned in the Woods. A Tale of Early Days in the West.
Down the Mississippi.

The Last War Trail.
Ned on the River. A Tale of Indian River Warfare.
Footprints in the Forest.
Up the Tapajos.

Ned in the Block House. A Story of Pioneer Life in Kentucky.
The Lost Trail.
Camp-Fire and Wigwam.
Lost in the Wilds.

Sixpenny Story Books. By well-known Writers. All Illustrated.

The Smuggler's Cave.
Little Lizzie.
The Boat Club.
Luke Barnicott.

Little Bird.
Little Pickles.
The Elchester College Boys.

My First Cruise.
The Little Peacemaker.
The Delft Jug.

Cassell's Picture Story Books. Each containing 60 pages. 6d. each.

Little Talks.
Bright Stars.
Nursery Joys.
Pet's Posy.
Tiny Tales.

Daisy's Story Book.
Dot's Story Book.
A Nest of Stories.
Good Night Stories.
Chats for Small Chatterers.

Auntie's Stories.
Birdie's Story Book.
Little Chimes.
A Sheaf of Tales.
Dewdrop Stories.

Illustrated Books for the Little Ones. Containing interesting Stories. All Illustrated. 1s. each; or cloth gilt, 1s. 6d.

Tales Told for Sunday.
Sunday Stories for Small People.
Stories and Pictures for Sunday.
Bible Pictures for Boys and Girls.
Firelight Stories.
Sunlight and Shade.
Rub-a-dub Tales.

Fine Feathers and Fluffy Fur.
Scrambles and Scrapes.
Tittle Tattle Tales.
Dumb Friends.
Indoors and Out.
Some Farm Friends.
Those Golden Sands.
Little Mothers and their Children.

Our Pretty Pets.
Our Schoolday Hours.
Creatures Tame.
Creatures Wild.
Up and Down the Garden.
All Sorts of Adventures.
Our Sunday Stories.
Our Holiday Hours.
Wandering Ways.

Shilling Story Books. All Illustrated, and containing Interesting Stories.

Seventeen Cats.
Bunty and the Boys.
The Heir of Elmdale.
The Mystery at Shoncliff School.
Claimed at Last, and Roy's Reward.
Thorns and Tangles.

The Cuckoo in the Robin's Nest.
John's Mistake.
Diamonds in the Sand.
Surly Bob.
The History of Five Little Pitchers.
The Giant's Cradle.
Shag and Doll.

Aunt Lucia's Locket.
The Magic Mirror.
The Cost of Revenge.
Clever Frank.
Among the Redskins.
The Ferryman of Brill.
Harry Maxwell.
A Banished Monarch.

Eighteenpenny Story Books. All Illustrated throughout.

Wee Willie Winkie.
Ups and Downs of a Donkey's Life.
Three Wee Ulster Lassies.
Up the Ladder.
Dick's Hero; & other Stories.
The Chip Boy.

Raggles, Baggles, and the Emperor.
Roses from Thorns.
Faith's Father.
By Land and Sea.
The Young Berringtons.
Jeff and Leff.

Tom Morris's Error.
Worth more than Gold.
"Through Flood—Through Fire."
The Girl with the Golden Locks.
Stories of the Olden Time.

"Little Folks" Painting Books. With Text, and Outline Illustrations for Water-Colour Painting. 1s. each.

Fruits and Blossoms for "Little Folks" to Paint.

The "Little Folks" Illuminating Book.

The "Little Folks" Proverb Painting Book. Cloth only, 2s.

Library of Wonders. Illustrated Gift-books for Boys. Cloth, 1s. 6d.

Wonderful Adventures.
Wonderful Escapes.
Wonders of Bodily Strength and Skill.

Wonders of Animal Instinct.
Wonderful Balloon Ascents.

The "World in Pictures" Series. Illustrated throughout. 2s. 6d. each.

A Ramble Round France.
All the Russias.
Chats about Germany.
The Land of the Pyramids (Egypt).
Peeps into China.

The Eastern Wonderland (Japan).
Glimpses of South America.
Round Africa.
The Land of Temples (India).
The Isles of the Pacific.

Cheap Editions of Popular Volumes for Young People. Illustrated. 2s. 6d. each.

In Quest of Gold; or, Under the Whanga Falls.
On Board the *Esmeralda*; or, Martin Leigh's Log.

The Romance of Invention: Vignettes from the Annals of Industry and Science.
Esther West.
Three Homes.

For Queen and King.
Working to Win.
Perils Afloat and Brigands Ashore.

Two-Shilling Story Books. All Illustrated.

Stories of the Tower.
Mr. Burke's Nieces.
May Cunningham's Trial.
The Top of the Ladder: How to Reach it.
Little Flotsam.
Madge and her Friends.

The Children of the Court.
Maid Marjory.
The Four Cats of the Tippertons.
Marion's Two Homes.
Little Folks' Sunday Book.

Two Fourpenny Bits.
Poor Nelly.
Tom Heriot.
Aunt Tabitha's Waifs.
In Mischief Again.
Through Peril to Fortune.
Peggy, and other Tales.

Half-Crown Story Books.

Margaret's Enemy.
Pen's Perplexities.
Notable Shipwrecks.
Wonders of Common Things.
At the South Pole.

Truth will Out.
Pictures of School Life and Boyhood.
The Young Man in the Battle of Life. By the Rev. Dr. Landels.
Soldier and Patriot (George Washington).

Cassell's Pictorial Scrap Book. In Six Sectional Volumes. Paper boards, cloth back, 3s. 6d. per Vol.

Our Scrap Book.
The Seaside Scrap Book.
The Little Folks' Scrap Book.

The Magpie Scrap Book.
The Lion Scrap Book.
The Elephant Scrap Book.

Books for the Little Ones. Fully Illustrated.

Rhymes for the Young Folk. By William Allingham. Beautifully Illustrated. 3s. 6d.
The Sunday Scrap Book. With Several Hundred Illustrations. Boards, 3s. 6d.; cloth, gilt edges, 5s.
The History Scrap Book. With nearly 1,000 Engravings. Cloth, 7s. 6d.

Cassell's Robinson Crusoe. With 100 Illustrations. Cloth, 3s. 6d.; gilt edges, 5s.
The Old Fairy Tales. With Original Illustrations. Boards, 1s.; cloth, 1s. 6d.
My Diary. With Twelve Coloured Plates and 366 Woodcuts. 1s.
Cassell's Swiss Family Robinson. Illustrated. Cloth, 3s. 6d.; gilt edges, 5s.

The World's Workers. A Series of New and Original Volumes by Popular Authors. With Portraits printed on a tint as Frontispiece. 1s. each.

John Cassell. By G. Holden Pike.
Charles Haddon Spurgeon. By G. Holden Pike.
Dr. Arnold of Rugby. By Rose E. Selfe.
The Earl of Shaftesbury.
Sarah Robinson, Agnes Weston, and Mrs. Meredith.
Thomas A. Edison and Samuel F. B. Morse.
Mrs. Somerville and Mary Carpenter.
General Gordon.
Charles Dickens.
Florence Nightingale, Catherine Marsh, Frances Ridley Havergal, Mrs. Ranyard ("L. N. R.").

Dr. Guthrie, Father Mathew, Elihu Burritt, Joseph Livesey.
Sir Henry Havelock and Colin Campbell Lord Clyde.
Abraham Lincoln.
David Livingstone.
George Muller and Andrew Reed.
Richard Cobden.
Benjamin Franklin.
Handel.
Turner the Artist.
George and Robert Stephenson.
Sir Titus Salt and George Moore.

. *The above Works can also be had Three in One Vol., cloth, gilt edges, 3s.*

CASSELL & COMPANY, Limited, *Ludgate Hill, London,*
Paris & Melbourne.

www.ingramcontent.com/pod-product-compliance
Lightning Source LLC
Chambersburg PA
CBHW030116030726
47498CB00007B/2414